RACHAEL WAECHTER

Burning the Ashes

First published by Rachael Waechter 2026

Copyright © 2026 by Rachael Waechter

This novel is entirely a work of fiction. The names, characters, and incidents portrayed in it are the work of the author's imagination. Any resemblance to actual persons, living or dead, events, or localities is entirely coincidental.

Published by Rachael Waechter

Hillsdale, Michigan

www.rachaelwaechterauthor.com

Cover design by Joanna Beadie

Author headshot credit to Madeline Chenet

Printed in the United States of America

First Edition 2026

Library of Congress Control Number: 2026904813

First edition

ISBN: 979-8-9950149-0-4

This book was professionally typeset on Reedsy.
Find out more at reedsy.com

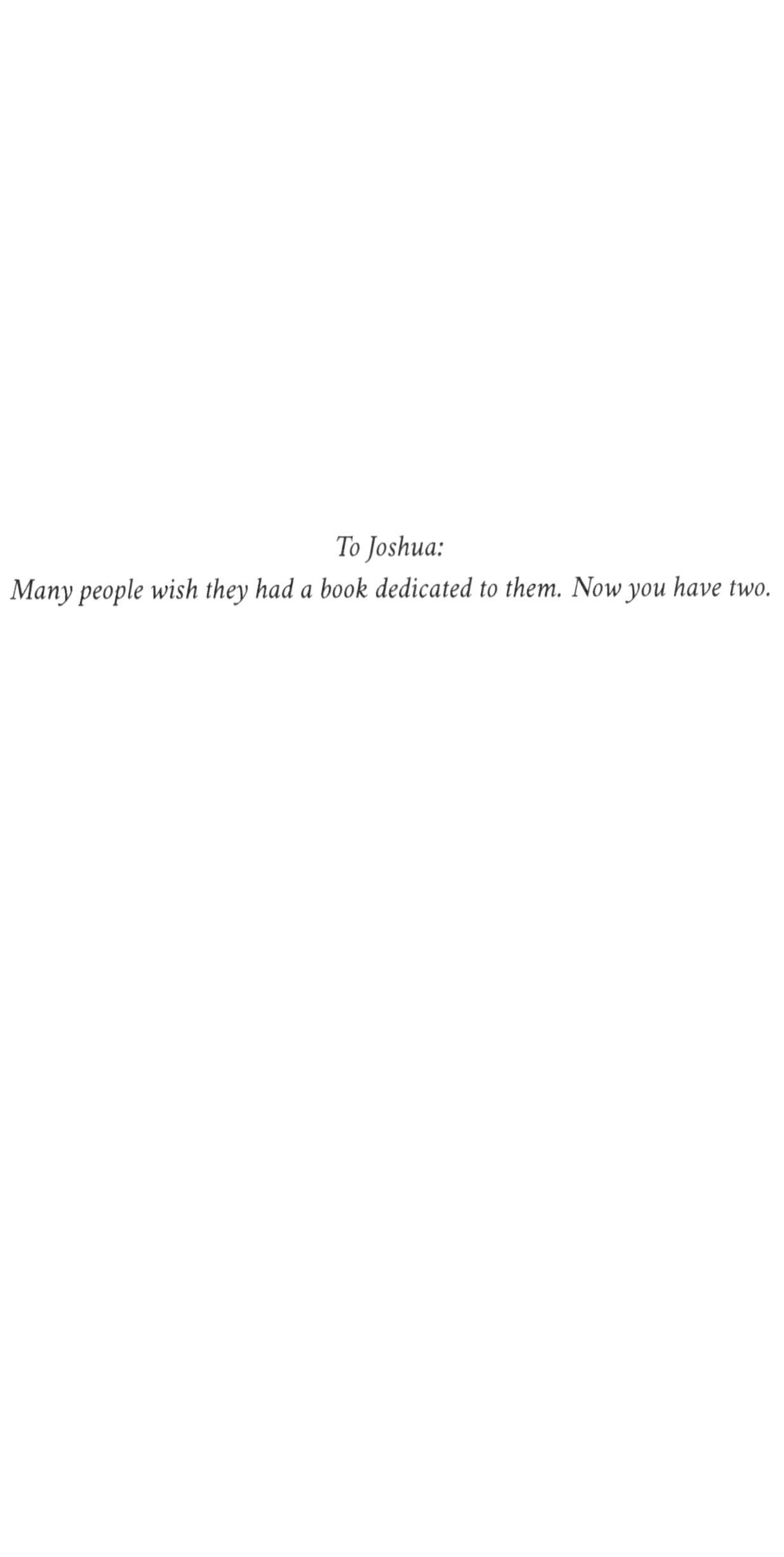

To Joshua:
Many people wish they had a book dedicated to them. Now you have two.

Contents

Content Considerations

This book is written for a young adult audience. Therefore, you can be assured that everything in this book is appropriate for those 14 and older.

All romance in this book is kisses-only. All violence in this book is action movie level, not overly gory or gross.

A character in this book deals with panic attacks and anxiety. This same character also has a difficult history with her family, leading to an uncomfortable meeting with her parents. These particular pages are not indicative of personal experience, but I hope they might help readers who have problems with guilt or psychological trauma caused by family, friends, or others from their past.

I hope that no matter what age you are when you pick up this book, you can enjoy the adventure in the pages ahead!

I

Part One

CHAPTER ONE

Alexandra

"I'm sorry ma'am, I don't think your bag's going to fit," the stewardess said, watching me use all my body weight in an attempt to cram my carry-on into the overhead bin.

"Well," I replied, "It's gonna have to." I kept shoving, hoping by some miracle the bag would reduce in size and slip in.

"We're going to need to check it."

"No, I really don't feel comfortable with that." Another push, still nothing.

Goodness gracious.

"I'm so sorry, it's airline policy," she said, pulling it down and calling for another attendant to bring a bag tag. "What on earth do you have in here? Rocks?"

"I seriously need my bag back; I don't like traveling empty-handed."

"It'll be at the gate when you arrive in Durango. Don't worry about it, honey," she replied, smiling. Then my bag was gone.

Dang it.

Defeated, I settled into my seat. Having only booked the flight the night before, I was lucky enough to have a seat by the window. I shouldn't have had a seat at all. I wasn't quite sure what she said, but I owed Jasmine for booking it for me.

I also shouldn't have been so surprised when she pulled it off. Anyone with the literal superpower of persuasion would be much more likely to get what they wanted compared to a normal person like me.

Sometimes I wondered what it would be like, being them.

I'd now spent several years of my life surrounded by these people, these incredible human beings.

Well, not all of them were the good kind of incredible.

I'd spent years with a man named Fadel. He just so happened to be a supervillain. Or at least he had the technology to make him one. Fadel carried a large staff, which held the superpowers of about a dozen heroes. Heroes like my friend, Bianca.

Bianca Williams, like me, had spent some time under Fadel's control. He cultivated her fire powers, using her as his own personal weapon of destruction. That was until the Victory supers rescued her. And then they rescued me, too.

And now, thanks to them, I was on a plane, finally returning home to Durango.

"Ladies and gentlemen, the boarding door is now closed. Please turn all electronic devices to airplane mode and fasten your seatbelts."

As I powered down my phone, a text from Penny Anderson, one of my other friends from Victory, lit up the screen.

PENNY: Safe travels! Hope to see you soon!

I tucked my phone into my jacket pocket as the plane lurched to life. Within a few minutes, we were in the air.

An hour into the flight, my stomach growled. I pulled a granola bar from my pocket. At least I still had *something* on my person. Thinking back over the last few hours, I hesitated.

I should probably clean my hands. I did go through security...

Shuffling past the others in my row, I made my way to the restroom. Pushing open the small metal door, I stopped in my tracks.

A tall, thin girl with long brown hair stood facing me, arms crossed over her chest. She wore a stomach-dropping smirk on her face.

"Alexandra! So good to see you again!"

My heart stopped.

In front of me stood Margaret Andrews, former friend and current follower of Fadel.

"Maggie, you shouldn't be here. Why on earth are you going to Durango?"

She laughed.

"Oh, that's cute, you think we're actually going to Durango? You of all people should know better! Dr. Fadel has other plans for us."

CHAPTER TWO

Bianca

"You're a terrible driver, you know that, right?"

"I am not. I'm just tired, I've been behind the wheel since Youngsville."

"And whose fault is that?" Theodore Martin asked me, in all seriousness. Seriousness was one of Theo's most rarely seen traits.

"Yours! You fell asleep hours ago and I didn't have the heart to wake you. You should actually be thanking me for doing all the work here."

He glanced over at me with a mischievous gleam in his eye I knew all too well. "See, that sounds like *your* problem. Despite having the temper of a volcano, you're too timid."

"Absolutely not. You're thinking about Penny again. She and I are very different, and you'd do well to remember that."

We'd only been in the car for eight hours or so and we were already bickering like siblings.

"Take the next exit and we can switch places. I bet you could use a nap," he said, pulling our conversation back down to that uncomfortable level of solemnity.

While I wanted to put up a fight, I had to admit that he was right. I thanked him and turned on my signal. We rode in silence to the nearest gas station.

"It's good timing," I said, putting the car in park. "We needed to fill up anyway."

I opened the car door and hopped out, losing my balance slightly as my legs wobbled beneath me.

This was going to be a long journey out west.

Truthfully, we weren't entirely sure where we were headed. Our guiding star was merely a memory; one I had just regained. However, having spent so long unable to remember two full years of my life, I felt that this memory was one worth following.

That memory had a name: Eric Vardoger.

Eric and I had worked for Dr. Fadel together. He was the one who first discovered our boss' real motives and chose to leave. As far as Fadel knew, Eric went south, hoping to move to warmer weather. I was the only person in the world given the truth. But still, I only knew a part of it.

I knew Eric went west, but to where? I knew he grew up in northern Utah, but I couldn't be positive that he'd returned home. He had mentioned knowing a place out west that needed his help, but he never gave me the name of the city. And after scouring the news for weeks on end, I could never find any reports of a city like the one we'd defended. No reports of people like us.

Search records only uncovered two such places: Victory and Durango.

Durango, Fadel's first target location, was the first place superheroes emerged. Unfortunately, Fadel got the better of them. According to the records and stories from my friends, every last one of them perished, and so did hundreds of innocent civilians. This included Sebastian's entire family.

Sebastian was not born a super, but he certainly has become a hero. He valiantly led all of us into battle, rescued the Meadows children from Fadel's grasp, and saved Victory from those who wished to destroy it, and us. All of this done without any powers.

But Theo didn't know that. In fact, none of our friends knew Sebastian's secret. They all remained under the impression that their leader was just like them. That he had the power to turn any object he touched into a weapon. But in reality, he just rocked with numbers.

Theo had already brought up Sebastian's name multiple times on the drive, and each time, I dodged any mention of his powers. And any other troublesome questions Theo thought would be fun to bring up. He especially liked to bring up Sebastian.

I assumed it was because he missed Penny already. They were never given a proper chance to express their true feelings for each other before separating for this journey. Part of me felt terrible, as though it was my fault that Theo and Penny were pulled away from each other to separate corners of the country. However, I had to remind myself that this mission was bigger than all of us.

Returning from the restroom, I settled into the passenger seat. Theo had been right; my body had been entirely drained of all energy. To put it simply: I was exhausted. My body ached and my head felt full, pressure flooding from my sinuses up into my head. I reached behind me and pulled a fleece jacket, one I'd borrowed indefinitely from Jasmine, from my backpack. Pulling it over myself, I cozied up and fell asleep to the sound of the car humming, heading west towards who knows what.

* * *

Before

"Have I ever told you about where I grew up?"

"No," Eric smiled. "Tell me about it." The night sky shrouded the woods around us, but this close together, I could still see his smile. His eyes glistened, maybe even sparkled, as I spoke. We stopped walking, just for a moment, and looked at each other.

"Well," I said as Eric tucked a strand of hair behind my ear. "It's nothing like this. Indiana is so flat. It's green, to be sure, at least in certain parts. But I grew up near a lot of farmland. Elevation was practically non-existent. My sister and I knew of a single hill outside of town. That's where we would sled in the wintertime."

"So, mountains are new to you?"

"Yes, absolutely. It's why I appreciate our walks. These trails twist and turn and show me views I never thought I'd see with my own eyes."

Eric laughed and my heart soared.

"Oh, Bee, you haven't seen anything yet. Just wait. When this war is over and we move on to the next city, I'm going to ask Fadel to give us a break for a while. I want to take you home and show you some real mountains."

This caught me off guard. I hadn't thought about what was next.

"You think there will be another city? Another one we have to protect? Like Victory?"

"Sure. I mean, first there was Durango, remember? And now Victory. But I know that other places like this exist. Other people like us. I knew of one place near my hometown. That's how I first discovered my own skills. I knew the people there."

"You did? Do you think they're doing what these so-called Victory Defenders are? Are they destroying that city, too?"

He went quiet for a moment, clearly bothered by my incessant questioning. My smile faded.

"You know, I don't really want to talk about it right now. I shouldn't have brought it up."

He looked straight ahead, his face hard to read. He began walking again and I hastened to catch up.

I'd touched on a subject that upset him. Or worried him. Or angered him. I couldn't tell. So much about Eric remained a mystery.

Everyone labeled him the "nice guy," keeping everything light and positive. But I always had this gut feeling that something lived beneath the surface, something that just felt off.

"Ok we don't have to talk about them. We can talk about something else."

"Like what?" he said into the empty space around us. He kicked a rock down the path. I reached out and grabbed his hand, rubbing my thumb across his knuckles.

"I want to hear more about the mountains, if you're willing to share."

He finally smiled again. His tone of voice shifted, back to a more joyful one. Much more 'Eric.'

"Imagine red, as far as the eye can see. I mean it: everything is red except for the sky. The sky is a gorgeous blue, not a cloud to be seen..."

CHAPTER THREE

Night one. The first night in just about two years I'd spent without hearing Theo's thunderous snores echoing through the wall into my room.

But I couldn't sleep, I found the silence far too loud. My brain screamed for attention. No way would I be able to shut it off long enough to rest right now.

Rolling out of bed, I grabbed my phone and opened the door to the living room. Jumping a bit at the unexpected presence beyond the door, I found Jasmine, sitting on the couch, alone in the dark. The opening door startled her, too. Her hand silently and urgently shot up to her mouth. Upon realizing it was just me, she settled back in. She looked as though she wanted to say something snarky but came up short. I gestured to the couch.

"Mind if I join you?"

I expected her to say no, but instead, she scooched over and patted the spot next to her.

"Honestly? Please do. I could use the company. It's far too quiet in here."

"I was thinking the same thing." I flicked on a lamp and joined her on the couch.

"It's funny because since we all met, we've always been in the same place. Every single night, four of us went to bed under this roof. Five, once Bianca showed up. It doesn't feel right, Theo's bed being empty."

"I thought Theo annoyed you," I quipped, trying to hide my growing smile.

"He does," she tossed back, "You all do. None of you are special, I'm just easily annoyed."

"Even Penny? I don't think Penny could annoy anyone," I challenged, amused.

"She's far too chipper all the time! How does that *not* get on your nerves? And the whole ordeal with her and Theo. They just need to kiss or something, I don't know. I'm tired of them dragging out the 'will they won't they' thing. We all know you like each other; just let it happen and stop making it our problem. It's been years for goodness' sake."

I laughed, wondering if Bianca and I had also been that obvious before we began dating. We tried to keep it under wraps, but at a certain point, that just seemed so unnecessary. So complicated. So childish.

Jasmine, for once, was right. Theo and Penny really needed to have that all-important conversation. If only they hadn't been pulled apart to different regions of the country.

That was, practically speaking, all my fault.

My idea to send Bianca with Theo instead of taking her myself led to the pulling apart of not just one, but two couples.

"I wish they'd gotten the time to talk about it before they left," I said, letting the guilt sit in the driver's seat for a moment too long.

"They've had years to talk about it, Sebastian. You can't beat yourself up over the decision you made. You seemed so clear-headed about it yesterday. Why change your mind now?"

"I haven't changed my mind. I stand by my decision."

"Then why do you seem so torn up about it?" Jasmine's intrigue cut a bit too deep for my ego to bear.

"I'm not torn up about it."

"Tell me why you're upset."

The words sat on the tip of my tongue. Realizing why and fighting it, I replied.

"Don't do that. It's unfair."

She smiled, almost sadistically.

"You're going to talk one way or another," she shrugged. "I don't want to use my Voice, but I will."

"I'm not upset."

"Sebastian, I'm not stupid. You're stubborn, but so am I. Just tell me what's up."

I refused to cooperate. I didn't need a heart-to-heart with Jasmine. I didn't need to talk about my feelings, especially with a woman who wasn't my girlfriend. But then she put a hand on my knee and spoke to me with her actual voice, a voice that was much more persuasive than the powerful one she tried before.

"We need to trust each other, Seb. You, Penny, and I only have each other right now. You have to rely on us. How can you expect us to rely on you when you won't talk to us?"

Maybe she was wrong. Maybe I could handle the burden of my thoughts myself. I didn't want to make them her problem anyway. But still, this deep sense of frustration bubbled to the surface, and I knew it might be best to trust her with my inmost thoughts, or at least some of them.

Besides, as annoying as Jasmine could be at times and as often as we found ourselves in a battle of wills, she remained one of my best friends. I needed her just as much as she needed me. And if I couldn't show her that I trusted her, how the heck would she know that she could trust me, too?

"I sent Theo with Bianca because I wanted her to be well-protected."

"But that could have been you protecting her on the road. You know that, right? That can't be the only reason. Besides, Penny and I would have done just as well here with Theo. As much as I hate to admit that."

The words were on the tip of my tongue.

I can't protect her. Not really...

I just had to say it. Four simple words.

I don't have powers.

But I couldn't tell her the whole truth. As much as I cared about her, I didn't want her to know that in reality, only two people currently under this roof had powers, and I wasn't one of them. Penny was Jasmine's only true source of protection. I could fight, but only as well as a well-trained martial artist, nothing exceptional. Not super.

"Theo's better than me. And he's bigger. He's got an intimidation factor."

She didn't buy it; I could tell by the incredulous wrinkle in her eyebrows.

"Yeah, that's not a real excuse. Why are you actually upset that she's gone with Theo and not you?"

Jasmine always knew how to get right to the heart of the matter. I wouldn't tell her about my lack of powers, but I could tell her something true, something that hurt more than my well-guarded secret.

"I can't help but wonder what will happen when she gets there. You know, when she sees her friend again. Her more-than-a-friend again."

Her lips formed a knowing smirk.

"Ah, I see. You're feeling insecure."

I opened my mouth to correct her use of the word "insecure," but she raised a hand to silence me. My mouth snapped shut.

Dang her internal Voice—the power she could use without saying a word—

was getting good.

"You're worried that Bianca will fall in love with him again, and you'll be out of the picture."

She released her Voice and the words spilled out of me.

"Again? Has she told you she loved him?" My pulse quickened at the thought.

"No," she hastily corrected herself. "Sorry, bad phrasing. I just mean to say that you're worried she will reignite some sort of feelings for this guy."

"I'm not worried that he's better than me or stronger than me. I regret not going because I want her to have a reminder of her new life, her life with us. I just worry that when she's with him, she will fall back into a state of comfort from her past and might even want something different than what we all have planned. I don't want her to stray from our plan."

"Our plan or us?"

"Both, I guess."

"And what will you do if the worst-case scenario happens? If she falls in love with him, he refuses to leave, and she ultimately chooses to stay with him? What would you do then?"

"Geez, Jas, this is getting really dark. I thought you said you weren't sure she ever loved him."

"What would you do?"

"I… don't know. I've lost my entire family, all the people I loved. I don't want to think about losing her, too."

We sat in silence for a beat or two.

"I love her, Jasmine."

She patted my knee again, softly. Her touch warmed my leg and calmed my heartbeat. She had gotten really talented. Maybe the sincerity behind her motivations strengthened her powers more than she knew.

"I know you do. That's why I want you to be ready for anything. Bianca might remember her past now, but we don't know anything about these people or her relationships prior to meeting us. I just care about you and want you to have something stable ready if things go south."

"And what would that be?"

"Us. Penny, Theo… me."

"I know I have you all, but—"

"I know it's not the same kind of love. But you need to know you have something. Please don't forget that whatever you do."

"I won't."

"Swear?"

"Swear."

"Because I can use my Voice to make sure."

"I'm good, Jas. I promise," I laughed a little.

"Besides, you forget she didn't go alone. There's no way Theo will let her forget us. There's especially no way he'd let her stay there, even if she wanted to."

CHAPTER FOUR

Bianca

"I wish I could stay here forever."

"The bed cannot be *that* comfortable."

I rolled over onto my side, overjoyed to finally stretch out on a hotel bed and not sit crammed in the car.

We'd booked two conjoined rooms in a hotel just off the expressway. While Theo drove, I texted Jasmine and asked her to call and make a reservation on our route, just outside of Jameson Heights. She certainly came in clutch once again. I wasn't sure I'd ever slept on a king before. The night ahead looked heavenly. But it wasn't just the bed that made me hesitant to get back on the road.

"I wish we could just hide from all of it."

"From what?" Theo twirled in the desk chair and began tearing into the complimentary chocolate bar and bottle of water he'd gotten from the front desk.

"Fadel, this mission, our real lives," I laughed. "Take your pick."

"*You* want to hide from all responsibility? Wow, after a day stuck in the car together, you're really starting to sound like me."

"I understand it's our duty to follow Fadel and take him down before he unleashes mayhem on another city. But sometimes I just wish things could be normal."

It sounded so cliche, being a super girl who just wanted to be normal, but I couldn't help it. Sometimes I dreamed of settling down with my friends, starting a family, and maybe raising some chickens or goats. The vision seemed appealing, at least in my head.

"Normal is severely overrated. Normal people don't get to live in a house with their best friends, fight supervillains, blast fire out their fingers, and chase bad guys on a cross-country road trip. Name one normal person whose life is more envious than yours right now."

I didn't hesitate.

"Alexandra."

He actually laughed out loud.

"Alexandra's life is anything but normal, are you crazy? I know you lost your memory once, but you obviously must remember that she was the secretary for a supervillain for years. Then, after she stopped working for Lord Evil Staff, she was beaten and left for dead, discovered by us, and then had to face him yet again. All this before returning home, likely with tons of trauma."

"But that's the thing: she *is* going home. It's all over. She can finally have her life back. I don't want her past, I want her present."

"Ok, one: did you not hear me say *trauma*? And two: what on earth is worth going back to now that you have us? This is your life now! And it's great!"

"I love my life and I love you all. But I do miss my family sometimes."

Theo stopped spinning the chair and smiled at me, a bit dazed.

"And you'll see them soon. All will be well after we complete our mission. Then you can finally have it all: them, us, all of it."

I smiled. In nine days, we would be back with Sebastian, Penny, and Jasmine. Then we would defeat Fadel once and for all. And finally, after all that, we could try to begin our lives again. The third version of mine… each one better than the last.

I imagined that house with Sebastian and my friends. I imagined introducing him to my parents and them accepting him right away as one of our family. I imagined a wedding, with Penny and Jasmine by my side. I couldn't help but smile at the thought.

But then I remembered where I was going.

I'd be looking Eric Vardoger in the eyes in only a matter of days. And not only that, but I'd also hopefully be bringing him to meet Sebastian. No matter how badly I wanted to run away from old versions of myself, I continued to get cornered by my past. I would never really escape the life I lived with Fadel. If the third version of my life came as a result of the second—this life I was living now—it also contained the first. You could never really wash away the past—not entirely.

"I'm gonna head to bed," I said. "I'll see you bright and early for day two."

Theo wished me goodnight and left through the door connecting our rooms.

He was right. Alexandra had trauma she couldn't shake off, just like I had trauma I couldn't escape. But at least her trauma wasn't connected to powers. Your past clings more when you have powers. Trauma was like a tattoo, and physical powers flexed the muscle showing it off.

Despite Theo's correct assertion, as I laid in bed, listening to the sound of his snoring through the wall, I couldn't help but once again imagine what it would be like to be Alexandra right now...

CHAPTER FIVE

Alexandra

My fear of flying began at the age of six, when I'd first experienced basic turbulence.

I'd gripped the seat and screamed, which caused my father to scold me for being too loud. But I couldn't help it: I cried uncontrollably and felt my hands shake for the entire two hour and fifteen-minute flight.

Planes were undoubtedly the bane of my existence, always causing some sort of panic attack. Something about the enclosed space and the thought of hurtling through the air in a combustible metal tube always made me wary of flying. When I moved from Durango to Victory, I took a series of buses. Everyone made fun of me for it at the time, but standing in the tiny airplane bathroom with a literal supervillain and two hours to go in the flight, I once again had been validated in my prior decision.

The locked door pressed against my back; Maggie stood less than a foot in front of me. If only I could reach back and open the latch...

"I wouldn't think about going back out there if I were you." Her eyes trained on my hand as it slipped behind my back.

She was right, of course. Even if I got out of the bathroom, where would I go? I was trapped at 40,000 feet.

"Who's flying the plane?" My voice shook as I spoke. I was not ready to die in a fiery plane crash.

"Oh, don't worry about that. The pilot isn't going to *crash* the plane, silly! We have precious cargo on board."

She continued to use a tone I wasn't used to. I'd known Maggie for years and her voice always came across as sarcastic and dry-humored. But this voice had a higher pitch, the kind a popular high school girl would use to give the new girl in school a backhanded compliment she'd be thinking about for weeks. What had I done to her? We were friends. Fadel and his cronies abandoned *me*, not the other way around.

"You, me, Lawrence, and a gentleman in seat 22E will be getting off at our *actual* final destination, where we will be joining the doctor," she continued. "Now of course, the gentleman in 22E is unaware of this… let's call it a 'change in itinerary,' shall we? In fact, he is unaware of many things."

She smiled, leaning on the wall to her left and crossing her arms across her chest.

"For one, he doesn't know that he's seated right in front of Lawrence. For another, that Lawrence continues to teleport between his seat and the cockpit, informing the pilot that we *must* land at the new destination or something bad will happen to everyone on board. And guess what? That gentleman also lacks the knowledge that his unexplained ability to change the weather at will is in fact, real."

The reality hit me like a ton of bricks.

The guy in 22E was a super. Another one. Someone Fadel had been tracking down. Someone he'd chosen to abduct. It was like the Meadow kids all over again. Like Bianca. It became harder to breathe, lightheadedness took over. My lungs seemed to snap shut, which caused my head to fill with fog. My vision began to blur.

"He'll know all of this soon enough. Dr. Fadel has been *very* eager to meet him," Maggie laughed and looked at herself in the mirror. "Goodness, these plane mirrors are not the most flattering."

"Why the plane? If Fadel's known about this guy for a while, why get him in the air? Why not send Lawrence into his house and teleport him back to Fadel? The theatrics seem to be a bit much, if I'm being honest."

She rolled her eyes.

"The guy travels for work pretty much constantly. Chasing him down has been a major headache. But when the Doctor hacked into the airline database to track his movements, he noticed that someone else would be on this plane today. Two for the price of one seemed like a no-brainer. Plus, he was able to remove his own name from the do-not-fly list. That was a very successful day, in my opinion."

"So is Lawrence just going to teleport us down, or what?" I tried not to sound as terrified as I felt, but in all honestly, I was shaking in my boots.

"No, he can't get that far with his teleports. Better to just land the plane where the Doctor wants. Then he can collect you both himself."

So the plane wasn't going to crash. But still, I had no intention of getting off where they wanted me to. This plane needed to land somewhere else, and fast.

"So, what's your role in this?" I asked, trying to see how much time I could buy myself before coming up with a brilliant, or at least half-brilliant plan.

"To keep you out of the cockpit. We don't want you actually crashing the plane out of some ridiculous act of heroism."

Crashing the plane.

Oh goodness, that was it.

"You and I both know I'm not the heroic type, Maggie. That was Bee. I just want to go home to my family. I don't want to be killed by Fadel for abandoning him. As a friend, I hope you can understand that and have mercy on me."

She laughed at my use of the word 'friend,' but said nothing.

I began spiraling for dramatic effect, hoping somewhere deep down, Maggie still had a soul.

"I didn't want to leave him because of Bianca. I missed my family. I didn't want to be a part of the drama between the two of them. You know I wasn't there that day. I stayed home because I didn't want to be dragged down. Please understand, I just wanted to go home."

Forced tears welled up in my eyes and I blinked rapidly, forcing a single tear down my cheek.

"Alexandra," she said, her tone changing from snark to at least partial sincerity. Her mean-girl expression faded and morphed into something softer. "He's not going to kill you. You know I would never let him. I know you don't believe me, but I fought him about leaving you there in the hotel. In fact, it was my idea to collect you and bring you back, so you could repent and rejoin us. I promise he's not going to kill you. He's going to give you another chance. Besides, you have information he needs."

My stomach flipped, and not at the slight turbulence that kept me gripping onto the counter.

"What kind of information?"

"The whereabouts of Eric Vardoger."

My mouth went dry and my throat clenched. Only one option remained at this point: to lean further in.

"Ok."

"Ok?" She looked confused.

"I'll go with you and talk to Fadel. But then I want to go back to my family. Please, Maggie. Please do this, as my friend. I don't want to be a part of this world anymore. Can you please ask him to consider this compromise?"

She nodded quickly, and my body flushed with relief. I knew she would take the bait.

"Good," she smiled. "I knew you would come around!"

But my heart continued to thump. We weren't in the clear yet.

"Now that we've settled that, can I please go back to my seat?"

I tried to sound innocent, focusing my breathing and my facial expressions to match the lies I told.

"We really should get out of here, shouldn't we? I know someone is bound to need the bathroom soon. And I, of course, still need to use the restroom myself before returning to my seat. If that's alright with you, of course."

She sighed.

"Sure, but straight back to your seat. I don't want Fadel thinking I'm betraying him in any way, you know? I want to make sure everything goes exactly according to plan."

Oh, it will. But according to whose plan, that's the real question.

She pushed past me and finally left me alone. Locking the door again, I frantically dug through my jacket pockets, looking for a pen.

The best thing I could find was a tube of lipstick. Unrolling the toilet paper, I wrote a scribbled note in cherry red.

Plane hijacked. Need to land ASAP. Looks like lightning. Please.

As I walked back to my seat and approached row 22, I prayed that what Maggie told me about this man and his powers wasn't a lie.

"Oops!" I tripped over my own feet right in front of an Asian gentleman in his mid-to-late late twenties. He just so happened to be sitting in 22E.

"So sorry about that!" I said, hopping up. "Oh, look! I found this on the ground; I think you might have dropped it."

I handed him the folded toilet paper and looked him straight in the eyes. He held my gaze for a moment, unsure what to say.

"Thank you in advance," I whispered, breaking eye contact and shuffling to my seat.

I buckled in and pulled the strap tight, bracing myself for what I hoped was coming. Looking ahead of me a few rows, I could see the man reading my note. Meanwhile, outside the window, flashes lit up the sky.

Even my fear of flying couldn't stop me from smiling.

CHAPTER SIX

Penny

Piqué, *piqué, piqué hold, arabesque, balance, balance, down, entrechat quatre, tour jeté, and turn, two, three, four, and...*

I fell out of my turns almost as fast as I got into them. My head was not in the music. It wasn't anywhere in the room. Frustrated, I slumped over to the mirror and slid down it onto my back. Reaching for my phone, I stopped the music and panted into the air.

"What's wrong with me today?" I said aloud to myself as I lay on the floor, pathetic as ever. My body was in shape, but my mind was not.

Time in the studio typically equaled time alone— the only time when I could get out of my head and into the rest of my body. The time when I didn't have to think about who I was outside of this room, the *super* version of myself.

I knew I should be helping Jasmine pack up things at the house, preparing to leave in a few days, but I couldn't bring myself to do it. Even thinking about it gave me a headache.

For one thing, I did not, under any circumstances, wish to leave Victory. I knew Sebastian had a big plan and everything, but something about leaving our home to go follow Fadel wherever he went did not sit right with me.

But of course, I had to go along with it. One, because Sebastian was my leader and I would always do whatever he told me to, out of loyalty to and trust in him. But two, because smiling through it was what I did best. That's what I've been doing my whole life.

Smiling through the pain.

And if I even thought about doing otherwise, I would disappoint the others. That was the other thing I was really good at: making other people happy. I couldn't dare fail them when they needed me most!

But I was scared…

I didn't want to leave home. I didn't want to risk life and limb anymore. I wanted to have that normal life I always imagined: a little house and a white picket fence. Theodore Martin coming home to me after a long day…

I thought about Bianca and Theo in a hotel room in the middle of nowhere, confused about where to go and what to do. They needed me here… Theo needed me here. I had no right to be scared when they were risking it all to bring Fadel down.

They needed me on the ground with Sebastian and Jasmine, figuring out Fadel's location and how we could stop him. They needed me at my best.

Thinking about them made me want to cry. I missed Theo more than I wanted to admit. Long before anyone else came to this city, long before we became known as the Victory Supers or the Defenders of Victory, Theo was already by my side. He'd been with me for so long and cared for me in my weakest moments. I could at least fight for him in return.

My eyes welled up with tears, but I sniffed them back.

Pull it together, Penny! You're better than this!

I reset my music and took my starting position again: arms out, chest open, breathing calm. As the music reached my cue, I pushed up into pointe and began to piqué again. This time, when I reached the pirouette sequence, the blood in my body pumped warm and steady.

They see you as the strong one. The smiling one. Why aren't you smiling?

The music sped up and I matched the counts with my breaths.

You're a performer for goodness' sake. If you can't keep up with the show, then what on earth is your value to the team's performance? You're the happy one, so be happy! Do it for Theo! He needs you. You cannot fail him!

I slipped out of my turns again, this time falling on my hands and knees. Breathing into the floor, teardrop after teardrop fell, wetting my hands. As the sniffles turned into sobs, I curled downward into a child's pose and cried into my arms. I might be the supposed 'strong one' or the supposed 'happy one,' but in that moment, I was nothing more than the one who needed to be held. Unfortunately, I found myself alone, so as always, I was forced to hold myself.

CHAPTER SEVEN

Alexandra

If only I had gone my whole life without seeing those little oxygen masks fall from the ceiling of a plane…

I didn't even bother to put one on. I knew the moment of sheer chaos was my only opportunity to make a move. As people around me screamed and rushed around to buckle in, I shoved my way back up to row 22, hoping to talk to the man who started the storm. But that wasn't going to happen, at least not right away. I stopped dead in my tracks, noting Lawrence standing over the man in question. I quickly ducked into row 23, keeping my head low.

"Make it stop. Now, or I will tell the pilot to crash the plane," Lawrence said, yelling at the man and pounding his fist on the top of the seat in front of him.

"I have no clue what you're talking about," the man replied.

"I know you started the storm, Arashi. So cut it out or you'll kill everyone on board." Lawrence jabbed a finger in the man's face.

"Their blood will be on your hands as you go to your own early grave."

The man shifted in his seat but held firm to his story.

"Like I said before, I have no idea what you're talking about. Why on earth would you think I could produce a lightning storm with my mind? You need to get that brain of yours checked out, man."

Lawrence cursed and disappeared, presumably to the cockpit.

I seized the moment and reached around to the man, tapping his shoulder from behind. He jumped, startled.

"Hi, I don't have time to introduce myself, but so long as we don't die, find me once we land. That guy and his friend plan to take you hostage and you can't let them. Find me and we will run. I know about people like you and I know how to help you. Please trust me."

Before he could respond, I booked it to the front of the plane, finding a gap in row five I could hide in. I seemed to be just in time, as Lawrence reappeared next to Maggie outside the front bathroom.

"The pilot refuses to take us all the way to Baton Rouge," Lawrence said, running his hands through his hair. "He says the plane needs to get on the ground immediately. He's landing in Charlotte."

"That's so far from the rendezvous though," Maggie said, biting her lip in thought.

"I know, but I'd rather not die by making him crash the plane. And Arashi is being uncooperative, so I don't think the weather is going to let up."

"It's fine. Once we get on the ground, we can hold Arashi and Oliver here and contact the doctor. He can probably get us on a new flight from Charlotte. Either that or we can rent a car. I know the doctor said he's desperate to get his hands on Arashi, but what's another day or two? It will be fine."

"Yeah, says you," Lawrence rolled his eyes. "If Fadel wants someone's head for this, I'm giving him yours."

Maggie nodded, her eyes wide and fear palpable.

"We just can't let them get off the plane."

The pair took their seats in row one.

My mind raced, trying to think of any way I could to get both myself and this Arashi fellow off the plane without being noticed.

As the plane touched down in Charlotte, I immediately pulled out my phone and called Jasmine.

Please, please pick up.

I called her four times before she finally answered.

"Hey, Alexandra! You landed ear—"

"No time to talk," I whispered. "Book me a flight from Charlotte to Durango, and fast. Two seats. One under my name and one under Arashi. That's A-R-A-S-H-I. Pick whatever first name you want. I need it *now*."

Jasmine didn't question me. As we taxied, she talked to me quickly.

"There's one boarding out in ten minutes, but I doubt you'll make it."

"No, that's perfect, book it. Call the gate. Whatever it takes, please. I'll call later and explain, gotta run," I hung up the phone.

While everyone was distracted grabbing bags and such, I crawled back to row 22, apologizing to every person I pushed past. Without thinking about how inappropriate it looked, I climbed over the man's lap and crouched in the middle seat.

"You again," he said, surprised.

"Me again," I replied. "Are you ready to run?"

"I'll do whatever you need me to if it gets me away from the psychopath up front."

Now that was an attitude I could work with.

"What's your name?"

"Robert. Robert Arashi."

I nodded, making a mental note.

"Ok Robert, you were great at making lightning, but how good are you at making wind?"

"Does wind count as weather?"

"It does today."

He didn't look like he believed me, but I grabbed his arm and pulled him to follow me anyway.

We flowed down the aisle with the crowd. There at the front, watching each passenger get off, stood Maggie and Lawrence, acting as steward and stewardess. It would be impossible for us to exit the plane without them seeing us.

"How fast are you?" I asked Robert as we got closer to the front.

"I'll be able to keep up, don't worry."

"I'll stay behind you. You push and then we run."

"Roger that."

Right before we reached the front, I gave the signal, and Robert blasted a huge gust of wind towards our captors. Their bodies hit the wall and then the floor, with deafening thuds.

Then we were running blind down the jet bridge and through the airport.

We got three gates down before I saw the two of them over my shoulder. Robert ran ahead of me and weaved through the busy crowd. I followed closely, dodging in and out. Any second now and Lawrence would appear; I just knew it.

The crowd behind us was thick enough now, so we hooked a sharp left and fell into two seats near a busy gate. I couldn't tell if Lawrence saw us or not. Hopefully, he would run right past the gate. And if he didn't...

He appeared almost immediately, only a few yards from where we crouched, looking around wildly. Maggie ran in his direction.

Please don't see us.

As he looked around, I knew only a matter of seconds remained before Lawrence saw our shocked faces. We'd be done for.

His hungry eyes scanned the gate.

But right before hitting us, Robert grabbed my face and twisted me, turning our backs to Lawrence. I thought he intended to duck us both down, but instead, his mouth covered mine and we were suddenly kissing passionately. Without meaning to, my hands slipped around his waist and he pulled me closer. The perfect distraction: no one would dare look that closely at two faces pressed up against each other in a moment like this. I knew I needed to focus on the act, but I couldn't help but get lost in the moment. Robert Arashi was a darn good kisser.

Thankfully, the loudspeaker snapped me out of it.

"Last call, passengers Oliver and Arashi to gate B17, flight to Durango. Last call, passengers Oliver and Arashi to gate B17. The boarding door is about to close."

I heard someone curse and opened my eyes to see Lawrence grab Maggie's arm, causing the pair to disappear.

They were gone. And better yet, they thought we were gone too. They'd get to gate B17 just in time to see the plane pull away, with us presumably on it.

Jasmine had done it again.

Suddenly I realized Robert and I were still pressed up against each other, no longer kissing, but still close enough that I could feel his breath on my cheek. Pulling away, I laughed awkwardly.

"That was quick thinking," I said, feeling my face flush.

"So," he replied, not acknowledging the kiss. "What's your name? I can't just call you my hero."

I blushed.

"Oh yeah, silly me," I took an extra breath to calm my pounding heart. "I'm Alexandra. And I'm no hero, believe me."

"Ok, well, No Hero, what do we do now?"

I hadn't thought this far ahead.

"Well, I don't exactly have a plan," I admitted. "But while I think of one, I guess we can go back to the gate to grab our checked carry-ons. It's like I told the stewardess earlier, I prefer not to travel empty-handed."

CHAPTER EIGHT

Jasmine

"Let me get this straight: you're in North Carolina?"

"Yes," Alexandra replied, her voice screaming impatience. "The pilot emergency landed the plane in Charlotte. The good news is that we were able to recover our carry-ons."

As I listened to her story, I paced around the living room, switching my phone from my right ear to my left.

"And you didn't get back on the plane to finish the flight to Durango? Or the other flight I booked you?"

It didn't make sense to me why they wouldn't have actually finished the journey, whether that be on the same flight or a different one.

"No, because that's where Fadel thinks we've gone. It would be far too risky to land in Durango. He's probably got someone staking out the airport at this point. He thinks we got on the flight I had you book."

"Got it," I replied, still not really getting it but pretending I did so we could just move on and make a new plan. "So, are you going to drive to Texas then?"

"We can't go back to Durango right now," she said after a long pause.

"So, what's your plan then? Are you and this random guy you just met going to hang out in Charlotte until things settle down?"

She sighed on the other end of the phone.

"I don't know. I truly thought that I'd be home with my parents right now. But since that's not the case, I don't know what I should do. I mean, we have Fadel's final destination now. We got the state right but not the city. It's Baton Rouge, not New Orleans. Or at least that's the airport he wanted us to land at. I presume he's there now. What scares me is that he sent his minions out of the way to abduct Robert. He obviously hasn't finished his collection."

"So, you saw Margaret and Zeke?"

"No, we saw Margaret and Lawrence. I don't know where Zeke is. Maybe on a separate mission? Or maybe he's with Fadel."

I was never the planner. We reserved that role for Sebastian. Since discovering my Voice, I never felt the need to plan ahead. All I needed to do was open my mouth and I had everything I ever wanted. I could be spontaneous, last-minute. I could change my mind as often as I wanted and whoever I was with would act as though I'd never had another opinion. Why plan when you could just act?

"I think the best thing for you to do right now is find a way home. One that doesn't require flying into Durango," I said.

Part of me felt a little guilty deciding on something like this without Sebastian. Another part of me could care less. He and Penny had both been MIA since their significant others left. If Sebastian cared to make the call, he would be around more instead of moping over Bianca.

But was I making the right decision? Should I be telling her to meet us in Louisiana?

"I think you're right," she replied before I could change my mind. "Robert and I both just want to be home."

She sounded hurt, like she really wanted to help but knew she couldn't do much more. It was not like me to be peppy, but Alexandra seemed to need the affirmation.

"You saved this guy, Alexandra. He's going to sleep safe tonight because of you. And now you can finally go home, just like you wanted."

Something didn't sit right with me, making this decision. But this seemed logical.

"Ok," she said, quietly. "We will spend a night here in Charlotte and then get a car and drive home. I can keep you updated as we go."

"Yes, please do. I can make you a reservation for the night, just let me know where you want to stay."

She didn't seem super happy to be returning home—something I thought she *wanted*. I really hoped I made the right decision.

Little did I know at that moment, my choice wouldn't matter in the end.

CHAPTER NINE

Bianca

By the evening of day two, I had already told Theo everything I could remember about my time with Fadel. We discussed the missions, the training, and most importantly, the people. He listened to stories about Maggie, Alexandra, and others I knew over my time there, but he wanted to know about Eric most of all.

"Would I like him? Is he a guy's guy?" Theo asked, badgering me as the sun set over the horizon.

"I don't know, probably?"

Theo laughed.

"Probably? Either I'd like him or I wouldn't. I'm not that hard to please. If you don't know, then maybe the dude actually sucks."

"No," I replied defensively. "He doesn't suck. He's really wonderful. So yes, thinking about it further, I think you would like him."

I hoped that this would end the conversation, but Theo would never let me win that easily.

"What's he like? Is he anything like Sebastian?"

It took everything in me to keep my eyes on the road and not react. Without even looking, I could tell a sly smile crossed his face.

How to respond to this?

"They have some similarities," I said, trying to remain as vague in my descriptions as possible. "They look different, if that's what you're asking."

"What about personality-wise?"

He really needed to drop this.

"Similar in some ways and different in others," I replied. Short, simple. But not enough for Theo.

"So who's hotter?"

My cheeks flushed.

"I thought we were talking about their personalities."

"Hey, I'm just curious." He shifted in his seat and leaned back, relaxing. "And you clearly have an answer. Your red face gave you away."

Ugh, Theo.

"Don't get too comfortable. I'm about to pull off for dinner. A sign back there said there's a town coming up in two miles."

We hadn't seen civilization in almost an hour— just miles and miles of cornfields and wind turbines. I worried if we didn't pull off as soon as we saw somewhere to eat, we would miss the opportunity entirely. Let alone a place to stay for the night.

When we finally reached the so-called "town" of Falcon Creek, it didn't strike me as the best place to stop. The entire town consisted of about eight or nine buildings, all a little worse for wear. There appeared to be a small supermarket, a barber, a gas station, a restaurant called "Bar," and a shady looking motel with a flickering Vacancy sign. The rest of the buildings appeared to be barns and storage facilities.

While it didn't look great, we were hungry and tired. And Theo had been complaining about needing the bathroom for the last forty-five minutes. This little compilation of buildings would have to do.

We pulled up to "Bar" and made our way inside. Theo booked it to the bathroom, and I found an empty table. Not that it was hard to find one; the place was practically deserted, just two other customers sat at the bar, having a drink. It was almost deja vu from the first time I met Alexandra over two years ago.

After a very lousy meal, we paid the bill and drove down to the motel.

"I don't see anyone here. And there doesn't appear to be a lobby. I wonder where we can get a key," Theo remarked as I looked around the property.

"The lights are on in one of the rooms and there are two other cars in the lot. There has to be someone around who can help us."

"Maybe the owner was one of the guys at the bar," he suggested, shrugging. "We could at least walk back down there and ask someone if they know anything about the motel and how we could get a room. It's right down the road."

That seemed sensible enough to me. The tiredness had taken over my ability to make decisions.

"Yeah, good plan. It's not even worth driving, it's so close. We could use the walk to stretch our legs anyway."

I locked the car and the two of us sauntered down the road, back towards the bar. Without streetlamps and light pollution, it was dark— so dark it made me anxious. Before the fear could overwhelm me entirely, I lit a flame in my hand. It didn't emit much light, but it made each step feel a bit better.

Suddenly, Theo's body tensed and his breathing picked up. He moved closer to me so our arms brushed each other as we walked. It was unlike him to be fearful like this.

"Bee, something doesn't feel right," he whispered.

Chills trickled down my spine.

"I feel like we're being watched," he continued, cursing under his breath and looking around wildly.

My heart did a loop-de-loop. My flame flickered and went out. A wisp of smoke drifted into the air.

"I— I think we should go back," I said, getting ready to run for it.

"Yeah, this place gives me the creeps. Let's get back to the car."

We turned around and started walking towards the motel, our pace significantly faster than before.

We heard a noise coming from our right, behind one of the barns.

"What the heck was that?" Theo yelped, grabbing my now empty hand and dragging me at a speed somewhere between a jog and a run.

The sound of quickening footsteps behind us caused me to panic. I tried to spark a flame as we ran, but the fear made it impossible.

"I swear, we are being followed right now, and I am *not* ok with that."

I'd never seen Theo this scared. And I couldn't blame him.

Approaching the car, I fumbled for the keys. But before I could get a grip on the fob, I heard a heavy thud next to me.

"Theo?" I asked, turning towards the noise.

Suddenly a sharp pain erupted across the back of my head and everything went black.

* * *

Before

The year was 2012.

I'd been sent to the principal's office for setting the bathroom trash can on fire.

I hadn't done it intentionally. None of the fires were ever intentional. In fact, I actively avoided fire out of fear. The fear seemed to dampen the effects.

I sat on a hard back wooden chair and rubbed my left palm with my right thumb, circling and circling and circling.

What would I even say? No one, not a soul, knew about my ability. And if they did, they'd think I was crazy.

The way things stood, I had two options.

Option one: tell the principal the truth. See how she reacts. Tell her that I have fire powers and that sometimes I accidentally let it loose when I get angry enough.

Option two: agree with the story she proposes and accept the consequences.

Which plan was more dangerous, I wasn't sure. The truth could burn me, but being pegged as a violent student? As a potential arsonist?

I could only think of one more option.

Option three: lie.

I wouldn't pin it on someone else, but I would make it easy enough to believe.

I'd found a cigarette in the bathroom. I couldn't believe my eyes. I didn't know what to do, so I panicked and threw it in the trash. But this set the trash on fire. That's why I ran to Dr. Mahoney's classroom to get help. If I'd set the fire, would I have run to get help?

Yes, this was what I would say.

The story was believable.

Too bad it wasn't true.

Too bad I had set the fire and then ran to get help.

Because the sad truth was, I knew how to start a fire, but not how to handle it when it got out of control.

CHAPTER TEN

Alexandra

J asmine had made a reservation at a hotel near the airport for Robert and me: two rooms right next to each other for a night. Not wanting to take any chances of being found by Maggie and Lawrence, the plan was to stay here overnight and then take a flight into Dallas. From there, we would rent a car and drive back to Durango. We'd spent a whole day in the room, ordering room service for meals and watching movies to keep distracted.

Like many older hotel rooms, ours had a locked set of doors between us. We chose to keep these internal doors cracked open, just so we could avoid using the open hallway as much as possible. As I settled into my bed for the night, I could hear Robert moving around in his room. He sounded restless. He'd barely slept the night before. What a shame he couldn't find rest now.

Having spent the entire day together, I now knew a good deal about Robert's personal life. It was nice getting to know another person with powers like my friends'. And besides, it could be considered sensible to bond with the man who both saved me from getting caught and melted my entire body with the best kiss I've had in my entire life.

A few years older than me and originally from the west coast, Robert was a fascinating human being. His personality, which reminded me a lot of Jasmine's, took a bit of adjusting to, since he was rougher around the edges than Sebastian and certainly more so than Theo.

To me, Theo had always been the big, intimidating guy with a teddy bear personality. His sharp and quick-witted banter kept us on our toes. Theo was the first to make us laugh and yet the first to jump in front of a bullet for his friends.

Sebastian's serious demeanor played a role in every aspect of his life, personality, and communication style. He remained steadfastly intentional in his mission and his relationships to his friends. I often noticed a quiet sadness in him that only came from overcoming some sort of tragedy. I found it fascinating that he and Bianca fit so well together, as her relationship with Eric looked like quite the opposite experience.

Eric was lighthearted, spirited, and romantic. He was sunshine for her when her days seemed cloudy. Meanwhile Sebastian was her safe space: protective yet encouraging. The boys weren't opposites, but they were definitely different.

Despite his rough-around-the-edges approach to conversation, Robert was kind to me. However, he didn't give away much emotion. Even when discussing his past, he remained stoic.

I learned that he'd discovered his powers a few years ago but never really accepted them until the moment on the plane. He had convinced himself for years that each instance was a mere accident or some sort of coincidence.

"I tried not to believe in magic," he'd said. "Little did I know that I was actually capable of it myself."

As he told me the story of his life, of his powers, of his plans, I couldn't help but reflect on all those people I recruited and how they told me the same thing. Every person had been unique, but each story sounded the same: simple life, shocking discovery, desire to use that discovery for 'the Good'. All except Robert. Robert's sole determination was to reject step two and avoid step three or die trying.

When I asked him what drew him to Durango, he admitted that the journey was more than coincidental. His move to Durango from California could be considered backwards from all the other supers I knew, ones drawn to action and seeking purpose.

After years of hearing about the city's supers and even more so about their defeat, he knew that Durango could no longer be considered a special place. As someone who sought to avoid feeling special in any way, it only made sense to go somewhere where he wouldn't run into anyone like him. Somewhere he could pretend to have a normal life. Where he didn't have to think about those 'accidents' that kept occurring.

While his powers were just an inkling and something he forced into the realm of the imaginary, he still couldn't take any chances. He had been living in Durango for two years up until this point, working a normal nine-to-five job and saving up to buy a house. That flight was intended to take him home, back to his forcedly normal life.

The most notable thing I learned about Robert was that he always seemed to be running away from something. If something good or special appeared in his life, he ran from it. It was almost as though he couldn't allow himself to have true happiness. I couldn't understand it.

We kept our time together simple, free of too many emotional conversations; one, because he didn't want to, and two, because we didn't have the emotional energy to do so after our chaotic travel day.

He forced me to watch three different James Bond movies and rank them based on how cool I thought the Bond actor was. I painted my nails and told him about my favorite coffee shops in Durango, the ones I couldn't wait to get back to once we returned home. He told me about his job, and I walked him through a Pilates workout. It was a simple day for two people who didn't know each other. We kept it professional.

We never discussed the kiss.

I rolled over in bed, struggling to sleep.

Did I have a plan? What was I going to do once I got home? What would my family think when I just rolled my carry-on up to their front door. What would I even say?

Hi Mom and Dad, I've moved across the country to work with a supervillain, almost died, teamed up with some superheroes, almost died again, and now I'm on your porch. Can I stay with you and pretend all that never happened? Also, here's this tall, attractive guy I met on the plane. Can he stay for dinner?

My stomach churned even thinking about that interaction.

I flipped over again and right before I settled in, I heard a loud banging noise. I shot up into a seated position.

"Robert?" I yelped. "Robert, what are you doing in there?"

A few beats of silence passed, interrupted by another bang.

"That's not me," Robert replied. But he didn't need to. The sound clearly originated outside my bolted door.

"Robert, I'm scared." I pushed myself up against the headboard and fumbled for my glasses. I was trapped in this room, no way out.

I glanced over at the conjoining door, wondering if it would be possible to slip into Robert's room and out his door without the intruder seeing me. But it was too late to act. The door broke open, the lock demolished. I screamed in shock and fear.

Only one person I know could have caused such destruction.

I looked up to see Zeke Nicholson standing in my doorway.

* * *

I'd never felt so vulnerable in my life. This moment may have been more terrifying than the day Fadel knocked me unconscious in a penthouse bathroom—worse than being cornered in an airplane bathroom. I may not have been in a bathroom this time, but I still knew I was vulnerable. I was not clothed enough for visitation. Trusting Robert wouldn't come into my room unless necessary, I'd gone to bed wearing a double XL "loyal Hufflepuff" t-shirt as a nightgown. My crumpled PJ pants were draped over a chair several feet away. This proved to be a massive mistake.

Moments from possible murder, the only thing I could think to do was pull my sheets up to my neck.

"Well, this wasn't the reception I expected," Zeke said, smiling as he observed my current disheveled state.

Before I could reply, Robert stumbled into the room, also quite disheveled. His glasses sat askew on the tip of his nose, like he'd just shoved them on his face without thinking.

"Who the heck is this?" he asked. He held his hands out in front of him like Bianca did before attacking someone. He was ready to defend us.

"Zeke, what are you doing here?" I blurted out.

"You didn't answer his question," Zeke casually smiled. "Don't you want to introduce me to your new friend?"

"She doesn't have to. You can tell me yourself," Robert replied, a rage in his eyes. "And you better hurry because I'm not a patient man."

"I'm one of Allie's former colleagues."

"Don't call me Allie," I snapped. He looked hurt.

"Sorry, I didn't know that would bother you now."

"You're not my friend anymore, so don't pretend to be."

He nodded and apologized again. So very Zeke of him, considerate as ever. Even as a minion of Fadel's, he still seemed to have a soul deep down somewhere.

But I needed to hold strong. I couldn't let emotion take over now. He *did* break into my hotel room in the middle of the night, after all.

"I'm one of *Alexandra's* old colleagues," he corrected himself and continued. "We are both former employees of Fadel. A little birdie told me you two had a run-in with some of his other employees a few days ago."

"Former?" I accidentally said out loud, not really believing it. Had Zeke left Fadel as well?

"Yes, *former*. I left him about a week ago. After the whole Meadows kids incident and with the move south, I found a way to slip out."

I might have been too trusting, but part of me actually believed him. I mean, the Meadows kids had been the reason I'd decided to end my time with Fadel, before he discovered my change of heart and left me to die on the bathroom floor, covered in my own blood.

"So why are you here then? If you're so reformed? Why not go home like a normal person? Don't you have parents and a sister to get back to?" I didn't mean for it to sound accusatory, but it did. I just couldn't be sure of his intentions.

"I planned to, but the more I reflected on the last few years, I knew I couldn't do it. Not yet. I needed to come find you, or Bianca, or someone."

"Why me? I was on my way home, Zeke. Why not go find Bianca or return to Victory and talk to Sebastian?" Even I was aware that what I suggested sounded ridiculous.

"Because you've always been there for me. You were there when I needed you most. And now I need you. Desperately."

My heart ached, remembering all those times that Zeke came to me, wanting to return home to his sister. Each time, I sat and comforted him. I showed him compassion when Fadel couldn't.

"I have something I'd like to propose, and I'd like you to hear me out."

"And why would we do that?" Robert cut in. He still looked prepared to attack.

"I want to hear it," I gestured for Robert to back off.

"I need you to introduce me to your friends. I need you to help them trust me."

"You mean Sebastian and the others?"

"Yes."

"Why do you want to gain their trust? Just to feel better about what you've done? Because honestly, Zeke, you should just go home. Reset your life. None of us can really take back what we've done. I've tried the whole redemption thing, and I still feel the weight of my past. We all have to push through that and just try to live like normal people."

"I'm not ready to move on, Alexandra. Maybe you are, but I'm not."

"So, what do you want them for? To apologize?"

"I want to fight with them. I want to take them to Fadel. But I can't gain their trust without you. I want you to coordinate a rendezvous with them."

Oh no. No no no, I'd been explicitly trying not to get more involved with all this.

"Zeke, no. Why can't you just let them execute their own plan? And honestly, why should they trust you? Why should *I* trust you?"

"He's too strong for the three of them to fight alone. And besides, I have Fadel's location, his real location. We can take him down, but we all need to do it together. Please give me a chance. You have to."

I looked at Robert for support, but he just shrugged.

"I don't know any of these people, it's up to you," Robert said.

"What are you saying?" I challenged.

He shrugged again. His eyes glistened with desire, like a fire had been lit in him that he didn't know how to control. I knew what he wanted to say, but he held back. I needed him to come out and actually say it, no matter how crazy it would be.

"So you think I should go with him?"

"I think *we* should go with him."

My mouth dropped open and he continued,

"No way I'm letting you go alone. If you're willing to do this, I am too. Home can wait."

"You're joking." I couldn't believe what I was hearing. "You've literally been doing everything you can to avoid confronting your powers."

"This Fadel guy had his accomplices hijack a plane to hunt me down. The reality is that I'm in the fight now, whether I want to be or not. So I might as well go get him before he gets me."

I looked from Robert to Zeke and back again.

"It's up to you, Alexandra," Zeke said.

I closed my eyes and took a deep breath.

You have got to be kidding me.

Opening my eyes, I sighed.

"Alright, you have a deal. But as soon as I get you and Robert to the rendezvous point, you're buying me a plane ticket back to Texas and you'll never contact me again."

I stuck out my hand for him to shake. He crossed the room to shake it, laughing at me for not leaving the bed. My other hand still gripped my sheets close to my neck; my knuckles had turned a ghostly shade of pale from clutching them so tightly.

"Deal. Meet in the lobby at 8:00 and we can get on the road."

He started to walk away but turned back at me at the last moment.

"And Alexandra? Thank you."

I nodded and he made his way out the door, barely able to get it shut with the broken lock. The metal frame made a horrible scraping noise as the heavy door slid back into place.

Robert and I locked eyes in the awkward silence that followed.

"Are you sure about this?"

"Nope, but here we are," I replied. "Now could you step back into your room? I need to get up to use the bathroom and I can't exactly leave the bed with you here."

He glanced from me to the chair and my pants.

Dang it, he'd noticed the pants.

"I could just turn around," he said with a smirk, which caught me off guard. Turning his back, he glanced over his shoulder playfully. "I promise I won't actually look."

"Go," I laughed, feeling my face go from fear-white to embarrassed-crimson. "I'll see you in a few hours. Try and get some sleep."

"How am I supposed to sleep when there's a strong chance I'll be murdered tomorrow?" He said, still looking over his shoulder.

"You will not," I shooed him with my hands. "Go to bed."

"And if I do get murdered, it will be your fault," he winked at me and left the room.

My stomach churned for the second time tonight.

What have I signed us up for?

* * *

Before

"You've gotta come with us," Maggie said, pulling my arm. "It won't be the same without you."

I shook her hand free and leaned deeper back into my rolling desk chair. Swiveling side to side nervously, I bit my lip.

"Maggie, you know I'm of no use. I don't have skills like you guys, so I'd just slow everyone down."

"You'd slow your team down, which is good news for my team," Eric smiled.

"Well maybe she'll be on your team and then you're doomed, too, Vardoger," Maggie laughed.

"Regardless," Bianca said, cutting off both our friends. "We'd love to have you join us."

I looked across my desk at the growing mounds of paper. I really wanted to join my friends in another round of their infamous capture the flag competition, but I knew I needed to stay late and finish some tasks.

I hated being the party pooper, but someone had to be.

"I have so much paperwork to finish, though," I frowned. Eric walked over and picked up a stack, thumbing through the pages, one by one.

"Ok, well can't you just sign them all quickly and move on?"

"Yeah, it can't take that long," Maggie replied.

I sighed.

"I mean..."

Eric picked up a pen and smiled.

"Idea: we help you." He began handing piles of loose papers to Bianca and Maggie. "Just sign Allie's name on the dotted line."

"Hey now," I tried to snatch a paper from him. "These might be important."

"Are they ever important?" Maggie asked. "To me, they look like reports from Fadel. This one just says '27947 Delivery, pipes and wire, 4 lb.' We can obviously sign that one."

I hated being a party pooper, but I hated breaking rules more. But the way my friends looked at me...

Maybe it wasn't the worst thing in the world to get a little help for once.

"Ok, fine," I nodded. "You all can help. But at least try to make the signatures look like mine."

"Yay!" Maggie clapped her hands together and started scribbling my name onto form after form.

We sat, filling out the paperwork together for several minutes.

"You know," I said, smiling. "You all may be the ones with special skills, but the Doctor pulled me aside the other day and told me that he was impressed by my work."

Maggie smiled at me.

"That's amazing, Alexandra! He's right, you know. You're the most accomplished, poised, and beautiful executive assistant this side of the Potomac."

I laughed.

"He says he's so proud that he's now going to be 'setting me up for greatness,' whatever that means. I wouldn't call what I do great or anything. But I'm happy to be here with all of you."

"Hey, I think you're great. You brought me here and I couldn't be more grateful for that," Bianca added.

"Here, here," Eric raised his pen like a glass. "To the best secretary in the land, Alexandra Oliver."

We all clinked our pens together, laughing. As we neared the end of our piles, Bianca held up one of her forms.

"I think this is one you definitely want to read, Alexandra."

I took the paper and read it over. And then I read it again.

"The Doctor is hiring again."

My friends swarmed behind me to read the form over my shoulder.

"Zeke Nicholson," I read out loud. "It says he's got 'strength.'"

"Wonder what that means," Eric said.

"Well," I replied, signing the last paper in my stack with a flourish. "We'll know soon. It says he starts tomorrow."

"Great, another player for capture the flag," Maggie laughed. "Gotta make up for Alexandra if you know what I mean."

"Hey!" I elbowed her, laughing. Grabbing my coat, I followed my friends out of my office and into the city below, ready to feel a bit special for once.

CHAPTER ELEVEN

Penny

Alexandra needed us on the road, and fast. Her middle-of-the-night call really lit a fire under us. We'd spent days waiting for some sort of direction. We expected it from Bianca and Theo, but since when had our plans ever gone as intended?

Jasmine rushed to pack the van, instructing boxes to load themselves into the trunk while she carried our personal bags and bins with snacks to the middle row. Sebastian sat on the back deck studying maps and researching lodging along our planned route.

It was a 16-hour drive (without stops) to Lenoir, Louisiana. If we left at noon, Sebastian said, we could reach Charlotte by five. That would put us only five hours behind Alexandra, who planned to leave Charlotte at noon as well. If we continued later into the night, we could burn a few more hours. We would all only stop for one night and would otherwise drive straight through, reaching our final destination about the same time late tomorrow.

Ludicrous as it appeared, the plan had been set. We were officially leaving Victory.

Jasmine continued packing like we'd never see this house again. And maybe that was the truth. There was no guarantee we'd return anytime soon, possibly ever.

As I dodged around a floating box of blankets, I followed Jasmine out to the van.

"Are you sure this is necessary? Packing up everything we own?"

She whipped around and shot me a freezing glare.

"That's a little dramatic, Pen. This isn't *everything* we own." She whispered to Sebastian's backpack, causing it to float up, through the van's open window, and onto the passenger seat.

"It just seems like we're really overdoing it. I get the personal bags and the toiletries and the snacks, but boxes of blankets, seasonal clothes, and dry goods? Jas, you packed a 10-pound bag of rice. Why on earth would we need that? Are you preparing for an apocalypse?"

She rolled her eyes and continued packing.

"We don't know what we're getting ourselves into. We don't know how long we will be there. Might as well pack out as much as we can."

"Yeah, but what about the house?"

"I mean, we own it, remember? We all paid off the landlord and took it over? So what does it matter?"

"I mean, it just feels weird to walk out like this. To just pick up our lives and leave. Doesn't that bother you?"

She whipped around to face me, ran her hand through her hair, and sighed.

"Pen, you've never left Victory, I get that. But this isn't my first rodeo. I've been moving around my whole life. I've never called a place home for very long. This is normal. And I know it's scary right now, but you'll find it easier than you think. The important thing is dissociation. You've just gotta let yourself move on mentally. Everything and everyone you love are going with you. That should make it easier, right?"

No, not right. Something still remained here that made it hard to leave. It wasn't the memories; it was the guilt.

"I need to go talk to Sebastian."

I rushed off to the backyard and found Sebastian on the step with two large maps laid out next to him. He traced down a highway with his finger and typed something into his computer, which rested on his lap.

"Seb, there's something I need to do before we go. And I need you to come with me. Or at least, I'd like you to come with me."

He looked up, startled. He said nothing, so I jumped right to the point.

"I want to go see my family. To wish them goodbye. It's important to do so before we leave town."

"I didn't know they still lived around here. You don't talk about them much."

"It's been a while since I've seen them," I shrugged. "We've been a bit busy."

"Ok we can stop by on our way. Go tell Jasmine we will plan to leave at eleven thirty rather than noon. Does that work?"

I agreed and made my way back through the slowly emptying house to find Jasmine.

I might not be able to move boxes with my words, but I could still assist her in packing the van. I didn't want to leave Victory, but since I didn't have a choice, I might as well make myself useful.

CHAPTER TWELVE

Theodore

"Bianca? Bee, dang it, wake up!"

Except I didn't use "dang."

I hadn't heard her move yet. She was still unconscious. Hence, the whisper-yelling.

"Bee, wake up," I whispered again, this time more yell than whisper. I finally felt her change positions.

"I'm awake," she whispered back groggily. "At least I think I am. Where are we?"

After a brief scan of the space, I knew we were in a barn: an abandoned, crumbling barn. It was dark as a cave, with small streaks of moonlight pouring through cracks and holes in the roof, dappling the dusty floor.

I hated the dark.

Oh, and Bianca and I were tied to a wooden post, back-to-back. So that was great.

"A barn. In that stupid town you decided looked like a nice place to stop in."

"How did we end up in a barn?"

"Doesn't matter right now, what matters is getting the heck out of here, ok?

I felt her attempt to pull away.

"Are we tied to a pole?" Bianca asked, the confusion in her voice mingled with fear. "That's seriously messed up."

"'Seriously messed up' is charitable. I would have used other words, all of them expletives. And once again, we don't have time to think. We have to *go*. Can you try and burn through the ropes?"

She moved a little from side to side.

"Negative. I think someone put winter gloves on my hands."

Of course they did.

I used one of the expletives.

"Ok, well maybe I can reach your hands and get them off." I fumbled my fingers behind me and searched for hers. I could only move them a few inches each direction. The rope cut into my wrists.

I swore again.

"I don't think I can reach. We need to think of something else."

But it was too late to think. The barn door slid open, bathing us in moonlight. Three figures walked in with flashlights.

"Theo," Bianca frantically whispered. "What was that?" She couldn't see the figures; her current position had her facing away from the door.

"Bee, don't panic," I whispered back, trying to sound as calm as possible, despite not feeling calm at all. "There are three people coming towards us. I think they're the kidnappers."

Now *she* cursed.

As the flashlights drew closer, I could finally make out the approaching faces.

"Two guys and a girl. A pencil looking guy, a short stocky guy who looks like he came out of a mob movie, and a kind of scary looking chick."

"Are they armed?" I don't know if I'd ever heard her so scared.

"Doesn't look like it but the skinny guy is carrying a snake."

"He's carrying a *what*?" she gasped, but I hushed her. I continued to stretch and pull at the glove on her right hand with my fingers. The rope cut into my skin so deep I could feel blood on my wrists, but I couldn't stop. We needed a way out of this, and fast.

"Our friends are awake," the stocky guy snarled, now only feet from us.

"Ohhh, can I finally play with them?" The girl giggled and clapped her hands together. Her twisted face looked dark and cold. She couldn't have been older than sixteen or seventeen.

"No, Rocco said that Angelica could have first crack at them," the tall guy said, holding up the long grey and black snake that wrapped around his arms.

"Shut up, both of you," their leader snapped. "You idiots stay quiet while I have a little chat with our guests."

He made his way around the back of the pole to Bianca. My hands froze in place, hoping not to tip off our kidnapper of my plan. I could hear Bee whimpering behind me.

"See, you're a pretty one," I heard the man say. "No wonder he wanted you."

I could imagine him reaching up to stroke her hair or touch her face as she continued to shake with fear. I wouldn't stand for that.

"Who the heck are you guys?" I demanded. "Why are you freaks here? Get away from her and face me like a man."

He hesitated, but ultimately came back around to me, smiling deviously. His eyes barely made it to my chest, but we probably weighed about the same. He was built like a fridge.

My hands froze on Bianca's glove for a moment, worried he might see, but realizing his angle would prevent that, I then let my fingers continue their work.

"*Freaks* is just the word he used, too."

"Who are you going on about?" Bianca cried out from behind me.

The creepy girl laughed.

"Your old master."

I couldn't believe what I was hearing.

"You mean Fadel?" I asked. "You know that guy?"

"Oh yes," the leader said. "We know all about him. How he picked and chose his army. How Bianca Williams was his prized gem. How she ran away from him, which made him so sad."

He mockingly ran a finger down his cheek like a tear drop and let out a snarling laugh.

"And what does that have to do with you?" I replied, stalling for time. Bianca's glove was now loose. With a few more tugs, I might have it off.

"Well, not all of us could be his little toys. Some of us weren't deemed worthy. Freaks banished to live a purposeless life."

"So, you're supers? Who tried to work for Fadel, but he rejected you?"

"Yes," the snake boy replied. I swore he had a bit of a lisp, almost a hiss. "He didn't think our skills were important enough. They weren't worth his time or effort."

"Well then they must be pretty terrible, seeing as he literally recruited a middle school girl," I smirked.

"Terrible? Ha!" The leader laughed. "Does Fadel have the power to call and command animals at will? Or the ability to twist and turn his body to fit through even the smallest shapes and crevices? How about the power to know the location of anyone on earth at any moment? Oh, most certainly not. If he did, he would know exactly where you were right now and would not be headed south towards who-knows-what."

"Animal control? Twisting his body? That doesn't sound like a power, that just sounds gross," I scoffed, taking one last pull at Bianca's glove. Her fingers wiggled free.

"No, Fadel needs us," the snake boy said, his eyes wide. "He doesn't know it, but he does." Yep, definitely a lisp.

"And he'll realize it soon," the girl whispered. "When we bring him back his jewel."

Enlightenment hit me like a punch in the face.

Holy. Nightmare.

They wanted to sell Bianca to Fadel in exchange for employment.

"Yes, yes," the leader said. "He will soon see that we are powerful. We've accomplished something none of his cronies could. Something not even he has been capable of."

"And what is that?"

"We've defeated the great Bianca Williams."

"Think again," Bee yelled out behind me. Suddenly the rope snapped and we were free. Wisps of smoke filled the air as Bianca came to my side.

We prepared to fight, seriously aware that we were outnumbered, two to three.

Two to four if you counted the snake slithering towards us.

* * *

Before

We'd fought a lot of bad guys, but we'd never been caught before.

Sometime during our first year as neighborhood superheroes, Pen and I spent weeks chasing the same bank robber to location after location. He had been fast— too fast— almost like he could teleport in and out of places. We always showed up right after he'd left. It frustrated Penny. It frustrated me more.

But the one time we made it there before him, the one time we planned ahead and did everything right, was the time he overtook us.

We'd staked out in front of the big walk-in safe in the back of the Commonplace Bank. Penny had stretched, I'd turned up the air conditioning. We were ready, but our target was more ready.

He appeared out of thin air and punched me in the face. I stumbled back, pulling my hand up to my nose and feeling the blood drip onto my fingers. He moved quickly towards the safe and latched on a small device the size of a baseball. It blinked three times, the sound of gears turning filled the room, and the door cracked open.

Penny ran at him, kicking at his waistline, but he dodged, sending her tumbling down. I reached for his arm as he slipped into the safe, but he was nimble and evaded my grasp.

I pushed open the safe's door and knew we had him cornered.

"The gig is up," I said, stumbling into the empty safe. Confused, I looked around, just in time to see him appear at the door.

"No!" Penny yelled and reached for the handle. But it was too late. We were locked inside as the door closed with a thud and a click.

The pitch-black darkness swallowed us whole.

Penny started to panic, her breathing rate increasing rapidly with each second.

"Theo," she gasped, "Theo, I'm scared."

I groped forward, reaching for her in the darkness. When my hand brushed fabric, I grasped her arm and pulled her into my chest. I couldn't see her face, but I knew she was crying.

"Hey, hey, it's ok," I brushed her hair gently. "I've got you."

"I'm really scared, Theo."

I didn't want to tell her about my fear of the dark, about the way my stomach was doing somersaults in my chest at that very moment.

I needed to be the hero here; I needed to take care of her.

I held her and asked her to match her breathing to mine, in and out in and out. She didn't know that I was using every ounce of my strength to calm my own breath so that she could recover hers.

In and out. In and out.

I stroked her hair, feeling the side of her face so I could tuck the loose strands behind her ear. I slid my hands down her shoulder and pulled her arms off my back, my fingers glided down and intertwined with hers. I pulled her hands to my chest.

"Feel my heart? Try and match the beat."

I couldn't see her, but I could feel her breath on my chest as her breathing slowly steadied.

"We can't get out. Our powers are useless here."

My heart sank. I never wanted to be useless, especially not to her. I wanted to blast my body into the door. I wanted to break it down and bring her to safety myself. I wanted to have any other power, something that could help us escape. Something that could have protected us.

But no, I was the dude who could float. Essentially, I was nothing.

"I know," I said, resigning to the fact that we had failed. "I know and I hate it. I'm sorry, Pen."

We waited a few hours in the darkness, until the first shift of employees arrived to open up business for the day.

When we finally stepped into the sun, I decided I now hated three things:

1. *The dark*
2. *Teleporters*
3. *Being too weak to protect those I cared about*

CHAPTER THIRTEEN

Sebastian

Penny's family lived on a farm in the countryside, not too far from Victory. A little stone house surrounded by fields and two large barns filled the scene as we drove up over a hill towards the address.

Penny made a point of never talking about her family. Neither Jasmine nor I had ever been introduced to them. It was possible Theo had known them back in his and Penny's high school days, but I couldn't be sure. Regardless, Jasmine and I were definitely walking into this interaction blind.

"Anything we should know in advance?" I asked as we pulled into the driveway. Chickens appeared, seemingly out of nowhere, running around the car. I gingerly steered the car around them in an attempt to avoid running them over.

"Always the planner," Jasmine muttered and I rolled my eyes.

"No, I don't think so," Penny replied unconvincingly. "I'm going to try and keep it brief."

"Why brief?" Jasmine asked. "Wouldn't you want to maximize time with your family before leaving town?"

"Just don't want to waste too much of their time," Penny said, smiling. The smile seemed anything but believable.

"Alright, let's get in there! We need to hit the road!" She forced the pep. I could tell. She didn't want to do this. I didn't know what the problem was, but something definitely felt off.

I wanted to stop her. I wanted to encourage her to change her mind, but before I could do anything, she hopped out of the car, smoothed her skirt, and approached the front door. Jasmine and I followed at a distance.

As the door opened, despite the smile plastered on her face, I swore I could hear Penny's sharp intake of breath. A middle-aged woman and a burly farmer stood in the doorway. Neither looked particularly thrilled to have us on their porch.

"Well would you look at that," the farmer spoke up first. "The prodigal daughter has finally returned."

Yep, they were definitely not happy to have us there.

"Hi Dad," Penny smiled gently. "Could we come in for a few minutes? I promise we won't take up much of your time."

Reluctantly, the couple backed away from the doorway and Penny entered, gesturing for us to follow.

"Where's the boy?" Her mother asked, crossing her arms over her chest as I passed her.

Apparently, Theo had met them before. Or at least they knew of his existence.

"Theodore's traveling right now, but he's still in the picture, if that's what you're asking."

Penny's voice still suggested a smile.

We made our way to the small sitting room in the back of the house. Their home wasn't large, but it had a very cozy cottage feel to it. A stone fireplace climbed the wall to my right and a mismatched collection of armchairs circled the room. A large Turkish rug tied everything together, creating a soft cushion for our incredibly uncomfortable steps. We all took our seats, Penny sitting between

Jasmine and me like we were the Swiss Guard or something.

"Thanks for having us in," she said, trying to launch some semblance of a conversation. "I don't think you've met Sebastian and Jasmine before, but they're friends with myself and Theo—"

"Why are you here?" Her dad cut in. No hesitation, no niceties, just dropping the bomb. I glanced over at Jasmine, who looked ready to pounce back.

"Well, we're going away for a while. I wanted to say goodbye before I left town. I don't know how long we will be gone and it didn't feel right leaving without giving you a proper goodbye."

Her mother laughed. I smiled, thinking things were finally taking a positive turn. But Penny had gone pale.

"Well, that's rich!"

"What's so funny about Penny wanting to say goodbye?" Jasmine jumped in, reading the situation faster than I could.

"*Now* she wants to say goodbye to us? What about the first time? What about when she showed up at home with the *boy*? When she ran off with all of you to play superheroes? When she abandoned this family by moving out, all without asking our permission?"

"I was a college graduate!" Penny exclaimed. "I moved out because I was an adult! Because I had a future I needed to pursue!"

"Oh, please. You chose that boy over this family. You chose these… these abnormal people over your flesh and blood." Her mother did not look like she intended to back off. But for once, neither did Penny.

"I chose to save lives instead of sitting at home doing who knows what. It wasn't about Theodore. It wasn't even about my friends. I never chose to abandon you; I chose to do the right thing and help people."

"You've never chosen this family." Her dad sternly snapped.

"Why can't I have both? Why can't I love my family and choose to live somewhere other than under this roof?"

"And what's wrong with this roof? Your grandparents lived under this roof, their grandparents lived under this roof. You have always been expected to honor this family by doing the same," her dad continued.

"You were supposed to marry a nice boy from college, Penelope. Marry him and return here. You knew that," her mother was now crying. "You promised that."

"See what you've done?" Penny's dad barked, gesturing at his wife. "You've hurt so many people as a result of your stupid decisions."

"I never promised anything," Penny said quietly, maybe to her dad, more likely to herself.

I didn't know where to look, who to focus on. This whole scene was extremely uncomfortable. As Penny's friend, I knew I had to say something.

"Mr. and Mrs. Anderson, I know it's been hard without her, but Victory's needed your daughter. We've needed your daughter. She's saved countless lives. Doesn't that mean anything to you?"

"This is all his fault," Mrs. Anderson challenged, refusing to look at me. Now she looked at Jasmine and shook her head. "That boy she met at school. The one who told her she was different. No one should have ever told her that."

"Please leave Theo out of this," Penny's eyes were now wet with tears that she refused to let fall.

"I knew from the moment I first saw him that you'd choose him in the end and we would never matter to you again." Mrs. Anderson was relentless. This conversation wasn't going anywhere. We needed to end it, and fast.

"Alright well this has been a great visit. I'm so glad Penny got this chance to say goodbye, but we really must be hitting the road," I said, slapping my knees and standing up. Jasmine and Penny silently followed my lead.

Penny's parents rose to their feet and showed us to the door. We made our way onto the porch as they lingered in the doorway. Her dad gripped the door, ready to close it. Before he could, Penny gave one last attempt at reconciliation.

"Please, you don't have to make me choose."

"Goodbye, Penelope," her dad replied and closed the door in our faces— in his daughter's face.

As the lock clicked. Penny's legs wobbled a little. She bit her lip and turned away from the door. I reached out to grab and steady her, just as she started to sink.

She gripped my arms and plunged her face into my chest, wetting my shirt with her tears. Pulling her to the ground, I held her as she sobbed. Jasmine sat next to us and stroked her hair, whispering for her to breathe.

"It's going to be ok, Pen. I'm so sorry you had to deal with this," I said. "You didn't deserve a single word they said to you."

Jasmine reached down and grabbed her hand and squeezed it.

"Let me go have a chat with them. Let me make them forgive you. Or have them forget this ever happened. Please let me help you."

Penny glanced up.

"Like wipe their memory?"

"If you wanted."

"Wipe their memory of me entirely? Do you think that would make them happier?"

Now I really was at a loss for words— we both were.

"To be honest, Penny," I cautiously responded. "I don't think anything could make them happier. They just seem like unhappy people. That's a choice. And it's one you've chosen not to make in your own life. That choice just makes them resent your joy even more. They're crabs in a bucket."

"Just let me know what you want me to do," Jasmine whispered, hugging her arms around Penny and leaning into me.

The three of us sat on the porch intertwined in silence for a few more moments before Penny sniffed and sat up.

"I don't want to make them forget. I just want to get in the car and go."

"Are you sure?" Jasmine asked, eager to do anything she could to help Penny rid herself of this pain.

"I'm positive. This was the closure I needed. Thank you both for bringing me here."

We slowly walked her to the van and helped her inside. As we backed down the long driveway and turned onto the main road once again, Penny curled up in the backseat smiling.

"What's that smile for?" I asked, unable to help myself from smiling too.

"I'm just really ready to see Theo again."

CHAPTER FOURTEEN

Bianca

I really tried to keep my eyes away from the snake, but it proved impossible. How on earth, after fighting dozens of villains over the last several months, was I this scared of a snake?

"Bee," Theo whispered. "Plan?"

"Working on it."

Where was Sebastian when we needed him?

Starting to panic a little, I did the best thing I could think of: I made a fireball and threw it at the snake. Hissing, it recoiled.

The tall boy yelled, "Don't you dare hurt Angelica!" Then, he spoke in a hushed tone, speaking not in English, but in some sort of snake language.

"This is some Harry Potter level freaky and I'm not here for it," Theo said, starting to back up. But getting closer to the wall wasn't going to help, it would trap us. We needed to get past them and out the door.

The boy's snake language turned into high pitched chirps. Two bats flew down from the rafters and started swooping around our heads.

"What the h—-" Theo cussed and swung his arms around wildly. With us distracted by the bats, our captors—not to mention the snake— slowly approached.

"I want you to think about this, Bianca," Rocco said, smiling. "You could end this now and agree to come with us to see Fadel. Or we could let Angelica take a bite out of your friend and drag you with us by force. Two fantastic options in my opinion."

I thought about this Rocco character and what he had said before. The tall guy could control animals, which was now quite obvious. The girl could apparently bend her body around, which was less of a power and more a result of flexible joints. But Rocco claimed to know anyone's current location. None of their powers were physical. It shouldn't be that hard to take them down.

The problem, however, proved to be the animals. They moved quickly across different spaces, two in the air and one on the ground. Get distracted by one and miss the other attacking you.

Fire wasn't going to work this time. At least not right now. Too many moving parts to worry about, let alone trying to hit targets above our heads. That would not be the best move if I wanted to keep Theo and myself safe. As Theo swung at the bats to keep them from attacking me, I crouched down and took a deep breath.

Only one shot to get this right.

I thought about Sebastian and exhaled, blasting a line of ice at the villains' feet.

The one trick they didn't see coming.

The snake's body looked like plastic, frozen in place and entirely immobile. The two men yelled at one another as I angled up and struck each of the bats, sending them clattering to the ground in small chunks of ice.

"My bats!" The taller boy yelled. "You'll pay for this!" But before he could make his move towards us, I hit him at the waistline, freezing his arms to his sides.

"Maryanne, get them!" he yelled.

"I can't," the girl fought back. "What do you expect me to do?"

"I don't know, something!" As he thrashed around, he desperately attempted animal calls: shrieks, whoops, and barks. It might not have been the kindest move, but I froze his mouth shut.

"Thank goodness," Theo laughed. "That guy was annoying as all get out."

I sensed movement to my left and swung around quickly, freezing Rocco the same way. Rocco continued to scream, even through the ice concealing his mouth.

The girl was not as easy to stop. She contorted her body and dodged several attacks, rolling and bending over and under my beams.

"Why attack me? I can't do anything to you," she pleaded. "We were just kidding! You should let me go. It was their idea anyway."

I continued to move with her, finally nailing a foot to the floor.

"Yeah, not gonna happen," I said, freezing up her legs. When I eventually had all three villains frozen in place, we finally made our move towards the exit.

"Can we leave them like this?" Theo asked.

"The ice will melt soon. I wanted to give us the best head start possible."

"Are you sure about that?"

"Nope, but I'm hoping it's true and they're not frozen indefinitely."

"Let's get out of here and never come back."

But before reaching the door, I realized something. Something of value remained in the barn. I gave Theo a quick "one sec," and ran back towards our captors.

Lighting a small flame, I held it close to Rocco's mouth. His eyes bugged out in fear, unsure of what I was doing to him. Slowly, the ice around his lips melted and his voice broke through.

"What do you want now, you disgusting freak?"

Ouch.

"Before I go, you're going to tell me the location of Eric Vardoger."

"And why would I do that?"

I lit another flame and danced it around his face.

"You wouldn't."

"No, maybe I wouldn't. But I *could* easily set this barn on fire. That at least gives you the chance of escape, slim as it may be. As the ice melts, you could still make a break for it. But at that point, it's not on me whether or not you make it out."

I liked the power I held here. All the months of trying to gain control of my powers, to make them appear at will, finally culminated in this moment. I had a bad guy within my grasp, and he was at the mercy of my powers, of my strength. Sebastian would be proud of me. I gave a little shrug and smiled innocently.

"How fast can you run, Rocco?"

His eyes sought to call my bluff, but I held strong. I moved the flame back in front of his face.

"Where is Eric Vardoger?" I tried again. As a bead of sweat rolled down his forehead and hit the floor, Rocco broke.

"He's sitting in a bar on 14th Street, in Crescent Ridge, Utah. Just outside of Salt Lake."

Utah.

If this guy was telling the truth, Eric was exactly where I thought he would be.

"Thank you for your service," I snuffed out the flame and ran from the barn.

Screams of "You'll be sorry!" and "I hope Fadel ends you once and for all!" echoed behind me. But by the time they reached me, Theo and I were already long gone.

Utah, here we come.

CHAPTER FIFTEEN

Penny

"How are you doing?"

The question I'd spent the last four hours and seventeen minutes waiting for had finally reached my ears.

Jasmine had fallen fast asleep in the backseat over an hour ago, so I knew Sebastian intended to use this as an opportunity to talk alone, rightly assuming I didn't want to deal with the potential of Jasmine's judgment.

"If it's ok with you, I don't really want to talk about it."

"Is that healthy? I mean, keeping something like that bottled up? I saw what happened there, Pen." He glanced over at me, hoping not to be caught in the act. Sometimes I really hated how straightforward he could be.

"I mean, has anything I've dealt with the past twenty-something years been healthy? I'm fine. None of this is new. Honestly, I'm just eager to get there so I can move my mind toward something else."

He didn't reply to this. I hadn't meant to upset him or snap back. He was only trying to be kind.

"I'm sorry," I said, backtracking a bit. "I know you're doing this because you care, but I would much rather not talk about this. I'm ready to move on."

"Ok, but how can you expect me to sit by and let something like that happen to you? I don't like seeing you get hurt. It's not like you haven't got enough on your plate right now with Theo gone."

Oof.

Hearing someone else state my burdens out loud didn't feel great. It took everything in me to control my reply.

"Your sense of justice is admirable, Sebastian. But really, it's ok."

"I just—"

"Sebastian! Really, please." I accidentally snapped.

I had to focus to slow down my breathing, the thumping of my heart ringing in my ears. We sat in silence for a little while, watching the exit signs count down.

"Have you heard from Bee or Theo?" I asked, trying to break the ice a little. Theo's name caught in my throat a little.

Sebastian's face made it clear that he didn't love the question.

"I thought you said you didn't want to talk about him."

I shrugged and he sighed.

"I heard from him a bit ago, but it wasn't much. Just a text or two letting us know that they locked in on Eric's location and are making good time. Should be there soon. Nothing special."

Missing Theo was harder than I'd ever imagined it would be, and knowing that Sebastian and Bianca were in the same boat made me feel terrible for both of them. This felt like an unusually heavy burden to bear. I wished that I was with Bianca and could talk to her about it, that I could console her.

I looked over at Sebastian again. His stone-set face hid something softer behind it, something that felt the same pain I did.

"I think I love him."

I didn't mean to say it, but once I did, it felt right. Sebastian didn't seem to react strongly to this statement, or at least that's what he wanted me to think. However, I swore I could see a small smile sitting on the corner of his mouth.

"Oh?"

I doubled down. If I was going to say something bold, I needed to stand by it.

"Yeah. I think I love him. I think I have for a long time. That's why I'm a bit on edge, I'm so worried about him. I have this… fear… that something will happen and that our hug in the driveway will be the last time… the last…"

"I understand, you don't need to say it," he gently replied, reminding me once again that we were in the same sinking boat together. "I've thought the same thing about Bianca. But you can trust me when I say they'll be just fine. I genuinely believe that. You and I both know that Theo's the toughest, strongest dude. He's unstoppable, his powers are incredible."

"How humble you are to admit that."

"His powers are great. I can't help but be impressed by how he's mastered them."

"Well, yours are great too. Don't sell yourself short!"

Sebastian's smile faded for a moment, which snuffed mine out as well.

"Hey, that was a compliment. You can accept it, you know. You don't have to be Mr. Humble all the time. It gets a bit old if I'm being honest."

He glanced over at me, mouth hanging slightly open and an unfamiliar flash of fear in his eyes. He fiddled with the wheel uncomfortably.

"Pen, I should probably tell you something."

"Ok?"

"I—"

"Guys I really need to go to the bathroom."

Jasmine's voice caused us both to jump. Sebastian gripped the wheel a bit harder and took a deep breath.

"Can you make it another half hour?" he asked, sending our previous conversation into oblivion. Some other time, perhaps.

"No."

"Are you serious? You can't go a half hour?"

"You try drinking two iced coffees and see if you can go multiple hours shoved in the backseat of a crappy car!"

"I'll have you know—"

"Shut it, Sebastian. Just find us a rest stop, or a Chick-fil-a, or something."

Sebastian smiled again. To see his emotions change so many times in a matter of minutes felt so relatable. So normal, not just for people like us, but for everyone.

Sometimes, it was nice remembering that your friends were human too.

CHAPTER SIXTEEN

Bianca

"Ok that's not terrifying at all."

The morning after leaving Falcon Creek, I sat on the curb of McDonald's parking lot, talking to Sebastian on the phone.

"Right? The dude had a snake. And bats. I didn't think I had a fear of either, but it turns out I have a fear of both. So I'm definitely not sleeping tonight."

"You must be exhausted."

"I am. Physically and emotionally." I meant this more than he could possibly know. My body needed a vacation, and this road trip sure didn't count.

We'd been making great time on our drive. Thanks to the all-night driving, we were ahead of schedule by almost a whole day. In fact, it was likely we'd be in Utah by mid-afternoon. I just needed Theo to get back with the coffee, and we'd be on the road again.

"It's only a few more days, then we will be back together again. You can make it."

"You're right. Thank you for reminding me that there's an end to all this."

"I know you gotta go. Definitely try and take a nap in the car, ok?

You were up all night dealing with snakes and whatnot. You need the rest ahead of your big evening tonight."

Big evening tonight.

He was right once again. But this evening I wouldn't be seeing him, I'd be looking at a face I'd not seen in so, so long. A chill trickled down my spine, the pain of knowing I wouldn't be seeing Sebastian and the fear of seeing Eric again colliding. Cold rushed through my wrists as a few ice droplets fell from my fingers. The grip of my other hand fused to the phone with a thin sheet of ice.

Dang it.

"Thank you for calling, Sebastian, I'll see you soon," I promised.

"Goodbye, Bee, I love you."

My heart soared, only coming back to land in my chest with a thud when I heard the line go dead.

I lowered my hand, still frozen to my phone, and tears flooded my vision.

Nope. Not now.

I blinked back my tears and mentally shifted my sadness into frustration. The warmth began to fill my palm. The ice keeping my fingers locked together slowly melted away.

I put my phone in my back pocket and made my way back to the car, praying that I'd actually be able to sleep a little before the big event looming this evening.

* * *

Rain soaked my dress and water pooled around my feet.

When did I put on a dress? Had I even packed a dress? Where were my shoes?

I looked around, the cityscape overwhelming my senses. Tall skyscrapers loomed in every direction; the sound of bustling traffic filled my ears. But there were no cars, just crowds of faceless pedestrians walking all around me. I was caught in a crowd of people, none of them even noticing my existence. This didn't look like Victory. It didn't look like what I'd imagined Utah to be, either.

"Excuse me," I said, trying to grab a man's arm. He just kept walking, not acknowledging me at all.

"Hey," I said, reaching for a woman. "I'm looking for someone."

She continued on, not even bothering to turn her head towards me.

"Has anyone seen Eric Vardoger?" I yelled into the crowd. The rain was coming down harder now.

"Please!" I cried, but no one would look at me. The rain burned me with its icy touch as it relentlessly slapped my skin. I wiped the flow of water from my face, just in time to see a tall, lean blonde-haired boy walking past me.

"Eric!" I yelled racing towards him, the water around my feet getting deeper and harder to move through with each step.

"Eric, stop!" When I finally reached him, I seized him by the shoulders, twisting him around to face me.

My goodness, it actually was Eric. His face changed, confused, but more awake than the others on the street around us.

"Eric, it's me, Bianca. I've come all this way to find you!"

"Bianca?"

"Yes! It's me! Eric, I've missed you so much!" I cried, warm tears mixing with the cold rain. I'd finally, finally found him. But his face remained stony.

"Go home, Bianca," he snapped.

"Excuse me, what? I drove all the way across the country to find you and bring you back with me. We need your help to defeat Fadel. You were right all along; he's not the man we thought he was. He's evil and we need you to

help us take him down. Please!"

I kept pulling on his arms.

"Go away, Bianca. I can't help you."

He kept trying to walk away from me, but I maintained a firm grip on his hands.

"I can't help you because the cause is lost. You're not powerful enough to stop him."

"But that's why I want you to come with me! We have a team; we just need you to join us."

"Why would I do that?"

My heart ached to say it, unsure if it mattered anymore.

"Because you care about me. Because you loved me once."

"Loved you? Are you serious?" Eric scoffed. I'd never seen him like this before. The kind, quiet boy I once knew seemed completely different now.

"Yes, you said you loved me."

"That was a lie. I never loved you."

"Please don't be cruel," I cried.

He yanked his arms from my grasp.

"I never loved you, and how could I? You're not powerful enough to defeat Fadel. I want to be with someone strong and brave."

"But I am! I can prove it!"

I tried to light a fire, but the rain made it impossible.

"What did I tell you?"

"No, no, I can do ice too!" I said, trying to freeze the rain around me with a lift of my hands and a flick of my wrists.

Nothing.

"No, I swear, I have powers! If I have enough sadness or anger, I can control the elements. Fire, ice, maybe other things too! I'm still learning!"

He laughed.

"Sadness? Anger? Why would you ever want to fuel those emotions?"

"They're not bad emotions, they just need to be controlled," I explained,

wiping the water from my face again. "I can control my emotions now. I'm so much more powerful than you remember me being!"

"Impossible," he said, turning away again. I pulled at his arm one last time.

"Please, please reconsider. Come with me and—"

Eric spun around, grabbed my waist, and smashed his mouth on mine. All the air in my body snuffed out as I melted into him, water pouring over both of us.

It was the same heartbreaking kiss that he'd given me over a year prior, the day he said goodbye.

We pulled apart and I stood there, mouth hanging open as he turned and walked away into the crowd.

"Eric!" I called after him again. But he was gone.

I turned around to walk away and smacked straight into another man. This one was tall, dark, and carried an all-too-familiar staff.

I gasped and suddenly sat up.

Theo was fast asleep on the fold out couch across the room, snoring like a hippopotamus.

I settled back in and stared at the ceiling, dreading the reality of what was waiting for me in Utah and trying to push away the images my sleeping brain just conjured up.

CHAPTER SEVENTEEN

Jasmine

"Y ou see, we just need the room for a few hours. We don't need it overnight, so it wouldn't make sense to pay for a night," I crooned, leaning on the motel counter smiling.

"It's not normal policy to allow guests to come and visit a room without paying," the boy working the desk replied.

"He looks like an easy target," Sebastian had said.

Yeah right.

He *really* didn't want to make eye contact, which made things even more difficult. I scanned him up and down as he typed on his old, dusty computer.

He had to be what, twenty? Twenty-one? My friends weren't going to be happy with me, but since when did I care?

"Listen, I know," I said. "But we really need the room. See that girl over there?" I nodded towards Penny, leaning against the wall, checking her phone. Probably catching up on texts from Theo.

"Yeah, the blonde one?" He asked, as if there was any other girl standing around.

"Mhm, the beautiful blonde over there. She's with me. And if you would so graciously lend us a room for a few hours, we would sincerely appreciate it. In fact, she would probably be so grateful that she'd want to thank you herself. We both would."

"Really?" His eyes darted to mine.

Finally.

"Oh yeah," I twirled a small piece of my hair between my fingers like Penny sometimes did. I smiled at him as softly as I could manage.

This is so gross.

"You could come by later," I said, really trying to lean into my Voice. "But you'd have to give us a little while. We need some time to freshen up. Give us a few hours and then come on by. We can all… hang out and then maybe get some dinner."

"So you just need the room for a few hours then?" He started typing even faster than before.

"Only a few hours. Thank you so much…" I glanced at his name tag. "Ryan."

He handed me a room key, and I gave him a little wave as we walked out. He smiled wide. Relief took over, making me glad to be done with that conversation.

When Penny and I got out to the parking lot and met Sebastian outside the car, I filled them both in on what had just transpired.

"You promised him *what*?" Penny gasped.

"Oh relax," I rolled my eyes. "It's not like we will still be here when he comes knocking. I told him to give us a few hours. We're just going to use the room as a rest stop for a little bit before we meet up with Alexandra."

"That poor kid thinks he gets to hang out with two pretty girls later. What a shame."

I smirked at Sebastian and batted my eyelashes as dramatically as possible.

"You think we're beautiful?"

Now he rolled his eyes.

"Oh shut up, you know what I mean. Show us to our room."

I laughed and led the way to our temporary hideout.

After a few moments, Sebastian laughed, too.

"I can't believe we're in the same city as Fadel again. And in a few hours' time, he's gonna know it."

* * *

Before

Sebastian punched the guy in the face.

I tried not to yelp, but I couldn't help it. I still wasn't used to watching people get demolished.

The man withstood his punch. He scanned the storage room, looking for a way out of this mess. Before he could move towards the door, Penny ran in and roundhouse-kicked the man in the chest, sending him tumbling to the floor.

I jumped out of the way.

I should have stayed in the car.

He pushed up off the floor and ran at Sebastian again. This time, Sebastian was more prepared to use his powers. He held a thick binder between his hands and swung it at the man's head. The man ducked it almost too-easily, but that was Sebastian's plan all along. He broke the momentum of the binder's swing and at a new angle slammed the binder against the back of the robber's head.

This now knocked the man forward, dazed. Penny kicked him with a force I'd never seen, directly in the hip. He spun around at least twice from the impact. Before he could regain his bearings, Theo came barreling into the fray and tackled him. Theo pinned the man to the floor and yelled at me to get backup.

I scrambled out the storage room door yelling.

"Has anyone called the police?"

The shop patrons all muttered to themselves.

"I guess I have to do everything myself," I said, shoving the man crouched at the cash register aside and grabbing the phone.

He stood up quickly, like he hadn't just been cowering for his life under the counter. His accent was slightly French and likely fake.

"Ma'am, we can't have you touching that—"

"I don't care about the rules, pretty boy. I'm stopping a literal robbery. You can thank me later."

I dialed 911 and relayed our location.

Hanging up the phone, I sighed, looking back at the faux-Frenchman.

"So do you own this jewelry store, or do you just work here," I said in all earnestness.

"You," he replied, "Are terrifying. You and all your friends, you're never welcome here again."

"But we literally stopped an armed robber. He had about $750,000 worth of diamonds in his pocket, you know that, right?"

"You broke my long cabinet and smashed right through my Ophelia collection," he said matter-of-factly.

"Ok first of all, I did not smash anything, that was Theo and he's a dumb klutz. Second, did you not hear what I said before? We saved your shop. What's some broken glass compared to almost a million dollars of stolen jewelry?"

He glared at me, sizing me up and down with his eyes. I stood firm and glared back. I could use my Voice to shut him up or even to punch himself in the face. But I let my eyes do the damage instead.

"You're an idiot if you think we're the bad guys here."

As the police came storming into the shop and the patrons began to flee from the building, the jewelry shop owner looked at me once more.

"I don't like you," he said in his offensively fake accent.

I didn't even bother replying. I just rolled my eyes and rejoined the others

in the back.
"Didn't like me?"
Ha.
Him and pretty much everybody else.

CHAPTER EIGHTEEN

Theodore

Crescent Ridge was lame.

I'd lived in the Victory City area my whole life, so that was my standard. Reliable public transportation but also walkability, an extensive selection of restaurants and shops, the ability to live in anonymity. This was one of those small towns where everyone seemed to know everyone. Bianca and I probably stuck out like sore thumbs.

At least this town was better than that stupid Falcon Creek nightmare. Holy heck, I was ready to get back to Victory already. Or at least somewhere I didn't feel like everyone's eyes were glued to me.

We'd parked on Main Street, which cut through the heart of the small downtown. The whole town was maybe a few miles wide in each direction, mostly residential besides a few streets that qualified as "downtown." The street we walked down was busy, a serious contrast to our last new town experience. But we did stand out, or at least it was clear that we weren't from the area.

We were stopped a few times by a friendly, "Are you lost?" from a passerby.

The first two times, we kindly thanked them and told them we were fine, just looking around. But by the third, I had had enough of pretending we were just tourists.

"Yeah, actually, do you know a guy named Eric? We're here looking for him."

The women looked startled. Bianca, even more so.

"I would need a last name, I know several men named Eric."

I guess this town wasn't as small as I'd thought.

"Uhhhh, Bee?"

"Vardoger. Eric Vardoger," she added, timidly.

"No, I don't know any Vardogers. How funny, a Nordic name all the way out here in Navajo country!"

I laughed awkwardly.

"Yep, pretty funny. Ok, well thank you." I walked past the woman and Bianca came scurrying after me.

"What was that about? We can't just *ask* people where Eric is."

"Yeah, well how else do you plan to find him? Do you expect to find him just strolling down Main Street?"

I stopped and turned around, realizing Bianca was no longer at my side. She stood frozen, staring straight ahead. Her mouth hung open slightly in shock. I followed her eyes to see a man, just about our age and exactly as she had described him, walking this way.

Oh my...

CHAPTER NINETEEN

Bianca

After months of being unable to remember my past, the first glimpse of his face practically thrust me into a time machine. His hair was that same shaggy blonde, a little floppy and curved at the part with a little cowlick. His eyes were blue like ice—the first thing I'd noticed—and his build was thin.

As he walked towards me, I realized I'd forgotten how he walked—how he looked—so different from Sebastian and Theo.

I wondered how stupid I looked, standing in the middle of the sidewalk, gaping at this approaching man. But it didn't matter. The only thing I worried about at that moment was his smile.

"Bianca?" He picked up the pace and jogged towards me.

Do I run towards him? Do I open my arms for a hug?

His body collided with mine as he picked me up and spun me around. I laughed, trying to figure out what to do once my arms were no longer pinned to my side.

He put me down and looked into my eyes, smiling. He looked like he wanted to kiss me. I took a small step back, hoping the movement would be obvious enough to prevent any intimate contact. I wasn't ready to think about that just yet. That dream last night scared me a little too much. Luckily, my hesitancy didn't seem to bother him.

Thank goodness for nice guy Eric.

"Bee, I can't believe you came! I can't believe you found me. How did you know I was here?"

"Well, there was this encounter with some bounty hunters, one had a snake, one could tell you people's locations. It was a whole thing. But I figured you were out this way. I knew you'd gone west, and I assumed it was to find your family."

He nodded.

"I did, I found them and sent them north to the mountains. I wanted them to get out of here and find somewhere safe. I knew it was only a matter of time before he would discover my lie."

"Tell him I've been dreaming about an island," he once told me.

"No, no, he fell for it and went south. We've tracked him to Louisiana. We think he went after you but did it all wrong. That, or more likely, he found a new community of people like us. He keeps taking more and more people with him. But we're working to stop him."

"We? Did Alexandra and Maggie come with you?"

I stopped smiling, remembering that Maggie was with Fadel and Alexandra was now who knows where.

"No. They didn't leave with me. Fadel eventually threw Alexandra out, so she's now home safe. At least I think so. Maggie is still with Fadel."

"So, who is 'we?'"

I'd almost forgotten Theo was standing there until he thrust a hand out to Eric.

"Hello, I'm We. Nice to meet you."

Eric looked confused.

"My friends call me Theo."

"Theo," Eric said, like he was trying to determine if the sound felt right coming out of his mouth. He shook Theo's hand, bewildered.

He then looked at me, concerned.

"Oh yeah this has to be awkward," Theo laughed a little. "No, we're just friends. I have a little blondie back home who's probably dying to see me."

I smiled at his confidence.

Eric seemed to relax, at least a little. But that didn't make me feel much better, since I was eventually going to have to explain my relationship with Sebastian.

"There are several of us," Theo continued. "Some went south to follow Fadel, and I came this way with Bianca. The 'went south' team is my girl, Penny, a handsome fella named Sebastian, and Jasmine, who's great but sometimes comes across a little—"

"Theo," I snapped, quickly changing the subject. I turned back to Eric.

"Is there somewhere private the three of us can go chat?"

* * *

Before

Orange and red leaves covered the ground and a cool breeze sent my hair flying in my face. I fought to contain it, pulling through the knots and twisting it into a bun.

"No, stop, it's so nice when it's down," Eric said, pulling at my hand to release my hair.

"No, it's a mess, I need to put it up. At least until we're out of the wind."

His hand still pulled at mine, so I relented, letting my hair fall back in my face.

"There," he smiled and brushed a lock behind my ear.

"I feel so messy."

"I like you messy." His smile warmed my heart, and I let it flow all over my body, down into my toes.

I curled up against him as we sat, looking out at the pond. I had dragged him out here, on the back of the property, insisting on getting some alone time.

"You've been so busy lately," I said.

"Well, I want to train so the doctor will let me do more. I want to see more action, so I need to improve."

"That's fair, but I think you could take just one little break." I rubbed his hands between mine, trying to pass on some warmth.

"I don't really know if I can slow down. I came all the way out here. I want all that effort to be worth it."

"You've already passed your final test, Eric. What more do you need to do? The doctor knows you're talented, otherwise he wouldn't have passed you."

"Yeah, but what if we could do more, you know? So we passed this big final test to become his sidekicks or cronies or whatever. What if we could go out and do good work ourselves?"

"Like missionaries? We find cities that need our help and go help them? And then just keep bouncing from place to place?"

I didn't love the sound of that. At least not at first. Our lives had become so non-stop since arriving at Fadel's doorstep. I wanted to see my family, to take a vacation once in a while.

"I think that's the dream for me," Eric replied. "Helping as many people as possible, all over the world."

"No home, then? Just always on the move?"

"Who needs a home when you're seeing all the world has to offer?"

I fundamentally disagreed. It was great traveling and all, but putting down roots meant something to me. I wanted a home, a family.

But I smiled anyway, because there was something different about the idea of travel when Eric spoke of it. His words, his tone, made it sound magical.

Like I could hop on his flying carpet, and he could take me anywhere I dreamed.

I snuggled my head into his chest. His arms tightened around me like a shawl.

"If you could leave here right now, if you could take me anywhere, where would we go?"

"How realistic are we going here?"

"The sky's the limit. Magic carpet, teleportation, anything."

"Teleportation is the same as magic carpet now?" He laughed. "Seriously?"

"Hey shush, no rules. Plan a date."

He thought for a minute. His warm breath on my hair gave me chills. His lips grazed my hair as he considered his options.

"Hmm... I think maybe I'd take you to Italy."

"Italy?"

"Yeah."

"Have you been?"

"No, but it sounds great. Florence, Italy. We'd start by going to dinner at some fancy place with nice pasta."

"We'd start with dinner? I thought we'd at least go dancing or something first."

He broke away from me.

"Excuse me, this is my date being planned right now."

"Sorry! Sorry," I laughed, hugging him in an attempt to get him to wrap around me again. I succeeded and he held me tight.

"We're at dinner. You got carbonara, I got a nice smoked chicken penne. We share both, obviously."

"Obviously," I giggled.

"We then go get gelato."

"Of course."

"And then we take a long walk down the river, under the lights and the stars."

"That sounds nice."

"Wait! I take it back. We do your magical teleportation and after we get gelato, we teleport to Paris."

"Paris? Isn't that a bit cliche?"

"Shhh... my date."

I laughed. He pulled out his phone and started typing something in.

"We go up on the hills above the city and watch the lights come on the Eiffel Tower. And while it's sparkling, I play this song."

A slow waltz played from his phone speaker.

"Mmm," I smiled. "I like that."

"And then I ask you to dance."

He stood up, bowed at the waist, and offered me a hand. I took it and he pulled me in. We danced clumsily, without saying a word. I could feel the thump of his heart through both of our coats.

He twirled me under his arm and I laughed. As the song wound down, I looked up at him, and he smiled down at me.

"What happens next?" I whispered.

"I ask to kiss you."

I nodded, and he leaned down, his lips barely grazing mine. It was taunting, tantalizing. I wanted more. I stood on my toes, closing the gap between us. He looked startled, but closed his eyes again and deepened the kiss. His fingers hooked the belt loops on my jeans and my hands wandered up his neck.

We'd been flirting, cuddling for a while. Many people at the compound would say we were dating, but we hadn't kissed yet. This moment had been worth the wait.

My hands grazed up and down his back, moving from his shoulders into his hair. He used my belt loops to pull me in until our bodies were pressed up tight against one another. I could really feel his heartbeat now. Could he feel mine?

The song changed again, this time to a jazzy number. We took this as our cue to break apart, slowly. He smiled down at me again.

"Thank you for this lovely date," I blushed.

"Thank you for asking me out to the pond. Maybe someday I'll repay you and take you to Europe for real."

"I'm holding you to that."

I dreamed of all the places we could go together. All the places where we could dance and kiss, just like this.

CHAPTER TWENTY

Alexandra

After surviving a plane hijacking, escaping Fadel's minions, and driving across multiple state lines with two men I didn't trust, we finally made it to our destination.

This particular destination just so happened to be one of the scariest looking places I'd ever seen. Zeke directed Robert down a back road, banyan trees drooping their mossy branches on both sides of the car like curtains. The sun hung low in the sky now; the first stars had become visible. I was so used to light pollution from living in cities, I never saw the stars in their full glory. My heart warmed at the thought of watching the sky tonight with Penny and Jasmine by my side. Only minutes remained until I'd be with my friends again.

As we pulled up to a large boat shed on the edge of the river, Robert turned off the headlights, plunging us into a dusky darkness.

"Is this it?" I whispered to Zeke.

"Yes. I was given the address by Maggie last night. The place hasn't been used for years— hurricane damage or something like that. Fadel likes the space. According to Maggie, he's been working here in the day, prepping to use it like he did the barn in Victory or our office space in Durango. You know, staff platform, testing equipment, all that stuff. He's staying in a shack down the river, so he shouldn't be back until morning."

"We can go in and get a look around, feel out the situation and map out a plan of attack," Robert rolled up the sleeves of his flannel. His arms were a little more muscular than I'd realized. I felt myself blush and quickly turned my head away.

"I'll text the others and tell them they should come now." I typed up a text to Penny, Jasmine, and Sebastian, informing them of our arrival and sending them the address.

"They'll be here in ten," I held up my phone, smiling.

"Let's get a head start," Zeke said. "I'd cover your ears if I were you guys."

Before I knew what he meant by that, he slammed his body into the door, sending it crashing down to the dirt. Zeke hadn't even broken a sweat.

"Man, you people freak me out," Robert muttered, shaking his head in awe.

"Says the guy who literally changed the weather on us," I whispered in return. He shrugged and led us inside.

We crept through the dark, fumbling around for some sort of light switch. A sound behind us startled me and I grabbed Robert's hand. Realizing it was just Zeke making the floor creak under his weight, I relaxed and embarrassingly tried to pull my hand back. But Robert just gripped it tighter.

Was he flirting or also terrified?

Up in the distance, I observed what appeared to be a small room, maybe a closet of some sort. A dim light shone from the crack in the open doorway. As we crept towards it, I worried that someone was inside.

We approached the door, and I couldn't hear anything behind it. Robert let go of my hand, braced himself, and yanked the handle, revealing a practically empty room. A desk and chair sat in one corner and a single armchair sat in another. A light bulb with a string-pull was the only source of light in the room.

"Weird," I wondered aloud. "Why's the light on?" Feeling around outside the door, I found a plate with three switches. Flipping all of them upward, the boat house lit up. It, like the office, was entirely empty. No boats, no people, no sign of Fadel having been here.

"I'm confused," I said. "There's nothing here."

"Don't be confused," Zeke replied, his voice sounding a lot less sure than usual.

I turned to look at him just as something—or someone—knocked me backwards. I looked up from the floor to see Maggie standing over me, smiling.

"See, this never gets old," she laughed. I turned to see Robert, now in a headlock from Lawrence, the teleporter.

"Zeke," I cried out as Maggie disappeared and shoved me down again, reappearing next to him. "Help us! Do something!"

But he didn't move.

No. This couldn't be right.

"Zeke, I trusted you."

His gaze shifted down to the floor like a hurt puppy.

"Zeke, please help us. You don't have to do this."

He looked up at me again, this time with wet eyes. His hands trembled.

"I'm sorry Alexandra, but I do. He took my sister."

I pushed myself off the ground and started to run at him, unsure what I planned to do, but knowing I needed to make him pay.

"I trusted you, you coward! I trusted you!"

I raised my arm to hit him, but was thrown off balance once again by Maggie, who grabbed me by the forearm and dragged me into the office.

"No!" I yelled as Robert was thrown in with me. The door slammed shut and the click of the lock sealed our fate.

"Let us out!" I screamed as Robert pounded the door and pulled the handle.

"Oh shut up in there!" Lawrence yelled.

"Yeah, be quiet," Maggie added. "We need this place to be nice and comfortable when our other guests arrive."

Other guests...

I fumbled in my back pocket for my phone, but upon pulling it out, I realized there was no cell service in here. There was no way I could warn Sebastian.

They were about to walk into a trap.

CHAPTER TWENTY-ONE

Sebastian

We walked right into a trap.

After years of dealing with a major supervillain, we should have known better. But mistakes were bound to happen, and this mistake just so happened to trap us inside an office the size of a closet with Alexandra and some guy named Robert, who apparently could control the weather.

When we'd arrived, we made our way inside, looking around for any clues and calling out for Alexandra. We heard muffled yelling from behind this metal door, but before we could open it, Fadel's cronies jumped us. The next thing we knew, we were sitting miserably in the brig with the others.

"The Doctor will come see you all in the morning," Margaret Andrews yelled through the door. "I'd get some sleep if I were you. You're going to need it."

"Aghhhh!" I screamed and slammed my arms down on the desk. I threw my body against the door, willing it to open.

"Tried that already," Robert flippantly remarked. "It's super-proof."

I kicked the lock. Repeatedly.

"Can't you use an object in the room? You know, use your powers? Maybe the martial arts won't work. Maybe we need some super strength right now, you know?" Penny was just trying to be helpful, but it stung. No object, no math equation was going to get us out of here. But I didn't want Penny to know that.

I reluctantly picked up a stapler and executed a roundhouse. I nailed the lock at a perfect 36.5-degree angle, but still, nothing. I dropped the stapler in defeat and beat the door with my arms again, screaming out with rage.

"At least we're all together now!" Penny chirped, steering attention away from my obvious failure. "Oh, we definitely need to start with introductions since we have a new teammate! I'll go first."

She smiled at Robert and put her hand on her chest like she was taking an oath.

"My name is Penelope, but my friends call me Penny."

Robert didn't seem to be paying attention. Jasmine huffed and slumped down against the wall.

"If I get out of here alive, remind me to throw myself off a cliff."

* * *

My hands and forearms were bleeding by the time I gave up on trying to open the door. I attempted multiple modes of escape: slamming my body into it, twisting the lock, using a shoe to attack it at a 110-degree angle, and even screaming curse words at the lock. Jasmine took a turn and tried to use her Voice on the lock. Penny tried kicking it herself.

Alexandra and Robert were useless. In fact, Alexandra nodded off and Robert spent twenty minutes folding a gum wrapper into a paper crane. He tossed it to Jasmine's feet, and she glared up at him. One thing had become clear: we were not going to get out on our own.

I sank down to the floor next to Jasmine. Tipping my head back against the wall.

"Are you sure you don't have magic key powers or something? Or like super-burglary?" I asked her, closing my eyes and drumming my fingers on my knee.

Penny and Alexandra had fallen asleep, Penny on the chair and Alexandra at her feet, so I'd decided to quit using force to get the door open. Robert had moved on from his origami and began fiddling with his car keys at the desk, zoning out into what resembled a trance.

"Ugh I wish. I really did think my Voice would work. I hate when it doesn't cooperate, or it's not powerful enough, you know?" She whispered and stared at her hands, as if they had been the offender.

"When you're not powerful enough?" I replied in a hushed tone. I didn't mean to say it aloud, it just sort of popped out.

"Yeah, exactly."

I sighed and slumped even further down the wall. "Don't I know it."

"You compare yourself to Bianca, don't you?"

My head snapped over to face her.

"No, actually. What makes you say that?" My pulse quickened. I wasn't lying. I didn't compare myself to Bee. But I did compare myself to the idea of Bee, of all my friends, really. I compared myself to the textbook standard of *superheroes*.

"Sorry, I didn't mean to assume you were weak. Something seems off with you lately. You seem a lot less sure of your powers and couldn't help but wonder if you were starting to think more like I do. If you also compare yourself to everyone around you."

Before I could reply, she continued.

"And I get it! I'm so grateful that she helped me discover my own strengths. I owe you all for giving me that gift. But it's hard not to compare, especially when I live with the hero who scares the crap out of a literal supervillain."

I smiled softly and laughed a bit.

"Yes, Jas, I'm just like you. But for me, it's not the comparison that really bothers me. I'm happy for you all and I recognize that your strengths are all valuable and unique. That's what makes us all a good team. For me, I have this… concern that my powers aren't strong enough. Like, to be a real hero."

I really didn't want to take this conversation any further, but I knew where we were headed. It had been on the tip of my tongue since I'd told Bianca. I'd almost spilled to Penny and Theo multiple times. Never did I think I'd be having this conversation with Jasmine of all people.

"Jasmine, I have to tell you something. And I don't want it to worry you or the others, so please take it with a grain of salt, ok?"

Concerned flooded into her brown eyes, making them look almost green for a second. For all the times we'd bickered and disagreed, Jasmine felt like a sister to me. I wanted to protect her and Penny almost as much as I wanted to protect myself.

"If you have a secret, I promise I won't tell anyone. I might be a loudmouth, but I know when to keep that mouth shut," she smirked. I believed her.

I waited a few seconds, not exactly sure how to reply, how to accurately justify the words I was about to say. But after brief deliberation, I decided it would be best to keep it simple.

"Jas, I don't have powers."

I let that hang in the air for a moment before continuing.

"I'm just really good at math. And I have a lot of drive and sometimes a little too much courage for my own good. I like getting myself into trouble and I love trying to get myself out of it."

She kept her eyes trained straight ahead, avoiding my gaze.

"Does Bee know?"

"Yes. I told her. But she's the only other person who knows."

I waited for her to ask me the inevitable "Why didn't you tell us?" or "Why have you lied to us?" but those questions never came.

Instead, she snuggled up against me. It was entirely unlike Jasmine. But then again, we were all acting a bit different recently, more vulnerable whether we liked it or not. So maybe this actually *was* like Jasmine, a more authentic version of her.

"So how are you going to get us out of this room?"

"You're not mad?" I replied, a bit surprised to not receive a tongue-lashing at minimum. "You don't have some quick-witted commentary or some insult you could throw at me?"

She laughed. She actually laughed.

"Ok yeah, I'm not going to lie, I feel a little bit betrayed, since you kept something so important from me. But also, I get it. If I were you and I'd taken a leap of faith, pretending to have powers and driving across the country to fight bad guys with my bare hands, I'd be pretty quiet about it, too. So yes, I'm mad and I worry what else you're not telling me, but I also see your passion, and I know your real skills. I know *you*, Sebastian. I can't be mad at that part."

She paused before quickly adding, "You're the best man I know."

"That's generous."

"Well, you are. You're a really good guy, Sebastian. Even if I pretend you aren't. I just like keeping you humble."

I smiled and she smiled back. But then a wave of guilt hit.

"I didn't intend for this lie to continue on for so long. And I promise there isn't anything else. You know everything now."

She nodded.

"You're honorable. If you were lying to us, there must have been a reason. If you can promise that there won't be any more secrets between us, I will stop being mad at you. And you have to tell Theo and Pen, eventually. You can do it on your own time—I won't tell them—but you have to do it. They deserve the truth, too."

"It's very unlike you to accept everything so easily."

"Yeah, well Penny's rubbing off on me."

My smile returned, relieved that my secret was finally out in the open. Or at least, more out in the open.

"So how are you going to help us escape?"

My on-and-off smile faded again. Had she heard a single word I said?

"I just told you, I don't have powers. I can't get us out of this mess."

"I'm not talking about your math skills or your fighting ability. I'm talking about your leadership. How are you going to coach your team out of this? Use that big brain of yours!"

She ruffled my hair and I shoved her hand away.

"Don't do that again," I snapped and she smiled.

"There he is."

I looked around the room, eyes glancing over the sleeping women and landing on Robert.

"Hey," I said out loud, startling him out of his meditative state.

"Yeah?"

"What did you say you could do?"

CHAPTER TWENTY-TWO

Theodore

You know what's worse than being stuck with two people who obviously love each other? Being stuck with two people who obviously *used* to love each other. Or maybe worse, one person who *used* to love the other and one who *still* loves the other. This was my living nightmare.

Bianca had been right, Eric Vardoger and Sebastian Caswell were very different men. Where Sebastian represented the brawn, Eric looked to be the brains. Sebastian was smart, obviously; he was our leader for a reason. But Eric *looked* the part. I couldn't see him in battle, but I could see him planning it.

However, there was one strong similarity between the two: they both looked at Bianca like she was the only girl in the world. And that was bad.

Bianca, on the other hand, seemed more bewildered than anything. I couldn't get a fair read on her emotions, if there was anything still left in the old love-tank for Eric. But seeing the way he acted around her, I got a bad feeling that something awkward was coming down the pike.

As he led us through downtown, turn after turn, his eyes sparkled and his stupid face didn't stop smiling. I wanted to hate him, since he was a threat to my best friend's relationship and because he was a freaking teleporter, but I also saw why she liked him. He was just plain *nice*.

"Ok, so the apartment is right down here," he said, taking us down one last street. Little row houses lined the block, with polished benches and glowing streetlamps dotting the way. It was Americana at its finest. Small town America, and in a much better way than that stupid Falcon Creek. I would never stop hating that place.

He unlocked the door to townhouse #104 and led us inside. The place wasn't large, but it was more furnished than our entire house. Wooden bookshelves lined the walls and rugs covered every square inch of the floor. Oversize armchairs and little mismatched side tables dotted the room, hugging the literature-covered walls. There was even a fireplace— a huge stone one that climbed up to the ceiling. It was like I had walked into a twenty-something girl's fantasy.

Maybe Sebastian and I should *both* be worried about this guy.

"I don't think anyone else is home," Eric said, taking his shoes off and hanging his jacket up on a wooden coat rack.

"Anyone else?" Bianca asked. "You live with others?"

"Yep. My cousin Benjamin and his wife, Marie. And their eleven-year-old daughter, Sophia. They took me in when I got back here."

Of course he has a niece. Women love men who are good with kids.

"I thought you said you sent your family north?" Bianca settled into one of the plush chairs.

A small tabby cat came plunking down the stairs and Bianca gasped. *Geez, this man has everything.*

"That's Paris. He's Sophia's." Eric grinned proudly.

"I had a cat, back in Victory. Or at least we had one living in our backyard."

"Well, there you go, a new friend to remind you of your old home!" *Oh, come on.*

"Ok, so you live with your family, but they also apparently went north?" I cut in. I couldn't take any more of the goo-goo eyes.

"Yes. My parents are a few hours from here, north as I said before. I didn't know of any… others… in my hometown. But I did know of some here, so I reached out to Ben, and he told me I could crash. He wasn't going to leave, even with my parents insisting. His work is important to him."

"That's so nice of him to let you stay," Bianca replied.

"It was, but I think having me here helps them feel safe, too. Sophia is starting to show some skills, if you know what I mean."

"Oh man," I leaned back in my chair. How many of us were out there?

"Yeah, she's been talking to Paris. And birds. And all sorts of other animals."

"Do they talk back to her?" I asked, genuinely curious, forgetting for a moment that I was supposed to be hating him.

"I wouldn't know," he shrugged. "But they sure do like her. They're constantly showing up at the door."

"Sounds like it could be something," Bianca replied. I loved that Penny's optimism seemed to have rubbed off on her. Either that or she was extra agreeable around Eric. I hoped it was the former.

"Ben thinks it's all just a game. He says she's going through 'a phase.' But Marie thinks she's…well…like me."

"And what do you think?"

"Well, I can't know for sure, but at the very least, I can help keep her hidden here."

We nodded and let silence hang in the air for a moment.

"Let's get right to it," I finally said, jumping into the thick of things. "We're here because Bianca thinks you can help us take down Fadel. She wants you to come with us to Louisiana or some other mosquito-infested hellscape to meet up with our friends. From there, we'd come up with some completely insane plan and then use that plan to off Fadel so he can't torture kids anymore. What do you say?"

I stood up and extended my hand to him to shake. He didn't take it. "Yeah, that's a no."

Bianca's head snapped towards him faster than a bullet from a gun. "What do you mean, no? We came all the way out here to get you."

Fire on the way! Get out the popcorn.

"Get me?"

"Yeah," she said, pushing her hair back behind one ear. But this time, she wasn't flirting, she was agitated. "We want you to come with us. We need you to come with us."

"I was under the impression you came out here because you were following me and wanted to stay here with me. Like we'd talked about back in Victory."

I tried so hard not to laugh. Was this guy for real?

"If I was coming all the way out here to stay with you, why would I have brought Theo?"

That one got me. I broke out laughing.

Bee's eyes snapped towards me, pleading for assistance. A part of me wanted to say, "forget it," get back in the car, and leave. That was the part of me that wanted to help Sebastian. But I knew that this whole ordeal was bigger than just my friends' love lives. We had a higher calling than small-town hero stuff, complicated relationships, and friendship. Whether I liked it or not, Eric mattered in the master plan. Losing his support wasn't an option.

"Ok I know it sounds absurd, but we need as much help as we can get," I said, supporting Bianca. "We've tracked him to a new location; we have friends tailing him right now. We've even got a guy on the inside who's confirmed the location. All we need now is to hop in the van and go."

"I have a life here, Theo," Eric was starting to get a bit heated too, but he definitely covered it better than Fire-pants Williams or myself.

"We get in, defeat the bad guy, get out. You could be back here in two weeks, tops," I said, in one final attempt of persuasion. *Maybe we should have brought Jas.*

"Bee, I thought you understood that I came here to protect others. I'm here for their defense, not to go on the offense. I can't abandon them."

"I did the same thing for a long time. I spent months protecting Victory from Fadel and his minions," Bianca replied. "But when he left, I knew I couldn't just sit back and let him destroy another city, take more hostages."

Her voice shook, causing me to look back at her, concerned. Tiny flames skirted around her fingers. Eric saw them, too. What Eric probably didn't see, however, were the few tiny beads of ice that hit the floor, only noticeable if you knew what you were looking for.

"He took *children*, Eric. We got them home safe, but if it hadn't been for us, who knows what would have happened to them. Would you want him to take your niece?"

"No," he argued, frustrated. "That's why I'm here and not in Victory or Louisiana or who knows where. I'm here to protect her."

"Ok but sitting around waiting for him to show up doesn't make you a hero, it makes you a coward," I added, pushing back.

He stood up sharply and glared me down. He didn't intimidate me. Nice guy trying to play tough guy didn't really suit him. I was used to dealing with Sebastian, or Jasmine for that matter, not a nice kid with glasses.

"Excuse me?"

"I just don't think you're actually helping anyone," I continued, shrugging coolly. "Fadel's across the country, he's not in small town Utah. Everyone here is safe. The only reason he went south anyway is because he thought *you* went south. He doesn't even know you're here."

"But he *does* know where I am," Eric replied.

Bianca and I listened, confused. This pulled her back together, back to reality. Both the fire and ice disappeared from her hands.

"But how?"

"I keep seeing him, I swear. I think he's watching me. He never seems to notice that I've also seen him. But he's definitely been following me."

"I don't understand how that's possible. I told you before, he's in Louisiana, we know this for a fact."

"He learned my teleportation. Or at least his staff did. Maybe he's in two places at once."

"Can your powers take you that far?" I asked, specifically avoiding the exact word for his power. I still hated teleporters. Maybe that's one of the reasons I hated Fadel so much. Other than him being the evilest villain on planet Earth.

Eric settled back into his seat.

"No, only a mile or two at a time. But maybe his is more powerful."

"He does have another teleporter now," Bianca said, closing her eyes and thinking it through. "Maybe Lawrence's powers combined with yours and gave him that ability."

"Maybe. But I'm serious. I've seen him at least half a dozen times. He knows I'm here."

Suddenly, the sound of a key in the front door's lock jolted us to attention. In came a man, maybe in his mid-thirties, a woman about the same age, and a young girl.

"Hey, Eric!" the man said. "Who are your friends?"

"This is Bianca. I've told you a bit about her."

"A bit? You haven't shut up about her since you got here!" The woman gushed, and Bianca's face flushed red.

"And this is her friend," he gestured towards me.

"Theo," I held up a hand for self-identification. "Bianca and I drove here from Victory to see Eric."

"Wow," the woman replied. "You're pretty popular, Eric! House guests! And a note! Both in the same afternoon!"

Eric looked confused.

"What note?"

"We just found a note taped to the front door with your name on it," she held up a half sheet of lined paper, folded.

Eric reached out for it.

"That's weird, it wasn't here when we got home a little bit ago."

He unfolded it slowly and then read it over a few times. We all sat in silence for a moment.

"What is it?" Bianca asked impatiently, getting up to read it over his shoulder.

"You know how I said Fadel knew I was here? I think he knows you're here too."

He handed me the note.

5273 Downley Road Upton Valley, UT

Reservation under Williams

Tomorrow night, 8 pm in the lobby. Don't be late.

CHAPTER TWENTY-THREE

Penny

"Y ou've gotta concentrate a little more, man."

Sebastian's coaching style had always been the same: nothing short of relentless. But even though we were used to it, this particular training was getting to be a bit much.

"I really am trying my best here. I don't know how to do these… things… you guys do."

Robert shifted his weight and rotated his wrists like he was about to perform a magic trick. He seriously had no clue what he was doing. I myself blushed from second-hand embarrassment.

"Ok, well, focus on being grounded," Sebastian said, running his hand through his hair.

"Trying…"

"Have you tried locking focus on the door? That's where we want to—"

"Yes, I said I'm trying!" Robert snapped back.

"Sebastian!" I spat out, a bit louder than I'd intended. Luckily, it got his attention, and he took a deep breath. "The poor man is wearing khakis. He's trying his best. Maybe it's just not going to work."

"Maybe we should start thinking through alternative options," Alexandra said, ever the voice of reason.

Sebastian nodded a few times.

"No, you're right. I'm sorry, Robert."

"Let's keep going. I can do it," Robert replied, steadying himself again.

"Ok if you're sure," Sebastian replied, putting a hand on his shoulder. "I don't want to force you."

"You're not," Robert looked up at the ceiling. "I think I'm just concentrating on the wrong thing."

"What do you mean?" I asked.

"Well, they want us alive, right?"

"Yeah, I guess so? But how does that help us?"

"They wouldn't let us die in this locked room. So, if I caught the entire building on fire, they'd take us outside."

"My gosh, you sound like Bianca," Alexandra said. "I knew you two would get along."

"If you can get a lightning strike on the building, we could start a fire and force an evac," Sebastian said.

"Exactly, and once we get outside, we can make a break for it. Fight them off if we need to, but essentially, we'd be out so we could run."

"Alright, well if you're up for it, let's try," Sebastian rolled up his sleeves.

"Tell me what to do, coach."

I smiled. Few things in this world brought me more joy than seeing my friends in their element. This time, something inside me knew that Robert and Sebastian's plan was going to work.

"Focus on your core. Everything you want to make happen on the outside starts with a spark on the inside. Let it warm you and build upwards and outwards. Concentrate on that core, not your hands."

"I'm feeling it," Robert said, clenching his fists a bit. I took a step back towards the wall, giving him more space.

"Great! Now move that energy up and out. Concentrate on your target. We don't need it to hit the door. Think of a bigger target, imagine the roof."

Robert closed his eyes and clenched his jaw.

"That's it, concentrate, Robert. You've got this."

Suddenly a deafening *crack* shook the room. Robert's eyes shot open.

"What was that?" Alexandra gasped.

"I think I hit the roof."

"How do you know they'll get us out?" Jasmine asked, clearly panicked. "How do you know we didn't just lock ourselves in a burning building?"

"Because the only thing scarier than being stuck in a burning building is the wrath of Fadel," Sebastian answered. "His minions wouldn't risk our deaths."

"Oh gosh, I hope you're right..." Alexandra wrapped her arms around herself in a comforting self-hug.

But he'd been right. Within a minute or two, the sounds of scurrying feet outside drove our attention to the door.

"Get ready, guys," Sebastian said. "Alexandra, get in the back. Robert, you join her back there, just to be safe. Jasmine, take the middle. Penny, move up by me."

I skirted around Robert and moved up next to Sebastian. I positioned myself into a stronger stance, bending a bit at the knees and rocking onto my toes with a slow pulse.

When the door opened, we attacked.

* * *

With every kick, punch, and piece of metal flown across the room by

Jasmine's Voice, we slowly yet steadily made our way outside.

Luckily, we only had to deal with Margaret and Lawrence. Zeke had disappeared. With an essentially three-on-two battle, it was not pre-determined that we would succeed. The two minions put up a fight, and their powers made it difficult to get more than a few steps in at a time. I'd been knocked down at least three times and poor Alexandra was in tears, begging them to stop and let us go.

Right outside the door, we could see Alexandra's rental car and our van, right next to each other, waiting for our escape. We could taste freedom.

"Alexandra, Robert, you two should make a break for it," Sebastian swung at a disappearing Lawrence.

Robert nodded and grabbed Alexandra's wrist, dragging her along behind him as he made a sprint towards the vehicles. But suddenly, Zeke appeared and stepped in their path, almost as if he'd teleported there like Lawrence.

Robert stopped quickly, causing Alexandra to crash into him from behind at full speed, knocking both of them to the ground. I turned to see Sebastian and Jasmine in the thick of it and made the impulsive choice to turn and run towards Alexandra and Robert instead.

"No!" I screamed as Zeke moved towards them.

"Zeke, please!" I heard Alexandra cry. "Please don't do this."

Maybe three yards from them, I stopped dead in my own tracks. Zeke wasn't moving towards them; he was moving past them.

"Get up and run," he said to them in a low voice I could just barely hear. "I'll hold them off."

"Zeke," Alexandra replied in a whispered, choked cry. "Come with us. Please, we can help you get your sister back. But please don't return to Fadel."

Zeke ignored her.

"When I run at them, I want you to go."

"No—"

"Go!" Zeke snapped and then sprinted towards the group. Before she even had a chance to consider any other option, Robert grabbed Alexandra's upper arm and pulled her up off the dirt. I ran towards them and snatched her other arm at the wrist. While she sobbed, we dragged her towards the car.

As we shoved her in, I looked back to see Sebastian and Jasmine coming our way.

"Start the van!" Sebastian yelled.

I felt in my jacket pocket and fumbled for the keys, running around to the driver's side of the van while Robert got in the sedan. I threw myself into the seat and started the engine. Sebastian and Jasmine ripped open the sliding door and jumped in the back, tumbling on top of each other.

We didn't even bother to shut the sliding door behind them. I just threw the van in reverse and sped off, trailing behind Robert as we drove through the winding bayou and away from yet another burning building.

CHAPTER TWENTY-FOUR

Bianca

A casino.

5273 Downley Road, more commonly known as Lone Wolf Casino.

"There's no way we're actually going to meet up with Fadel, right?" Theo exclaimed, as flustered as I'd ever seen him.

Eric said "no" the exact same moment I said "yes." Every head in the room whipped around to face me.

"If Fadel is here, we need to figure out why."

"So, you want us to walk into a trap?" Theo actually seemed mad at me at this point.

"There are three of us. And besides, he says to meet in the lobby. It's a public place; we will be fine."

I didn't know that for sure. In fact, I doubted the validity of my own statement. But Theo needed to agree and if that required me to lie to him, so be it. Eric looked both uncomfortable and frustrated.

"So first you ask me to get in the car and come with you to find Fadel in Louisiana and now you want me to get in the car and come with you to find Fadel in Upton Valley?"

Theo and I both stood for a moment in silence.

"Yeah, I mean, I guess so," I shrugged. "Look, it needs to happen.

You said you wanted to keep Sophia safe, right? Well, if Fadel *did* write this note, that means he knows where you live. In that case, she's no longer safe anyway. The best thing you can do for her is face him. So yeah, I don't want to do it, but at the very least *I* am going to the meet-up spot."

"I'll come with you," Theo sighed, putting a hand on my shoulder. He really didn't want this, but I knew he'd have to come around if I threatened going alone. "I promised I'd help you, so if this is what you want, I'll come."

I smiled up at him.

"Thank you."

He squeezed my shoulder and released it, returning his arms into their classic no-nonsense fold across his chest. His eyes now locked on Eric.

"Fine."

"Really?" I asked, surprised to see him agree so easily.

"Yes to the casino meet-up. No to the Louisiana trip."

I could work with that, at least for now. Besides, if it really *was* Fadel, we could deal with him now and maybe wouldn't *need* Eric to come with us back there.

But "need" was a strong word. Maybe I wanted him to come whether we needed him or not. Maybe he really would be a good part of our team. But on the other hand, maybe it was for the best to keep him and Sebastian apart.

My brain hurt, but my heart hurt more. Why was this so complicated?

"Ok," I said, shaking the negative thoughts away. "We will go to the casino tomorrow night and see what Fadel wants."

"Ok."

"Ok," I said again, not sure why.

Eric opened his mouth, presumably to say more, but shut it again and promptly left the room. I looked over at Theo, who shrugged. Heat filled my cheeks and my head began to feel a bit lighter as I booked it out of the room and followed Eric as he ascended the stairs.

"What were you going to say?"

"It doesn't matter," He continued climbing the steps, not looking back at me.

"Why does there have to be so much conflict? You were pretty happy to see me when we first found each other. Now, you seem annoyed that I'm here at all. What changed?"

"I'm just trying to process all of this."

"In a good way or a bad way?"

He stopped mid-step.

"I don't know."

"Are you happy I'm here or not?" I said, a bit bold, even for me.

He sighed and finally turned to look down at me. His blue eyes looked like the ocean, but with a depth of concern creating a grey-ish haze.

"Truthfully, I don't know about that either."

"And why is that?"

His face grew more serious, his mouth settling into a frown and his eyebrows furrowed. He lowered his voice.

"This reunion isn't exactly what I had thought it would be. You showed up here after so long, which is what I've been dreaming of. But you also came with someone else."

I laughed.

"Oh, *Theo*? No, no. Theo's just a friend. He's got it bad for our other friend, Penny. That's not something to worry about."

"No, I'm not talking about you being in love with him. I'm not blind, you obviously aren't attracted to him. I'm looking at the bigger picture here, Bianca."

"Which is?"

"You found a new home and new people. You seem… so different. But at the same time, I can't help but notice that you have the same smile, the same confidence. No matter how much my mind doubts it, my heart seems to know that you're still the same girl I fell in love with."

My heart skipped a beat and picked up speed. Something drew me to him, like something from our past bound us together. Like no time had passed since we said our goodbyes, since he'd held me in his arms.

"Bianca," he whispered.

His eyes darted around my face, from my eyes to my mouth, back to my eyes.

"Eric, I—"

But I couldn't continue, he teleported, just one stair down. But this step put our bodies inches from one another. He grabbed my waist, his hands pulled me up a step towards him, into him. Before I realized what was happening, his mouth landed on mine. Our bodies pressed against each other, the contact melting me against his chest. His warm, familiar embrace pulled me in, physically and emotionally.

We'd been transported back to Fadel's farm, young and foolish. He would pull away and give me a soft smile and I would giggle awkwardly. Then one of us would make a joke or propose a race back to the compound. And then we'd part ways, him back to his apartment in the city, me back to mine. And I'd go to bed thinking of him, that warmth still lingering on my lips, begging for more. All that in one kiss. It was so clear, our past, present, and future. My first love.

But then it hit me: Sebastian. Eric was my first love, but he hadn't been my only.

I pulled away.

"Eric, I can't. Not right now."

I couldn't look into his eyes. I couldn't handle that.

"I don't understand."

"I just can't."

Before Eric could say anything else, Theo appeared at the bottom of the stairwell.

"Hey, you guys down to get dinner? I just found out that Sophia *also* loves pizza. Definitely gotta do that, am I right?"

"Uh, yeah," Eric replied, clearing his throat "Sounds great. I need to go change my shirt." He disappeared, teleporting away, presumably towards his room.

Theo disappeared too, returning to the living room. I stood alone on the stairs, unsure where to go from here.

My whole body trembled. I felt hot, like I might pass out or set something on fire. I felt cold, like a sadness typhoon had just made landfall in my heart. I felt confused and angry and embarrassed, all at the same time.

I crossed my arms over my chest, trying to form a barrier between me and the outside world, between my heart and the man upstairs.

As my left hand crossed over my body, a little fireball shot out, falling to the carpeted step, setting it alight. I quickly stomped it out, cringing at the hiss and the icy footprint I'd accidentally created.

Maybe coming to Utah wasn't a good idea. Maybe seeing him again would break me. At that moment, I wished I'd also been blessed with teleportation powers so I could send myself all the way back to Victory.

CHAPTER TWENTY-FIVE

Theodore

Just as the note said, the front desk had reserved rooms under Williams. But they weren't just any rooms. The reservation happened to be the penthouse suite.

When we walked in, we were greeted by a small lounge area with a stone fireplace and massive windows on either side, facing the mountains. The sun set behind them, creating one of the most stunning red skies I'd ever seen. To the right, we found a kitchen and dining room, the table set with crystal and China. To the left, a series of bedrooms lined the hall. Each one had its own bathroom, complete with a Jacuzzi tub and a California king. The last time I'd seen a penthouse, it had been deserted and trashed. This, on the other hand: pure luxury.

"Guys have you seen this?" I asked, entering one of the bedrooms.

Laid out on the bed were two tuxedos and a floor length gown. On top sat a note card that just read "Welcome to Lone Wolf, Bianca, Eric, and Theodore!"

"This is kind of creepy," Eric said, picking up the note card.

"Everything about this has been creepy. The tux is the least of my worries," I ran a hand across the fabric. I wasn't one for getting dressed up. Very few times in my life forced me into a suit. I wasn't sure I'd even seen a tuxedo before. I was built for gym shorts and running shoes. But this was something different, something that drew me in.

"Well don't stand around unless you want to see me naked," I snatched the tux up by the hanger.

"Wait, you're not actually going to put it on?" Eric asked.

This guy was a bit of a buzzkill.

"Yep, and you should too if you want to blend in. Didn't you see those people in the lobby? Something big and fancy's going on and I'm absolutely going to be a part of it if it means free drinks."

After twenty minutes or so, Bianca finally emerged from her bedroom. I shot up, smoothing the tails of my jacket.

Bianca gingerly touched her rhinestone gown. The black dress fit her form perfectly. It curved around her waist and hips nicely. The neckline came up to her collarbone, but instead of sleeves, a light layer of sheer black fabric draped off each shoulder, exposing her long neck and freckles. The whole thing sparkled as she moved. She'd done her hair up in a little twist, with some front pieces curled to frame her face. A small pearl hairpiece in the shape of a bird sat above the twist. But despite looking spectacular, there was a sadness in her eyes, one that said, "I know I look beautiful, but it's Sebastian I want on my arm tonight."

Since that wish was nothing more than a fantasy, I extended my arm to her instead. She smiled softly and took it.

"You look wonderful," I whispered. I don't know why I decided to remain so hushed, but she whispered back, making it a bit less weird.

"Pen's a lucky girl. You're quite handsome yourself."

I flushed a little.

Eric came out and I felt Bianca's body seize up.

"You ok, Bee?" I whispered once again. She watched as Eric fastened his watch. He'd put on glasses, which when combined with the tux, made him look a little goofy. Not much of a Bond, but that was alright.

He wore the look with an endearing awkwardness. I could tell that Bianca definitely didn't mind.

She watched him closely, smiling. Her eyes scanned up and down his body, as if looking for some imperfection.

And then I noticed it. Her hands fused together, just for a moment. Her continence held firm, but her fingers gave her away. They twitched as she tried to pull them apart.

For Bianca Williams, ice only meant one thing.

Something had changed. I didn't know what, but something had happened between the two of them and it made her upset. This wasn't the Bianca I knew, and that terrified me.

"Yeah," she gave a little extra umph and pulled her hands apart, fumbling for her purse as a cover. "I'm good." She smiled up at me, daring me not to ask. I pushed the memory away and clapped my hands together.

"Alright ladies," I said, causing Eric to shoot me a confused glance. "Let's go see our favorite villain!"

CHAPTER TWENTY-SIX

After the initial panic settled, Jasmine and I coordinated via phone to meet an hour away, at a seafood place on the water aptly named "The Boondock."

"If I'm going to get chased down and killed by Fadel, I'd at least like to die with a drink in my hand," Jasmine had said. She wasn't wrong, that *would* be a much better way to go out.

As we sat around the table, sipping our drinks and eating our fried grouper bites, we also tiptoed around the elephant in the room: so, what now?

"Well first things first, I think we need to consolidate," Penny said. "You guys should join us in the van so we can all stay together."

"What about the rental?" Robert asked. "I don't have the money to pay the major fines associated with a missing vehicle."

"Jasmine will take care of it," Sebastian said, and Jasmine smiled.

We sat in silence again and I took a long sip of my Coke.

"So..." Jasmine started. "The real question is this: do we stake out around here or do we head west after Bianca and Theo?"

"Wait, go out to them? But they're supposed to be coming out to us," I replied. The whole point of their mission was to rendezvous here, with an extra soldier. What would be the point of going to them if the problem was here?

"I don't know if we *can* do anything until we hear back from them," Penny said, checking her phone again. "I'm worried about what they might have gotten into. We haven't heard from them for over 48 hours! I haven't gotten a good morning text or a goodnight call or even a photo of a stray cat in two days! Nothing!"

"They're probably fine," I said, trying my best to sound reassuring. Truthfully, I'd been worried too. "I think we need to let them finish their task and come to us."

"I just don't see the point in sitting around waiting for someone else to do something. I want to keep moving," Jasmine said, rather impatiently. At this point, I'd learned not to get offended when Jasmine disagreed with me, but it was still awkward. It was hard to push back against someone who could literally persuade you to jump off a bridge or marry your cousin.

"But we don't know if he's gone anywhere. He could be staying put. We need to be where he is, Jas, even if that means holding out here." Penny replied. "We can't get ahead of ourselves and assume he's heading west. Besides, he doesn't know that Bianca and Theo went out there to find Eric. As far as he knows, Eric is nearby, right?"

"I don't think he knows where Eric is. And also, I don't know if he cares. What's one disgruntled former employee compared to a possible population of them down here? He's obviously here for a reason," Sebastian said. "I'm guessing he has his eyes on something here. This is an oddly specific location for him to just magically select."

"He's probably staying here," Penny said, agreeing with Sebastian. I agreed with them too, but wanted to play mediator, as Jasmine was starting to get a bit frazzled with a 'everyone disagrees with me' attitude.

"But we burned down his hiding spot. He's going to have to go elsewhere, won't he?" I asked, trying my best to remain levelheaded.

I swallowed my growing fear that Fadel was on the move once again, possibly headed somewhere it would be harder to find him this time. But the truth was, I didn't want to leave, not until I knew Zeke and his sister were safe. If Fadel found out that he helped us escape…

I remembered the guilt I'd experienced when he went after the Meadows kids. Especially once he had gotten rid of me and took the kids somewhere I couldn't protect them. Thank goodness for my friends. I couldn't let Fadel take more children.

"Her name is Emily," Zeke had told me back that day on the farm. He'd finished a training session with Fadel, and I'd come out to help tidy things up. He stuck around to chat. I'd always wondered if there was a particular reason he'd been so eager to spend that time alone with me.

"She's twelve," he said. "It's just us now. We both lived with my aunt after my parents died. Well, actually, she's still with my aunt. I came here to help her. If I can use these skills, this strength, to prove my worth, maybe I can use this as a springboard. Maybe I can get a great job and can finally afford a place, just for the two of us. I could pay to send her to private school."

"Is she not happy where she is now? With your aunt?" I'd asked.

"She's fine there," he said. "But I'd love it if we could just be us. I love my aunt, but I've always known that I was supposed to take care of Emily. I'm the man of the house now, that's what my mother told me after Dad died. She knew that she was sick. She knew this would fall back on me. I need to step up and support her. Em's the only thing I've got now. I'm here because of her."

Zeke had always had the kindest heart. Where did it all go wrong? *Fadel.*

That's how it all changed. Fadel brainwashed him. Him and Maggie, and all the people I cared about. Fadel was the reason that Zeke could look me in the eyes and lie to my face, the reason Maggie could hijack a plane and not care if I lived or died. They'd been transformed by empty promises and their own desires for justice and peace.

Fadel promised them the moon and stars, and the only thing they had to do in return was to 'live virtuously and fight for a noble cause'. They'd been deceived and they still didn't know it.

But maybe Zeke did.

Yeah, he tricked us. He played Judas and handed us over. But in the end, he let us go.

"He has my sister," he'd said. He still did everything for Emily. But if Fadel had actually taken his sister… then he must know the truth. What he'd said to me in the hotel, in the car, it was all true. He really had woken up. There was still hope.

Penny was the first to notice my tears.

"Alexandra!" she cried. "What's wrong?"

"We need to find Fadel," I said. The tears kept flowing. My face started to feel warmer; my voice shook a bit. "We need to find him as soon as humanly possible."

"Hey, hey we will," Sebastian said, putting his arm around me. Jasmine grabbed my hand and stroked it softly, shushing me quietly. My body obeyed her Voice and a wave of serenity washed over me.

"We will find him," Sebastian said. "And we will follow him. Or we will stay and keep an eye on him."

"No," I said, wiping my eyes. "No, we can't do that. As you said earlier, he's here for a reason. For each location he's ever chosen, what had been the catalyst?"

"Each spot has had more people with powers he can take," Jasmine replied.

"Exactly," Sebastian replied. "There have to be more people like us here. And they're vulnerable."

"What if we tried to get them to fight with us?" Penny asked. "Maybe they would join us!"

"But think about it," I replied. "All the people who have worked for him fell for his lies. He promised them justice. He let them be heroes. He's persuasive, cunning. The longer Fadel is here, the more they are at risk."

"But I'm also persuasive, I can just talk them out of it," Jasmine said between bites of fries. "I can talk them onto our side."

"Ok so we build our army, but Fadel moves onto the next place. And the next place. Meanwhile, we are just pulling more young people away from their families to help us take down one man and his cronies. No, they're better off if we leave them alone and let them live their lives in peace."

"Are you saying you'd have been better off without Fadel coming into your life and without us rescuing you? Are you saying you'd rather not be here?" Jasmine asked, the bite in her voice stinging my whole body.

"No… I mean… yeah, my life would have been better if Fadel had never entered it."

"Even though now you're helping save people from him? What you're doing now isn't worth your comfort?" Jasmine put down a fry and locked in on me, her eyes piercing mine.

"Well, no, it's worth it. All of the pain was worth what I'm doing now," I replied, as calmly as possible. "But this isn't about me. I wouldn't wish what I went through on anyone else. Just because I came out of this better doesn't mean we should subject others to the same thing. Especially children."

"Children?" Sebastian asked. "The Meadows kids were a one-off."

"No," I said. "He took Zeke's sister. I don't know if she has powers or not, but he took her. That's one more innocent life he has in his clutches. I can't sit back and let him continue to hurt people. I'm tired of chasing him place to place, hoping each and every person he takes is the last. It's never the last!"

I could feel the salty sting of tears forming in my eyes again.

"First it was Eric. Then it was Bianca. Then it was Zeke, then Molly and James. Now it's Zeke's sister. All the while, he still has Maggie—my best friend. I *care* about these people, Sebastian. I know you care deeply about Bianca. Imagine that love you feel for her times ten. He didn't just take one person I love, he took so, so many."

The tears started flowing again.

"I'm not letting him take anyone else, and I don't have powers, so I need you to help me. We need to get him away from anyone else he can take and then we need to destroy his entire operation. Please," I begged.

Sebastian pulled me into a hug and I sobbed. The waitress tried coming up to the table, but Penny discreetly shooed her away.

"We won't let Fadel take more prisoners," Sebastian said. "And if that means getting him away from here, that's what we'll do. We'll enact Plan C. We won't stay here and we won't go out to Utah. Instead, we will lure him far away from what he came here for and get him to chase something else."

"How do you suppose we're going to do that?" Jasmine laughed. "You want him to chase after us again? I don't know if you remember, but that was freaking horrifying."

"Yes, actually," Sebastian said. "That's exactly what I want. We're going to keep playing cat and mouse. But this time, I want us to be the mouse."

"But I thought he came here for Eric," Jasmine said.

"He knows Eric isn't here," Alexandra said. "He has Zeke with him and Zeke's known that information for a while. He's here for someone else, likely multiple someones. Besides, he wouldn't pick up and come all this way just for Eric, especially since he has Lawrence now, who has the same powers as Eric."

"So why would we make a good mouse? Or one worth chasing. He left us in Victory, remember?" Penny asked, innocently. "He doesn't care about us."

"He cares about one of us," Sebastian smiled. "So much so, he was willing to make national headlines by downing a plane."

We all looked at Robert, who hadn't spoken this entire time. Sebastian had a wild look in his eye now, one that I knew meant a very big, very dangerous idea.

"Hey Robert, how do you feel about being bait?"

CHAPTER TWENTY-SEVEN

Bianca

The so-called "lobby" of this casino hotel was far more elaborate than what you'd normally see in a hotel, even a nice one. The check-in desks stood against a giant mural, embellished with gold and ivory detailing. It depicted various scenes from *The Odyssey*, with Odysseus' ship prominently displayed in the center. Chairs and couches were strewn elegantly throughout the main reception area. A full refreshment stand of not only coffee, tea, and water, but also cheeses, fruit, and chocolates, sodas, juices, and even decanters of wine and brandy covered an elaborate multi-tier display. A large bar and lounge area sat off to one side. This was where we decided to wait for Fadel.

I stirred my rum and Coke with a straw while Eric gulped down two glasses of water. Theo moved on to his second old-fashioned and checked the time on his phone.

"It's almost eight. He should be here any minute."

Eric nervously tapped his foot. His eyebrows furrowed as he looked at his watch, acting as though he didn't trust Theo's judgment of time. He looked more nervous than I felt.

"Hey," I said, "We've got this. We're a great team."

He looked at me expectantly, pushing up his glasses like he wanted to see me more clearly, not believing what I'd just said.

Oof, I hadn't meant to say, "we're a great team," or anything close for that matter.

I was still reeling from what happened back at Eric's cousin's place. The conflicting emotions sent me into a complex spiral. I felt guilty, letting something like that happen behind Sebastian's back. I felt angry at Eric for kissing me. I felt sad because someone, maybe multiple someones, would be hurt in the end. I felt scared, for many reasons.

Focus on the mission. Focus on the mission.

"I just mean that you, Theo, and I are all tough," I backpedaled. "We can manage Fadel. Especially in a public place like this. If anything goes awry, we just get out of here as fast as we can. We can get away."

"I hope you're right," he replied, perhaps disappointed by my verbal turn.

"She is," Theo said a little too defensively, before changing the subject. "I feel like Sean Connery in this suit, I could take Fadel on myself."

And it was at that exact moment that a lanky, thin, bearded man exited the elevator and began strolling towards us.

* * *

All three of us stood up. My brain gasped for air. He was here. In Utah.

He was also alone and without a staff. That made him defenseless. This might be easier than I'd anticipated.

Before I could speak, he cut me off.

"Take a seat, Miss Williams, I'm not here to fight you, I'm here to talk." His voice was gruff, gruffer than I'd remembered. He also looked tired, worn out.

"I'm not going to do anything you say," I snapped. My hands became heated now. I could end this conversation quickly, with one swift motion. But for some inexplicable reason, I gave him the grace of an explanation.

"I see the problem," he said, stopping in front of us, smiling. "You think I'm malicious."

"Well duh," Theo said. "We don't just think it, we know it."

"But you see, there's the rub. If you think I'm malicious, you must also think my name is Chakir Fadel. Which, I'm sorry to tell you, it's most certainly not."

CHAPTER TWENTY-EIGHT

Jasmine

Alexandra's hands shook as she dialed the phone. I concentrated on her trembling wrists and willed them to calm. Her fingers slowly found the courage with each button pressed, but her mind held her back.

"I don't know about this."

"Yes, you do, you're going to get on the phone and tell him where we're going. And if it doesn't seem to work, you're going to hand the phone to me, and I'll take care of it."

I didn't love the idea of getting on the phone myself. I'd gotten rather good at using my Voice face-to-face, and I'd spent a lot of time last year trying to perfect the over-the-phone style magic, but after I'd realized that I could move objects or even people non-verbally, I shifted my focus to that skill instead. That said, my over-the-phone Voice was rather rusty. Still, I believed that if Alexandra failed, which was certainly possible, if not probable, I could step in. But Alexandra was the best first choice for the job, anyway, seeing as her relationship may be more convincing than even my powers.

I willed her to hit 'call' and when her finger pressed the button, she gasped and looked up at me. I replied with a shrug.

"It's ringing!" she whispered. I urged her on.

Stay calm.

I heard the line click through the speaker.

"Alexandra?"

Zeke's deep voice sent shivers down my spine. We really *were* crazy enough to call the enemy and walk right into the trap.

"Zeke?" Alexandra whispered into the phone.

"Alexandra, what the heck are you doing calling me? Don't you know Fadel is looking for you?"

Alexandra's eyes flashed with panic. I willed her to keep talking.

"Yes, I know. But I'm worried about you. And I want you to come with us."

"You know I can't do that."

"I know you think that, but you have to. You've gotta get out of there."

"I can't just leave. He has my sister. You know that!"

"I know, but I have a plan. You're going to bring Fadel and your sister along."

"What?"

She took a deep breath.

"I want you to tell him where we're going. And that we have Robert. I want you to follow us."

"You *want* him to chase you?"

Alexandra paused and looked at me. I nodded and smiled.

"Yes, I do. I want you guys to follow us. And when we get where we're going, we can help you get your sister to safety. And you, too."

"You're insane," Zeke said. Simple, true. We *were* insane.

'I know."

"Why are you doing this? Why are you telling me your plans?" Zeke sounded like he was spiraling a bit now. "How can you even trust me?

I *betrayed* you, Alexandra. I sold you out."

"You did it for your sister. And I may not know her, but I care about her too. Because I care about you. So yeah, I shouldn't trust you, but I do. I want to give you a second chance. Please, just don't let me down this time."

Silence followed for several beats. For a moment I wondered if he'd hung up.

"Alexandra—"

"Please," she whispered. "Please, it's the only way out of this."

Another long pause.

"Ok. Text me your destination."

"I can do you one better, I'll share my location."

"Are you sure about this?

"No, but we're doing it anyway," she smiled a little. I could see tears starting to form in the corners of her eyes.

"Ok, well share your location and we will see you soon. I just hope you know what you're getting yourself into."

"Me too," she whispered as the line went dead. Then she burst into tears. I didn't try to stop her. Instead, I pulled her into an embrace and held her while she mourned the normal life she kept trying to go back to.

* * *

Clearly for Alexandra's sake, Sebastian organized a distraction. Unfortunately for him, Alexandra had not wanted to participate.

"I'll stay in the car. I could use a nap," she had said when Sebastian proposed a quick training session in the woods.

We'd driven several hours since Alexandra made the call to Zeke, doing so mostly in silence. Sebastian had me pull off a few miles outside of Kingsbury and then led a group of us into a clearing, blocked from the view of the road by a line of trees.

"Ten-minute training session," he said, rolling up his sleeves. I tried pulling my own sleeves further down around my wrists, as both a gesture of defiance and coldness. Despite being in Texas, a state I thought was supposed to be warm all year round, the late Autumn weather became more noticeable the further north we went. It wasn't Victory cold, but we certainly weren't in Louisiana anymore. The hills around us created more wind than I was used to. Theo would have loved it.

"Ok, so you kick us off, Mr. Leader," I said, immediately regretting it when his eyes latched on mine with a hint of betrayal.

Oops. Almost forgot.

"I want to see a bit more of what you've got, Robert," he said, taking the attention off himself.

Robert frowned.

"I don't really want to keep doing this. I don't love leaning into the whole power thing."

Sebastian wanted two things. One, he wanted to avoid his own powers, or lack thereof. Two, he wanted to feel useful, and training Robert would help with that. Sebastian's true powers came from helping others, not in doing great things himself.

"I want to see it, too," I pitched in. Penny looked at me horrified.

I'd just agreed with Sebastian. Not only that, but I was also adding fuel to the fire and making Robert angry. But I honestly didn't care.

"Show us a rain cloud or something. I want to be entertained."

Robert glared at me.

"My powers are not meant for your entertainment."

"Sure, they are. Now be a good student and listen to Sebastian."

Sebastian asked him to concentrate on the sky, the target, and his body. He worked him through the steps he wanted him to take and requested he practice each, one at a time.

Penny was in la la land, twirling around between the trees, kicking leaves as they fell like they were stray blasts coming from Fadel's staff. She executed a back walkover with grace, just for fun.

"Nice, Pen," I said, encouragingly.

"That wasn't me using my powers," she blushed.

"I know, I just thought it was cool. Would you teach me how to do that? I have pretty good balance from surfing, maybe I could figure it—"

Water began to flow over my head, like someone was holding me under a watering can.

"What the heck?" I looked up to see a single, grey cloud hovering over me, pouring gallon after gallon over my back.

I tried to step aside, but it followed me. I frantically looked over at my friends. They stood completely dry. Penny looked horrified. Sebastian looked impressed. Robert...

"Robert!" I barked. "Make it stop!"

He shrugged.

"Don't you shrug at me! *Make it stop!*"

I watched his arms lift up and silence the storm, completely under my control.

"Hey," he said. "Don't do that."

"You're the one who soaked me with your stupid rain cloud!"

"Well, you're the one who told me to make a rain cloud in the first place!"

"Sebastian told you to focus on your target! Were you even listening?"

"Maybe *you* were my target!"

Penny skipped over, landing between us like a wall.

CHAPTER TWENTY-EIGHT

"Hey, it was an accident. Let's keep practicing or go back to the van, ok?"

I grumbled and looked around for something I could use. I whispered to a rock and commanded it to float towards my target. I wiped my wet hair from my face and willed it to inch slowly, steadily towards Robert's stupid face.

"Jas!" Sebastian reached up and snatched it from the air.

"You're no fun."

"Sebastian," Penny interrupted again. "Don't you want to practice?"

He looked at me again, fear clearly visible in his eyes.

"No," he said. "I'm good. I got it all up here."

He tapped his head with his finger.

"But wouldn't it be good to work with some random objects? You know, just to get some real-world experience? It's been so long since you've used something in battle. You've been relying a lot on your martial arts lately. Maybe if you just—"

"I'm cold and wet!" I yelled, helping Sebastian as much as possible while also reminding Robert of how stupid he was for making that rain cloud. "Let's get back on the road. And someone else is driving. I've done far too much for all of you this trip."

CHAPTER TWENTY-NINE

Bianca

Not Fadel? But he looked just like him. Either my eyes or Fadel himself were playing a trick on me.

I mean, he looked a bit more worn than I'd last seen him, but he really did look like the man I'd spent so much time at war with.

This *had* to be Fadel.

"Please," the man gestured towards our seats. "Sit down and let me explain." I hesitated to put myself in such a vulnerable position, but after considering that he appeared defenseless himself, I ultimately chose to take a seat. Eric and Theo followed my lead. The man came and took the fourth chair.

"If you're not Fadel, which I still don't believe, by the way," Theo started. "Who are you?"

"My friends, I *am* Fadel, just not the one you want. Chakir is my older brother. My name is Charles Fadel. I own this hotel."

Charles Fadel?

Did we know Fadel had a brother?

"You're lying," Theo said flippantly and stirred the ice at the bottom of his glass.

The man waved his hand towards a waiter, who rushed over.

"Good evening, Mr. Faber, what can I get you this evening?"

"Could you please bring this lad another drink?"

"Another old fashioned, sir?" The waiter asked Theo.

Theo wordlessly nodded.

"Certainly. And for you, miss?" He looked at me.

"No, I'm fine, thank you." He scurried away and I looked back at the man.

"He said Faber, not Fadel," I noted. "That didn't prove anything."

"That's because here, I'm known as Charles Faber. I haven't gone by Fadel since I was your age."

"Why?"

"You and I have many things in common, Miss Williams. One of which is conflict with my brother."

"Why would Fadel— Chakir Fadel— have a problem with his own brother?" Eric asked. The man didn't respond, waiting patiently for the waiter to hand Theo his drink and leave again before continuing.

"I represented something he despised: the younger brother he never wanted."

"It can't be that simple."

"Things like this never are. No, no, he never wanted a brother, that's true. But more than that, since the day I was born, my life was one that he's always dreamed of for himself. I'm not saying this out of pride, it's just a fact. Chakir was the older brother, raised according to a strict heritage, high expectations placed upon him. I was the younger, more Americanized child. I was given more freedom, more attention."

"He hated you for being spoiled?" Theo asked.

"He hated me for many reasons, but most of all, because I was gifted."

"Gifted?" The word sent chills down my spine.

"You see that he carries a staff? One he fills with the special skills of others? Why do you think he has that?"

I knew the answer. We all did. We never questioned that Fadel would be powerless without his staff.

"Yes, we understand that," I said. "Fadel doesn't have any 'special skills' so he steals other people's. But you said you're gifted."

"Indeed. How else would he have known that he wanted powers?"

Powers. Fadel never used that word. Always "skills" or "talents." Never "powers."

"Because he was powerless, he found a way to make himself powerful. He diminished the value of others' and acted as though these things could be learned. He was determined to do what I could do and more. And I think that's why he was so interested in you."

He looked fiercely into my eyes. Despite being scared to do so, I held his gaze.

"You never told us what you can do."

"Oh yes," he smiled. "That."

He looked around to make sure no one was watching and then raised his left hand above the table, a flame hovering over his palm.

* * *

Charles Fadel was born in 1970, three years after his brother, Chakir. The boys' upbringings were practically polar opposites.

Chakir was raised in a strict Persian household. His father had high expectations for him, the stereotypical "American dream" mindset: Chakir was to be a doctor or at the very least, a lawyer. This was drilled into him from a very young age.

Charles had a radically different experience. He was the all-American baby, the first in his family born in the United States. He was raised speaking only English, encouraged to play baseball from age six, and told that he could do anything he wanted to post-high school graduation.

Charles' upbringing was not the only thing that made him different than his older brother, Charles caught the curtains on fire during his fifth birthday party, and not with the birthday candles. The younger Fadel boy was talented, *special*. And that only made things harder on his older brother.

Did Chakir have powers too? If Chakir had applied himself, could he have become a bit more like Charles?

I almost felt bad for Fadel hearing this history of his childhood. Almost, but not quite.

"What happened when you both left home?" I asked, stirring my drink with a small black straw.

Charles switched which leg was crossed over which and leaned back in his chair.

"Chakir did what my father desired and went to an Ivy, getting a doctorate in psychology. I went to a top university for business and financial management."

"Hence the fancy hotel you casually mentioned you owned," Theo chuckled.

"Yes. I've invested well and launched several businesses over the last few decades. But to be fair, I only own 51% of this one. A majority share."

He smiled slightly, obviously proud of his great achievement.

"Anyway, this attracted the attention of my dear brother. Suddenly, I appeared to be an asset to him. When we were 27 and 30, he showed up at my flat in Prague… yes Mr. Martin, I have a flat in Prague… and laid out a grand plan. He had ideas, dreams, of bringing together people with special skills to make a new sort of world power. He believed that a force like this could replace police or even military forces."

"That's wild," Eric leaned forward to rest his forearms on his knees.

"He wanted to use people like us as a protective force? He's literally doing the opposite."

"But he convinces his followers otherwise. You remember what he told us during on-boarding? That we are the heroes destined to bring lasting justice across the nation," I added.

"Exactly," Charles replied.

"Do you think he actually believes this? Do you think he genuinely considers himself the hero?" Theo asked.

"Maybe he did, but the version you've seen of him is not the one that sat at my kitchen table that day. In fact, that version of him did not last very long."

He closed his eyes for a moment, bracing himself for what he was about to share with us.

"That day, I told him no. I told him that I didn't want to do anything with my special skills. I wanted to focus on my business. I was making major investments, and I wanted to see them through.

"He told me that he wanted me as a financial advisor rather than just a hero for his team. I, of course, had already put this together. But I knew my brother. I knew his temper. I knew his ability to hold a grudge, to hate someone with every ounce of his being.

"His reaction had been quite volatile, as one would expect. He cursed me and told me I'd be sorry for not helping him. He reminded me that he was the elder brother and that I should have more respect. And after all this, he left. And I never saw him again."

"And that's it?" Eric asked. "Then how do you know so much about his recent endeavors? About us?"

"I said I never saw him again, not that he was out of my life forever."

He smiled a little, but something sad, something sober, dwelt behind it.

"Four years later, while I was living in Colorado, I got a letter in the mail with no return address. One single line written on crumpled paper: 'You're not the only one who can make the world burn.' I foolishly thought nothing of it at first. But that night, my house burned to the ground while I was asleep. Luckily, I woke up in time and made an escape into the woods. And even more luckily, the reporters went wild. The local newspaper reported me dead; my body burned to ashes. As far as my brother knew, I'd ceased to be a problem. I fled west, changed my name, and lived the rest of my life without sparking a single flame. Until tonight."

He raised his eyebrows, looking pointedly at me.

"So why now? Why upend your whole life, change everything you've ever known, just to show us your powers tonight?" Eric appeared invested in Charles' story, sympathetic to every detail. That was very Eric, to be connected to those he encountered. His relatability was almost a second power.

Theo and I, on the other hand, continued to hold a bit of skepticism. The details added up, but what was the point? What was his intention?

"I'm happy to keep living in obscurity. I've built a comfortable life. But sometimes something big happens that disrupts comfort, something too important to ignore."

He smiled and reached into his pocket. His hand reemerged with a very nice, very expensive smart phone. He swiped and scrolled before sliding the device across the table to me.

"Mr. Vardoger was not the first one to arrive at this hotel."

I picked up the phone and looked at the photo on the screen. It was a photo of Charles with two teens. One, a girl, looked about thirteen or fourteen. She wore cutoff shorts, a plain white t-shirt, and a Boston Red Sox hat. The other was a boy, who looked maybe seventeen or eighteen. He wore jeans and a grey Henley.

"Who are these two?" I asked, passing the phone to Theo and Eric.

"The girl is Monica. She's from Massachusetts. She can create these massive gusts of wind and power, 'pushes' she likes to call them. Came out here for a family vacation back a few years ago and accidentally pushed their tour bus off a cliff."

"Oh my gosh," I gasped.

"Thankfully, no one was in it at the time, but her parents were furious at the damages, both financially and to their reputation. They were also terrified for their own lives, so they selfishly left her here."

"They abandoned her?" Eric asked, rightfully angry.

"Yes, as did Luca's parents. Luca's a good kid. Came from Chicago. He can grow things. Plants. Trees, vines, the like. And he can control and bend the ones that already exist. Fascinating, but clearly a bit too 'freaky' for his lawyer father and small-business owner mother." Charles chuckled. He put air-quotes around "freaky" and smirked at the phrase "lawyer father."

"Divine Providence brought Luca and I together. He didn't know anything about me, but he came to this hotel after four days alone and without food. He said he needed help and begged for a room for the night. Said he couldn't pay me but that he could help me with the landscaping. Little did I know what he meant by that. I hired him on and offered him a room, where he stayed for two weeks while he transformed this hotel into a tropical oasis in the middle of a desert.

"Luca was such a good worker and clearly a wonderful kid. I remembered my brother and his work and worried that someday Luca, if turned out to the world, would be at risk. I just couldn't allow something to happen to him. So, I welcomed him into my home and to this day, he continues to help me out at the hotel in exchange for lodging and protection. He's the one who found Monica, who now lives with us as well."

"That's amazing," Eric said.

"Divine Providence," Charles said again. "And I believe that's what brought you here as well. But you aren't like the others. None of you are. I kept an eye on this one," he said, pointing to Eric. "I wondered if you needed my help as well. But you always seemed to disappear before I could make contact."

"Well, I did think you were your brother," Eric replied. "No offense."

"None taken," Charles smiled. "I'd done my research, knew your face, Miss Williams. Your friend, Mr. Vardoger, had posted pictures of the two of you on his social media, back when you were on the east coast together. I did a bit more digging and found newsreels with your face, with your fire. When you showed up, I knew that we needed to meet. I knew that you weren't here for protection. You weren't here to hide."

"So why do you want to see me?" I asked. "Did you just want to make contact with another person like you?"

"Oh no," Charles said, "You're on a mission and I know it involves my brother. You see, I want him stopped as badly as you do. I want to live in a world where Luca and Monica can be free to help others, to take advantage of their gifts without fear of a man like my brother. You appear to be an answer to that prayer."

I nodded, trying not to blush. Being the answer to Charles' prayer felt like the highest form of a compliment I could receive.

"That's what I want as well. We came to Utah to find Eric and bring him with us. We need his help," I said. Then a crazy idea hit me.

"You should come with us. We could use your help."

Charles gave me another soft smile.

"I cannot do that. My brother thinks I'm dead, and I'd like to keep it that way."

"But you have powers," Theo remarked. "Isn't it a bit cowardly to hide while there are people out there that you can help? That need people like you to save them?"

"Yes, maybe it's cowardly. But you must remember that I'm the only thing protecting two people I care very much about. I'm guarding them from the same fate that you all miraculously escaped. I don't see how that's any different than what Mr. Vardoger is doing for his niece."

A red flush poured into Eric's cheeks.

"Touche," Theo said, throwing back the rest of his drink and clinking the ice-filled glass back on the table.

"So now what?" I asked. "You aren't coming with us, but you want to encourage us to do what we are already doing. What's your angle? What do you want from me?"

"It's not what I want from you. It's what I want from Mr. Vardoger."

"Which is?" Eric asked.

"You need to go with them."

Silence. Theo's eyes lit up. I silently pleaded with him not to speak. Eric was the one who needed to respond. It was all in Eric's hands now.

"But you essentially just validated my decision to protect my family," Eric said cautiously.

"Yes, but I'm an old man and you're a young one. You are able to add more to the fight than I ever could."

"What about my family?"

"Consider it taken care of. I will make contact and work to protect them as I do Luca and Monica."

"I still don't understand what this really does for you," I said, before Eric could reply to Charles about his family. I wanted to give him time to think, which seemed like the fair thing to do, despite my deep desire for him to agree to Charles' deal.

"I told you, I want my brother defeated. But not only that, I want those poor kids under his control to find relief. I want them to be healed and taken care of. You could say that I finally found a cause I'd like to support, a place to put my fortune."

He reached into his pocket once again, this time pulling out a folded piece of lined paper. As he unfolded it and laid it down for us to see, he continued.

"I want to build a center for these kids, a school. Lodging, classrooms, training space. Like what my brother was doing, but instead of taking everything from them, it would be giving them everything they need to go protect their own communities, to fuel their own missions. They could master their powers on their own time while being taken care of and having a safe place to live. Then, they could go out to use them for a noble cause. Or they could go out and collect others like them, bringing them back to start the cycle again."

"You're building a headquarters for supers," Eric said, tracing his finger over the rough blueprints Charles had sketched.

"Yes."

"It's a genius idea!" I exclaimed, scanning the drawing over and over again.

I envisioned the school, a multi-story glass building, with classrooms full of dummies and rope courses, and simulators, bedrooms for everyone, a big communal kitchen and dining area where supers like Molly Meadows and Eric's niece could share a meal. There could be meeting rooms for planning and game rooms for relaxing over a game of cards. Heck, a pool could be built on the roof, with lounge chairs for reading and hammocks for napping. It could be a haven for people like me. I'd never longed for something more.

"I want to help you," I extended my hand to Charles. He took it gently and squeezed. His hands were warm and weather worn. It felt a bit crazy, two people, each with hands that could make fire, making contact like this. Charles represented who I wanted to be, his mission was one I not only wanted to support, but one I needed to support. This could be our purpose, our future.

"We will bring you more supers. I know of some kids in Victory who would really benefit from this. And if we can take down Fadel, we can send his minions to you for help and healing, as you expressed. When this is all over…"

I couldn't continue. I knew what I wanted to say but I didn't know how to say it.

"You'd be welcome here anytime. All of your friends would be welcome. You could come and go as you please. Maybe you all could help me teach the others or lead more rescue missions."

"That sounds amazing," Theo smiled.

Charles had sold us on the idea. The revelation that a future existed for us where we could help others gave us the boost of energy we needed to win this war. That is, if we could actually defeat Fadel. It had been so long, and he still continued to survive, to win. We needed Eric more than ever. As if he could read my mind, Charles turned to Eric.

"So, will you do it? Will you go with them?"

Eric sat in silence; eyes fixed on the table. He looked to be deep in thought, weighing all the options presented to him. Charles must have seen this, too.

"Come with me for a moment, Mr. Vardoger," he said, pushing out his chair and standing up, "We can take a stroll through the solarium and chat about it in private."

Eric stood to follow him, glancing over his shoulder at me with a 'I guess we will see' expression. The two walked under an archway and out of sight together.

"Another drink while we wait?" Theo asked me. "It's obviously on the house."

153

CHAPTER THIRTY

Penny

"I say we go up north through Dallas and Oklahoma City and then cut west through Albuquerque. And then north again," Alexandra said, holding a giant, unfolded paper map across our laps. She traced the proposed route with the back of a pen, ready to mark the journey once our leader approved it.

"Wouldn't it make more sense to go all the way up to Omaha and then cut straight west from there?" I said, looking over her shoulder and pointing at the highway I thought we could use.

"What's the faster route?" Jasmine asked, shivering. She had a giant towel wrapped around her like a blanket. Her hair was still damp from the training incident.

"I don't know, none of our phones have service here for some reason," I said, checking my signal once again. Still nothing. Maybe that was why we hadn't heard from Bee or Theo...

"Well, I guess we don't have to make a decision until we're in Oklahoma," Sebastian replied, smiling at us in the overhead mirror. "We can either head west from there or keep north to Omaha."

Alexandra pulled out her phone and checked her location app. She'd shared ours with Zeke, who, thankfully, shared his as well. Not only could they track us, but we would know where they were, too.

Currently, they were about five miles on our tail. It was a bit too close for comfort, in my opinion. However, Sebastian said this was a good thing, as it kept them moving and kept us motivated.

"We've got a toll about ten miles ahead," Robert said, pointing to a sign.

"Good eyes," Sebastian replied. "An extra own on Fadel, now he has to pay a toll." He laughed a little, but no one laughed with him.

As we got closer to the toll exit, traffic slowed.

"Guys, they're only about two miles back now," Alexandra said, scrolling in to see their exact spot.

"I don't like that," I said. "I don't want them to get too close." I pulled her hand away so I could see the screen as well.

"Once we get through the toll booth, we should be ok," Sebastian replied. "We can try to shake them off a little."

We slowly approached the booth and Sebastian searched for his wallet. As we got to the window, something didn't feel right.

"Heading north, huh? That'll be $4.25 or the man in your backseat."

All of our heads whipped up at once.

The attendant in the box was Lawrence.

* * *

Lawrence disappeared and reappeared outside the car window, grabbing at the steering wheel. Sebastian wrestled to keep it out of his hands.

"Holy—!" Sebastian yelled, yanking hard.

Lawrence could teleport within at least a two-mile radius, a mile more than we'd anticipated based on conversations we'd had with Bianca about Eric's powers. He must have teleported into the booth while Fadel's car was stuck in traffic.

"Punch him!" Jasmine squealed. I couldn't tell if she was using her Voice or just panicking. Regardless, it worked. Sebastian wound up and punched Lawrence square in the jaw, causing him to stumble backwards, away from the car.

"Now punch the gas!" Jasmine screamed. Sebastian slammed his foot on the pedal and plowed right through the toll arm.

We took off at about 70, recklessly merging onto the expressway. Unfortunately, Lawrence was quicker. He suddenly appeared in a crouched position on top of the console space, between the driver and passenger seats. He'd teleported right into our car.

Jasmine, Alexandra, and I screamed as Lawrence pulled himself over Sebastian's shoulder and grabbed at the wheel.

Sebastian elbowed him in the gut, but Lawrence put him in a choke hold. From the passenger seat, Jasmine reached over and grabbed the wheel to steady it. She whispered directions to the car, trying to keep it straight. Lawrence continued to pull, trying to steer us towards the shoulder.

As the two boys fought for power and Jasmine tried to keep us from dying in a fiery car crash, I unbuckled and moved forward, trying to take up a better position. I wanted to knee Lawrence, but Robert was in the way. I punched him repeatedly instead, which knocked some wind out of him, just enough to make him change his hold on Sebastian.

Alexandra sat petrified in the very back, squeaking and squealing with each blow Sebastian and I inflicted on the villain.

I pushed past Robert and grabbed Lawrence around the waist, which startled him. I intended to knee him, for real this time, when he suddenly let go of Sebastian, twisted, and turned back to Robert and me.

Regaining his composure, he smiled.

"I don't know why I'm wasting my time with all of you. It's him the doctor wants," he said, nodding towards Robert. Suddenly, he lunged and grabbed Robert's wrists. My fingers still held onto his belt loop: a massive mistake.

Before I could let go, the car disappeared.

CHAPTER THIRTY-ONE

The tall guy still had a grip on me when we skidded across the asphalt. I guess that should have been predictable, as our physical contact was the reason I ended up on the shoulder of the expressway to begin with. He'd teleported us out of the car, now covered in scrapes and bruises. I was definitely going to have a headache later.

I kneed the guy in the chest, causing him to release me. Once I finally broke free, I realized that we weren't alone. The small blonde girl— Peggy maybe— had been teleported with us. She looked frazzled, a little scared even.

"Robert!" She yelled to me over the sound of whizzing cars and rumbling trucks. The tall guy realized her fingers still clutched his belt and began trying to pull her off. His fingers clawed at her grip, but she squeezed all the tighter, her fingers turning white.

"Don't let go!" She yelled at me. I almost forgot that he was our only transportation out of here. I lunged forward and grabbed one of his boots. Knowing it was me he wanted anyway, it was clear that he wouldn't be trying to shake me off like he was with her.

He jostled us, which kicked up the dust around us, making it harder to see, not to mention breathe. The girl coughed. The tall guy saw this moment of weakness and let go of her hands, lunging for her neck instead. She gasped and released his belt. Realizing her mistake, she gasped as he shoved her off and we disappeared again. This time, we ended up in another vehicle. I assumed it was the one the tall guy originally intended for us to wind up in, rather than on the side of the road. And worse, the blonde girl was nowhere to be seen.

* * *

"Finally," a goateed man said, smiling. A quick glance around told me we were now in the back of a box truck, lined with moving boxes and dimly lit with a few electric lanterns. The man lounged dramatically in an armchair with a non-operational standing lamp beside him. It looked like a scene from *The Godfather*.

"I've been chasing you down for days, boy."

He smiled at the teleporter.

"Very good, Lawrence. See you've finally done something right for once."

I let go of the teleporter's boot and pushed myself to a standing position.

"We've gotta go back," I spat out, panicked. "There's a girl back on the shoulder. We can't leave her there."

"Well— Mr. Arashi, is it? While I've been chasing *you* down for days, I've been trying to shake her for well over a year. What a surprise to succeed in both simultaneously!"

I needed to get out of the truck. By any means necessary I needed to reach the girl.

The man continued to talk at me, noting something about me being an excellent addition to his team or collection or whatever. I wasn't listening, I was too focused on the door latch.

What had that Sebastian guy been saying before about making lightning? If I could conjure lightning, which I'd done a few times now, could I create other weather too?

What kind of storms could I make? Lightning wouldn't help now. Maybe a tornado? Could I make a windstorm? I did create that wind push on the plane...

I imagined a big gust swirling inside the truck. I visualized myself at the center of the churning wind, twisting and turning to make a tornado.

At first, I thought I was crazy, because I really felt it, a small breeze. It was only when the man's expression changed to a frustrated scowl and he asked, "What are you doing?" that I knew the storm was real. I focused all my attention on the wind and willed it to circle me.

"Stop that this instant!" the man yelled. He looked more and more panicked as the wind picked up.

"Not gonna happen," I said, and lifted my arms, the wind whipping furiously.

I backed slowly towards the door.

"What are you doing standing there, you idiot!" the goateed man yelled to the tall guy. "Get him!"

I made my move, pushing the wind in between us, using it like a wall. I backed up against the door and fumbled for the latch with one hand, using the other to keep the wind wall going. The tall guy moved along towards me like a monkey in quicksand. I gave the latch a turn and yanked it upwards, opening the entire back door of the truck.

The road beneath us sped by at a dizzying speed. It might have been insane, but there was only one way out and only one idea I could think of.

"See ya boys," I said before I leapt out backwards. As I jumped, I thrust my hands and threw wind ahead of me, angling my direction back towards the shoulder.

For the second time in less than five minutes, I skidded across the asphalt again. This time I ended up on my back. But I was on the shoulder, out of the road. I was safe. But the girl still wasn't. We must be a mile apart... at least. Without thinking twice, I took off running in the direction we came from, leaping over various road debris as I encountered it.

As I jumped over a large piece of blown tire, I had another crazy idea.

I ran back to grab the debris and tried to flatten it, at least enough to get both feet on it. I stepped on and spread my feet like I was on a small surfboard. I squatted and pushed a wind behind me. I moved a little. This could work.

With everything I had left, I pushed. I surfed along, riding the tire-board down the shoulder.

We were back in business.

CHAPTER THIRTY-TWO

Bianca

Eric and Charles had been gone for a good forty minutes. As they finally rounded the corner, I tried to get a read of their expressions. Eric's face gave nothing away. Charles smiled softly, a good sign.

Those forty minutes allowed Theo the time to drink three more cocktails. The boy could really hold his liquor.

"Are you coming with us or not?" he asked Eric. He stirred the ice in the bottom of his glass with his straw.

Eric continued to hold a straight face but nodded.

"Yes. I'll come with you as far as Louisiana, or wherever you plan to rendezvous with your friends. We can put up a fight against Fadel, but if he leaves and goes any further east, you're going to have to be on your own. I promised Charles I would fight, but I can't let this drag on forever. That is my compromise."

That wouldn't do. He couldn't give us a half-hearted effort; he needed to stick it out with us. I looked over at Charles to protest, but he silently held up a hand to stop me. Theo, now clearly intoxicated, did not seem to comprehend what Eric was saying. Instead, he shook Eric's hand enthusiastically, called him 'Old Sport,' and announced he was going to bed.

"You should all be getting to bed, you have a long drive tomorrow if you want to get all the way to Louisiana by your desired deadline," Charles said.

Eric nodded again and wished me goodnight. He reached down and picked up my hand, giving it a light squeeze.

"I'm going back to the townhouse tonight to pack my things, but I'll be back in the morning. We can head out as early as you'd like, just text me when you're awake."

"Oh!" I said, realizing I didn't have his number. Such a silly little thing, but he didn't have a phone when we worked for Fadel. He lost it on a training mission once. He never bothered to replace it, as he said it made him feel lighter— freer.

"Let me find my phone and we can exchange numbers," I said, releasing his hand and feeling my hips where my pockets usually were. I had forgotten that my dress didn't have pockets. My phone must have been in the room.

"Here," Theo pulled his phone out. "You can use mi— wait a minute." He raised it to his face to examine it more closely.

"I have a text from Penny! Multiple, actually. And like five from Sebastian. And here's one from Jasmine that just says, 'you idiot, pick up your phone.' And several missed calls. Maybe I shouldn't have left it on silent all day."

"Theo!" I gasped and lunged forward to grab the phone from him. "Why didn't you check your messages? Why did you have it on silent? They're trying to get a hold of us!"

"Why didn't you wear a dress with pockets? Or carry a tiny purse for your phone?"

I ignored him and scrolled message after message.

"We're not going to Louisiana anymore," I said. "They've left. They're heading west, towards us. We need to meet in the middle. They want us to choose a location."

I thought for a moment before turning back to Eric. There was only one place that made sense for us to use as a rendezvous. Only one place would give us the home court advantage we needed.

"How do you feel about returning to your roots?"

CHAPTER THIRTY-THREE

Theodore

When the night finally came to a close, we returned to our rooms, exhausted from the long day and a bit nauseous from all the booze, at least in my case.

And now that Eric would be joining us and we knew where we needed to go, I could take the foot off the gas for a bit and check in on the outside world. My phone died two days ago, and I'd neglected to put it on the charger. However, I continued to put it off, hoping to use the time off my phone to focus on the task at hand. Bianca wasn't the only responsible one this side of the Mississippi.

I struggled a bit trying to get the tiny charger into the tiny charging hole, thanks to Mr. Jack Daniels. But once I got the phone plugged in and started up again, I discovered more than a few missed calls and messages. Geez, could these people not function without me?

I expected the texts and calls from Penny, that was a given. But as I'd predicted, the frequency of her outreach fizzled out after a "I hope all is well. Text me when you can. I believe in you."

Penny understood the mission. She knew what we all signed up for, and as much as I knew it must pain her to not be able to talk for a bit, I knew she would understand.

What did surprise me, however, were the plethora of panicked, urgent texts from Sebastian. And a few really mean ones from Jasmine, too. They clearly did not get the same memo that Penny did.

SEBASTIAN: Dude, where are you guys? We can't get through to either of you and it's starting to become a concern.

SEBASTIAN: Things are bad. On the run. Heading out towards you guys. Call back ASAP with a rendezvous point.

SEBASTIAN: Theo, we need a meeting spot. Give me two minutes and call me back.

JASMINE: YOU IDIOT ANSWER YOUR PHONE! I AM SERIOUSLY GOING TO KILL YOU WHEN I SEE YOU NEXT!

And about an hour ago:

SEBASTIAN: Penny in trouble, Fadel. CALL ME BACK.

My heart stopped. Penny was in trouble. I couldn't dial the phone fast enough. In fact, I accidentally called the wrong number twice, my hands shaking as I tried to hit the right digits. Sebastian picked up on the second ring.

"Dude, where the heck are you? Why haven't you been answering the phone?"

Ok, now I felt really guilty for not charging my phone.

"Sorry, man, my phone was dead. But we're all good now. We have a location. But tell me what's going on with Penny. Is she alright?"

I tried not to sound too desperate, but internally, I prayed over and over again that she was safe. I also tried to sound as sober as possible, hoping not to let slip that I'd not only ignored my phone, but that I'd just finished an unexpectedly fun night.

"Fadel's minion, Lawrence, teleported into the van and took her and Robert. We don't know where they are," Sebastian said, an ache in his voice I couldn't quite place.

"Who the heck is Robert?"

"Doesn't matter. What matters is that Jasmine, Alexandra, and I took the closest exit to where we lost them. Hopefully, they can figure that out and find us. Penny has her phone on her but isn't responding. I think it's either dead or she doesn't have service. We are pretty remote right now."

I couldn't believe this was happening. I massaged my jaw and sighed.

"You said you'd take care of her, Sebastian."

"I did! It's not my fault the guy can teleport. I don't even think he was aiming for Penny, I think she was an accidental passenger when he left the van."

"I don't really care what his intention was. What I care about is making sure she's safe."

"And I'm handling that."

"How? You don't know where the heck she is!"

"She's gotta be within a mile or so of us. At least that's what I expect. Alexandra said Lawrence has about a mile or two radius for his teleportation. He also gets drained quickly, so it's unlikely he hopped more than once. The only way they're outside of the small radius we are in is if—"

"If they are in a moving vehicle with Fadel."

"Yeah."

This was bad. Penny could literally be anywhere. And coming out of a moving vehicle... was she even safe?

"At least we know where they're probably going, if they have Robert," Sebastian said. "He's the one they wanted anyway. They're probably heading to you now."

"First of all, I still don't know who Robert is, nor do I care that much. Second, we won't be *here* much longer. Bianca, Eric, and I are taking a flight to Durango tomorrow morning. Fadel's brother, Charles, got us all hooked up. First class and everything, baby."

"Fadel's brother? We have a lot of catching up to do."

"Yeah, we do, so you better find Penny and meet us in Durango, buddy. And honestly, don't bother showing up if she's not with you."

Maybe it was too far, but Penny was my number one priority. "Understood."

Sebastian was a good man. My anger sometimes took me over, a bit like Bee's, but without the cool powers. So many of my friends considered me the funny guy, the one with personality. But I considered myself to be the guy with grit. The guy who would fight until he has nothing left in him. If I cared about something enough, nothing could stop me. I wasn't the easiest person to deal with when I fell into those emotional grooves, and Sebastian knew that. We'd been working as a duo for years. He was my best friend, my brother. And despite what should have been frustrations for him, he always looked past my faults and pushed me in the right direction. He always made sure I ended up on the right track.

Even though I was angry that he lost Penny, I knew it wasn't entirely his fault. And, like me, I knew he would give everything to make sure she was ok.

I thanked him and told him I would go get Bee and have her call him to explain the plan in detail, but that I needed to go to bed.

This was a lie, of course. There was no way I would be sleeping. Not so long as Penny was missing. I knew she must be out there trying to find a way back to us. And if she'd be awake, I would be too, keeping a vigil and silently urging her on.

CHAPTER THIRTY-FOUR

O h my gosh, they were gone.
I was alone.
Alone.

On the side of the expressway in the middle of nowhere. My phone, destroyed from the fall. I left it in the dirt next to me, knowing it wouldn't be of any use now.

My breath caught a few times and I started to panic. My chest tightened and my hands trembled all at once, my head became foggier and my muscles locked. I couldn't breathe without gasping.

I was—*gasp*—alone. I—*gasp*—wasn't ok. I—*gasp*—would never—*gasp*—get home. I—*gasp*—would never see my friends again.

My body seized up, in too much shock to cry. I rocked back and forth and my knees. I desperately tried to get in a breath—any little breath.

My parents were right. What was the point? Why had I even bothered with this? Fadel was powerful and strong. Why did stupid little me believe that we could beat him? What were we going to use? The power of friendship?

Why was I so stupid?

I heaved over and over. I rocked faster and faster.

I—*gasp*—can't—*gasp*—do this.

All I wanted was Theo. Theodore Albert Martin. For so much of my life, I protected others. Now, I just wanted someone to protect me. I wanted *him* to protect me.

Where was he now? Was he still on the road, driving down a highway just like this one? Was he in a bed in a hotel somewhere, unable to sleep, worried about me?

Wherever he was, I knew that he wouldn't want me to give up. He would want me to keep fighting.

But what if I had nothing left to give? No fight left in me…

"I'm sorry Theo," I whispered to the dirt. "I'm so sorry."

The tears finally came, granting me a relief of breath. My body started to collapse, and I wasn't going to stop it.

What other choice did I have?

But then, over all the road noise, I heard something like a yell.

As I wiped my face and looked up to the horizon, a dark silhouette appeared on the shoulder, growing larger by the second.

It almost looked like a person.

I pushed myself to my feet and jumped up and down, waving my arms and yelling.

"I'm HERE! I'm here!"

I didn't care who it was. A stranger? Fadel himself? It didn't matter. I just didn't want to be alone anymore.

"I'm HERE!" I cried, hot tears hit the dirt under my jumping feet.

Robert came clearer into view. He was riding some sort of road debris.

"Robert! I'm here!"

When he got close enough, he jumped off and ran towards me. I ran at him and jumped in his arms. I didn't know him at all, but I didn't care. I was being rescued for the first time in ages, and I needed to feel every little detail of that moment.

"Let's get out of here and try to find someone to call."

"I can't," I said, pointing to my smashed phone on the ground.

"Do you have Sebastian or the other girl's number memorized? If we can get somewhere with service, you can use my phone and call them to come back for us."

"Not theirs," I said sadly. "I can't get them to come back. But I do know one person's. He hasn't been answering, but it would be worth a shot. A Hail Mary if you will."

Alright, well hop onto my magic carpet," he said, gesturing to an old piece of scrap from the road. "Let's get back to civilization."

* * *

"My gosh, Pen, I was worried." A twinge of pain hung on Theo's every word. Yet despite his clear frustration and relief, he still sounded levelheaded. He still sounded like Theo: very sure of himself and very stable.

I, on the other hand, was anything but composed. I cried. Hard. I needed both hands to hold Robert's phone.

Robert had wandered off to look for dinner. He clearly wanted to give me privacy.

"I'm fine," I said, trying to sound like the strong woman I needed to be. But did I? This was *Theo* I was talking to. He'd been with me through thick and thin. And not only that, he was the person I cared most for, maybe in the world.

Just hearing his voice again, after forever and a day, especially after thinking I was never going to see him again, really made it clear to me. I loved him.

I imagined running into his arms, never wanting to let go again.

My whole life was wrapped up in Theo's embrace. He was my joy. I couldn't delay things any longer. I needed to see him. I needed to be with him and never leave him again.

"Actually… I'm not fine. I haven't been fine since we left each other."

"Pen—"

"I started having panic attacks again."

"Oh Penny," he said breathlessly into the receiver.

"I hadn't had them in years. But I've had a few now, since you left. I've been scared and lonely. I've been panicking a bit. I didn't realize that you were the reason I'd overcome them all those years ago. You have helped me and healed me. And being without you… I'm scared. I feel alone. Especially now, my goodness. I'm *literally* stranded here. And I don't know what to do."

I wiped my tears with the back of my hand.

"I need you, Theo."

"I know," he whispered. "We will be together again soon. I need you to be strong, ok?"

I sniffed.

"Yes, I know. Everyone keeps telling me to be strong. *I* keep telling myself to be strong! But sometimes I need someone to be strong for me. I need someone to hold me up right now."

There was a moment of silence between us. A bit too long of a pause.

Had I made a mistake? Should I not have told him this?

"I'm sorry," I said quickly, cutting through the building tension. "I'm fine. I can take care of myself."

I panicked again. My hands started shaking and my eyes darted around before clouding over.

"Penny. No, you're not fine. Just breathe and listen to me. I just need you to hang on a bit longer. And then I'll hold you up as long as you need me to. I'll be all the support you need, and you won't have to be strong anymore. Ok? But I can't do that until we are together again. I know you're capable of taking care of yourself. I know how brave you are. I know you can make it just a little longer, ok?"

I didn't want to admit it, but he was right. I could make it a bit longer. And it would be ok. He was going to be there for me on the other side. I just needed to keep pushing.

"Bare minimum, ok?"

I nodded, even though he couldn't see me.

"Just do what you have to do to get by. Survival mode. And it will be ok."

"Ok. I can do that."

I started crying again, now for a different reason. He was there with me, even thousands of miles away. I knew in my heart, in that moment, he loved me in return.

"Good. So where are you now?"

That was a very good question.

"I don't know," I replied, honestly.

"Do you think you went more than an exit from where you got pulled out of the van? I know that's where Sebastian and the others are."

"I have no clue. I assume I'm not far. But I think Robert and I can keep moving. We all know where we're going now, thanks to you. I don't want to hold Sebastian and Jasmine up. I want us all to get to Durango as quickly as possible."

"Do you have your ID on you?"

"Yes, thank goodness. Robert and I could fly there and meet you all. That way the others don't have to come get us. And we also don't have to shove into the van again. It was a bit more than cramped—Jasmine packed way too much stuff."

"Are you sure?"

"Yeah, that way I can see you sooner." Despite the pains, the aches, and the bruises, I smiled a bit.

"In that case, I'll tell Seb to keep moving. I'll also ask our friend, Charles, if he can book some flights for you two and some rooms under his name in Durango. When you land, I'll send the hotel info to this number, which I'm guessing is this Robert guy's?"

"Yes, it is. That sounds like a good plan."

"Alright, well I'm going to hop. I'll get that booking settled and sent your way."

"Thank you. I hope you sleep well and we will see you soon."

"Goodnight, Pen. I'm happy you're ok."

An hour later, Robert got a text with the booking information for two hotel rooms in Durango and two flights from Dallas leaving in a few hours. Robert and I ate fast food burgers under a streetlamp and called a cab to the airport.

Before boarding our hopper flight across Texas, I sent a text off to Theo, wishing him safe travels. And that finally, finally I would see him soon.

CHAPTER THIRTY-FIVE

Jasmine

Penny and Robert were boarding a flight to Durango. Bianca, Theo, and this Eric hottie were also boarding a flight to Durango. And somehow, I drew the short stick and got stuck in a mom van with Sebastian and Alexandra, who were proving to be the least interesting people in the world.

Our current estimated time of arrival would put us into Durango tomorrow at noon, if we drove through the night.

Why was Texas such a massive state? It should not take a half day's journey to get from one side of the state to the other. I missed Hawaii. And at least California was short one way across. Like five or six hours tops, traffic dependent. Oregon, where I'd gone to college, was big. But I never drove through it. Flights were easier.

Alexandra and Sebastian chatted about the physics of teleportation or something absurd like that— Alexandra was also a math nerd. This trio was almost as bad as if I'd been stuck with Seb and Bee and they were making out. I couldn't stand to hear them use the word *velocity* any longer, so I popped headphones in and went back to my assigned task: keeping in touch with the others.

It had become my duty to coordinate a meetup with the other two traveling parties. I did not want this job, especially once I found out what it entailed.

Sebastian wanted me to text Bianca to monitor their progress, which was fine. The problem was, I then needed to relay information to Robert, whose number I got from Theo, since Penny had used Robert's phone when she contacted her boyfriend.

This is where I lost interest in Sebastian's plan.

Robert Arashi was, in short, annoying. Not in the way that I found Penny or Theo annoying, but in the sense that he didn't want to message me. I know that because he practically told me so.

Our texts started off just coordinating plans. I mean, what else would we talk about? We'd barely exchanged eye contact in our brief time together. Except when we were at each other's throats. But what did that matter to Sebastian? We were only texting about GPS coordinates! What did that matter in the grand scheme of things?

Just my sanity, that's what.

Our first conversation was short and sweet.

JASMINE: This is Jasmine. I was told I had to text you.

ROBERT: Why?

JASMINE: I don't know, but believe me, I'd rather not.

ROBERT: Can you give the phone to Alexandra?

Our next conversation wasn't any better.

JASMINE: Progress?

ROBERT: Fine.

JASMINE: As in you're both doing fine, or "fine, I'll send you a detailed update on our progress" fine?

ROBERT: Fine as in we're fine, please stop asking.

JASMINE: I'm sorry I want to know how my friends are doing.

ROBERT: We aren't friends.

And one of our more recent exchanges broke me, so I just chose to let it escalate.

JASMINE: Before you freak out on me, I was told I had to check in with you. How are you guys doing?

ROBERT: I'd be better if I wasn't getting texts every hour asking about my progress. We're fine, you can stop now.

JASMINE: I'm just following orders. I need to keep an eye on your location. So, like it or not, we have to check-in.

ROBERT: How about we don't and pretend we did?

JASMINE: You're insufferable.

ROBERT: Penny thinks I'm nice.

JASMINE: Penny thinks everyone is nice.

ROBERT: Does she think you're nice?

JASMINE: She knows I'm nice.

ROBERT: Lol.

JASMINE: Shut up and just respond when I check in next.

ROBERT: Great, can't wait to hear from you again in an hour.

Our conversations frustrated me. Maybe it was jealousy or maybe it was just pure annoyance, but it bothered me how he acted with Alexandra or Penny compared to me.

Men—or at least men I thought were hot—never took me seriously. I've always been smart and interesting and good at conversation, but it never mattered. They ignored me for some other silly, cute girl. I'd call myself fierce and loyal, but I've always been labeled as abrasive. Maybe worst of all, it didn't matter if I was pretty or not, no one ever acted like I was. I could always use my Voice to *make* them like me, but I shouldn't have had to.

It infuriated me to add to the growing list of men who didn't like me.

JASMINE: Why are you so cross with me?

ROBERT: I'm not.

JASMINE: Um, yes, you are. You're all flirty cutesy with Alexandra but have been a jerk to me.

ROBERT: I'm not being a jerk to you.

JASMINE: You've always been a jerk to me. Lest us not forget the rain cloud? The fact that you dumped several gallons of water over my head???

ROBERT: Oh, stop being dramatic, it wasn't that bad.

JASMINE: I hope you're not treating Penny how you've treated me.

I didn't think he'd reply—why would he? But my phone vibrated again.

ROBERT: Penny hasn't been pestering me via phone constantly.

JASMINE: You know I'm not doing this by choice. I'm the designated communicator. It's the task chosen for me because I'm the least important person in this car.

I might have crossed a line. I knew that whether or not I liked my powers, at least I had some. Alexandra, who sat mere feet from me, did not. And neither did Sebastian. I was the only person in the car with actual powers, which felt insane to admit, even to myself.

But maybe I was testing him. Maybe I was fishing for a compliment or an admittance that I wasn't just the random girl he was forced to text. That I mattered in this mission.

It took him a while to respond. The three "typing" dots appeared and disappeared multiple times. When the message came through, it did so as a big blue box of text.

ROBERT: I'm sorry. I don't mean to be cross. It's not you. I'm just frustrated to be isolated right now. The only reason I agreed to coming with Alexandra is because I knew she couldn't go alone. I knew something was up with that Zeke guy and I just didn't trust it. But now, I'm not even with her, I'm with this Penny girl who won't shut up about this Theo guy or her 'best friend Bianca.' It's lonely and it's hard because in all honesty, I'd rather be home right now. And before you say, 'you're literally heading home,' know it doesn't work like that. I don't get to just turn around and pretend that this never happened. Someone tried to kill me. My normal life is over, and

I feel like I can't catch a breath or even a moment to realize what's happened.

I read the text a few times but didn't respond. Another one came through.

ROBERT: I've been avoiding getting involved in this whole superhero business, so you have to understand that it's a bit messed up to now be in over my head with someone I don't know, heading back home but not in the way I intended. I get to go back home, but not really. You know? Maybe you can't understand.

I couldn't fully understand. I eased into this. I chose to join Sebastian, chose to get into this mess that was my life. It was a hard choice, but it was a choice, nonetheless. Robert didn't have that luxury.

JASMINE: I'm sorry. I don't know what else to say. But I'm sorry.

ROBERT: Don't be. I don't want your pity.

JASMINE: It's not pity.

ROBERT: You can stop texting me now. I'm done with this conversation.

I wanted to fight him. I wanted to keep it going. But instead, I tucked my phone under my leg and stared out the window.

Robert Arashi was frustrating and highly emotional. He had a temper like a ticking bomb. But I couldn't help but find a bit of enjoyment in setting him off. He might have been the one to admit loneliness, but he was speaking for both of us. And until I was reunited with Bianca and Penny, his volatile texts were my only remedy.

CHAPTER THIRTY-SIX

Bianca

Durango. I'd spent a lot of time thinking about this place. I'd heard so many stories from Eric, Alexandra, and Sebastian. Sebastian.

I often forgot that he grew up in Durango. That his family... that his family died in Durango. What happened here, the tragedy of it all, that's what inspired him to become the hero he did.

I admittedly felt bad about forcing him back here, causing him to face his trauma-stained past. And to drag Eric back here, too. Two people with horrible memories of this place, now forced to return. Because of me and my big ideas.

But where else was there to go? At this point, we knew for certain that Durango was superhero-free, thanks to the previous efforts of Fadel.

It was the only place we were certain he couldn't find new blood to join him. And besides, it was familiar territory for Eric and Sebastian, which could ultimately prove useful.

The wheels of the plane had barely touched the runway and Eric's tension was already palpable. As we rode in our cab towards the hotel, his stress took on a new sound as he tapped his foot with nervous energy.

"This has been a long time coming."

I glanced over at him as he stared forward at the road ahead. This was the first time he'd even acknowledged that we were back where it all began for him.

"Oh?"

We kept our voices low, so as to not bother Theo up front as he gave the driver directions from his phone. The driver spoke very poor English and Theo looked exasperated.

"How so? Did you ever think you'd be back?" I asked, genuinely surprised that the thought of returning here someday had even crossed his mind before I'd made this decision.

"I always imagined bringing you here."

I hadn't expected that answer. I'd imagined coming here as well, but not with Eric. It definitely felt a bit wrong being here with a man other than Sebastian. Trying to steer any conversation away from *our* history, I selfishly dug a bit further into his, at risk of putting a little too much pressure on his open wound.

"Why? Doesn't this place bring back unpleasant memories?"

He didn't seem to mind the question, thank goodness. But his eyes still showed a type of anguish.

"Yeah, but it's part of my story. And besides, I'd only been with Fadel for a few months before he moved to Victory. I was still considered a new recruit when you joined, remember?"

"Yeah, I remember."

Eric was the cool, talented, fit boy I couldn't take my eyes off of. I remembered the way he would teleport around me. The way he would disappear mid-sentence just to make me laugh, reappearing with a flower from the local gardeners to tuck behind my ear. I remembered the way he would hold me tight by a campfire I'd light in the woods. I remembered our special places, our little secrets.

Looking at him now, it was hard to see that same boy. It hadn't been long, but he looked like a different person entirely. He looked tired, war worn. His smile looked sadder, his eyes without that mischievous glint.

But his embrace was the same, like not a minute had passed since he walked me back to my apartment and kissed me in the rain one summer night. Like the clock's hands hadn't moved since we chased each other around Fadel's training facility, laughing so hard we cried as he caught me and we fell to the floor. If I closed my eyes and breathed in his scent, we were back in Victory, and everything was alright. There wasn't a worry in the world, we were just heroes, but also just kids.

It was funny how such tragedy, such loss of innocence, aged a person. Two physical years were like twenty mental years. Because things weren't actually ok. We were with a supervillain. We just *thought* everything was ok. We were young, naive. We weren't the same people anymore. All that innocence was gone, and no matter how much we wanted to reverse time and steal it back, it just wasn't possible.

As we pulled up to the hotel, memories of Eric were immediately wiped from the forefront of my mind. A blonde girl with dirty jean shorts and a tank top stood in front of the building and captured my whole attention.

Before the car even came to a complete stop, I'd already ripped off my seat belt and thrown the door open. I leapt out and ran straight to her as tears filled my eyes.

Penny and I collided and fell to the ground, hugging each other tightly. I don't know which of us was sobbing harder.

Holding my best friend for the first time in days reminded me once again of what time could do to a person. It hasn't been ten days, like we'd originally anticipated. It felt like so much longer. If it had actually been ten days, I don't know if I could have survived. I'd missed her dearly.

"Careful Bee," I heard Theo say behind me. "You'll freeze my girl if you're not careful."

"No, these are happy tears, not sad," I sniffed, but smiled. Still, I pulled off, so Theo could get a look at his girl.

His body stiffened upon seeing her face. His mouth hung slightly open, unable to find words. It was like watching a groom see his bride coming down the aisle for the first time. He suddenly blinked, shook his head a bit, and laughed.

"Wow, you're really dirty, I thought I wanted a hug, but now I'm not so sure."

But Penny only burst into tears again and sprinted into his arms. He stumbled back a bit, but reciprocated the embrace, stroking her hair. Overcome with those initial emotions once again, he planted a kiss on her head and whispered calming, sweet nothings to her. I could have sworn there were tears in his eyes, too.

After a few moments, they finally pulled apart. Well, not fully apart, because she still gripped his hand and hugged his arm like she would never let him go again.

I introduced Eric to Penny and Robert, who introduced himself to Theo and me. We sorted out our sleeping arrangements, with Penny and I sharing a king bed in one room, Eric and Theo each in a queen in another, and Robert on a fold out couch in the boys' room. We made plans for breakfast in the morning, before Jasmine, Alexandra, and Sebastian got in. Wishing each other goodnight, I finally pulled Penny away from Theo.

Penny and Robert had arrived with nothing, having apparently teleported out of the van and onto the expressway. Not wanting her to sleep in her dirty shorts and t-shirt, I loaned her pajamas. She took a shower, rinsing off two days' worth of dirt, and picked up a cheap toothbrush from the front desk. When we finally finished our wind down, I climbed into bed and squeezed her hand on top of the covers.

"I missed you more than you know, Pen."

"I missed you, too. I really did."

"I'm so happy you're here with me."

"In Durango?"

"Yeah. It feels really weird. Being here, I mean."

"Because of Seb?"

Sebastian. Not Eric. Sebastian.

"Yeah."

In less than 24 hours, I'd see him. I was thrilled but also a bit nervous. I was already feeling so fragile. Would I be able to support him how he needed once he returned to this place?

I was happy the lights were out so she couldn't see the tears in my eyes.

"Penny?" I asked into the dark.

"Yeah?"

"Do you want to run an errand with me in the morning before breakfast?"

"Of course, Bee. Anything for you."

I smiled and rolled over. I was finally with my best friend again. Tomorrow I'd be with my boyfriend. We would all be together again.

All would be well.

* * *

Penny and I arrived at Oak Ridge cemetery outside Durango at 9:30 the next morning. We'd stopped in a shop on the way and bought a small bouquet of flowers. Now, after an hour wandering around trying to find the right spot, I finally found the graves I was looking for.

EMILY AMELIA CASWELL
DAVID JOSEPH CASWELL

I knelt down, placed the flowers on Sebastian's mother's headstone, and said a quick prayer. Tears flooded into my eyes for these two people I'd never met. Thoughts of Sebastian as a child flooded my mind. What was he like? Did he cuddle up with his mom? Did his dad teach him how to wrestle? Did they all have family dinners together? Did they celebrate him every time he brought home a positive report card or when he made the varsity track team?

I didn't know them, but I was sure they were proud of him. I knew they loved him dearly. How could someone not? He was the best man I'd ever met.

So much about this was wrong, being here without him. Visiting the graves of people I'd never met. But one thing felt very right: the way I cared for Sebastian, the way I wanted to know everything about him. I wanted him to keep me safe, and for me to return that favor.

I wanted Sebastian.

"Thanks for coming with me, Pen."

She reached for my hand.

"Of course."

As we turned to leave, a figure in the distance began moving our direction. Penny noticed it too.

"Bee, is that…"

"Sebastian?" I whispered to myself.

As the figure got closer, I noted sandy brown hair and a tan zip-up hoodie.

My goodness, it *was* Sebastian. For a moment, I thought I'd willed him into existence. Just thinking about him seemingly conjured him out of thin air. Maybe I was imagining him. Or maybe I was seeing a ghost. The chills down my spine upon seeing him certainly made me feel like I was.

But reality told me that he must have gotten in earlier than expected and come straight here to see his parents' graves. He didn't know I'd be here, and why would he? I'd only gotten the idea last night.

I let go of Penny's hand and jogged towards him. It wasn't a ghost. He was growing more and more real as I approached. His soft hair, his strong build, his long, determined stride. It was definitely him.

Sebastian must have realized that I was also real, because he started running too. I laughed and cried simultaneously as I picked up the pace and ran faster over little hills and valleys. His face grew clearer and his smile more definite.

And then I was in his arms. The world melted away and nothing else mattered except my whispered name and the warmth of his embrace as his lips pressed tightly against mine.

II

Part Two

CHAPTER THIRTY-SEVEN

Sebastian

I held her for what felt like forever. I didn't even care that Penny was watching. Nothing could pull me out of that moment. Even if Fadel had shown up, I don't know if it would have mattered.

"Bianca," I whispered between kisses.

"Sebastian," she breathed, smiling. Oh, how I loved kissing that smile. My hand was in her hair, tangled, desperately holding on, scared to lose her again.

The flowers I'd gotten had fallen by our feet. She tried not to step on them, but I pulled her in closer anyway.

"Sebastian, the flowers."

"It's ok. This is what mom would have wanted. This is all she ever wanted for me."

"Sorry," she pulled away. Her hands had frosted. Her eyes were wet.

"Don't be sad, Bee. It's all ok, we're together now."

"I'm not sad over you. I'm truly so happy to be here with you right now. I'm sad because I never knew them."

She gestured to the graves around us. I stooped to pick up the flowers, and we made our way back to my parents. I leaned down to set the bouquet on the grave but was stopped suddenly by the sight of another bouquet leaning against the headstone.

"You brought her flowers, too."

"I did. It's what I would have done if I'd met them in person. Your mother deserved something beautiful, since she brought something beautiful into this world."

I couldn't help it; I hugged her again. She smelled like vanilla and lavender. She snuggled up against me; her cheek pressed on my chest.

"I love you."

"I love you, too. And I missed you."

I squeezed her and we pulled apart. Penny cautiously approached, taking advantage of our moment apart.

"Sebastian," she ran into my arms and threw hers around my neck. "I'm so happy we're all here! We finally made it!"

"I know, it's been wild. I'm so happy you're ok. Gosh, we were so worried when you disappeared from the van. Thank goodness Robert found you."

"I wouldn't be here if it wasn't for him. I'm truly so grateful."

"I can't wait to hear all about your adventure, Pen." I knew Robert had found her on the side of the road and got her back to the nearest town, but I didn't know much more than that.

"I'll have to tell you when Jasmine is around," she replied, smirking mischievously.

"Why?" Bianca asked.

"Because she's pretending to hate Robert. Once I make it clear that he heroically saved my life, she will have to admit she secretly loves him."

"You and your scheming. You need to stop playing Emma and let her be."

She just skipped over and grabbed Bianca's hand.

"Let's get going," Bianca laughed. "I'm dying to see everyone."

I turned and took one last look at my parents. Checking to make sure Bianca and Penny weren't looking, I took a few steps closer to the headstones. I leaned down and kissed my mother's stone. I saluted my father's.

"I hope I can make you proud, Dad. I'm going to get him back for what he did to you both. I just wish you could be here to see it."

CHAPTER THIRTY-EIGHT

Penny and Bianca were gone when we pulled up in the van. Disappointment didn't even begin to cover it. No, I was annoyed. The welcome committee that ushered us out of the vehicle and into the hotel were two of my least favorite people: Theo and Robert.

To be fair, I loved Theo. I could never tell him so, but I did. He was my friend and brother in all of this mess. But still, he annoyed me and I didn't want to see his over-enthusiastic smirk this early in the morning.

Robert, on the other hand...

He jogged out to the van alongside Theo as we pulled up. They must have been sitting in the lobby waiting for our arrival.

His long legs and tan skin forced my eyes to look him up and down as he approached. I couldn't help it, even if I didn't like him, he was fit. Fit and thoroughly attractive.

Maybe that made me dislike him more. Attractive people had a track record of ignoring me or fighting with me. Always the bridesmaid, never the bride. That was my eternal problem.

When Theo pulled the sliding door of the van open, he faked a frown.

"Well well, look what the cat dragged in."

"Shut up," I tried to push past him, but he seized me around the waist and pulled me out of the van. Lifting me into the air, he yelled."

"We're back in business, baby! All of us together again!"

"Put me down."

"Nope. We need to celebrate this momentous occasion."

"Put me down."

Theo obliged and set me on my feet.

"You're no fun."

"You missed me."

"Yeah," he smiled. "I kind of did. Just a little."

Theo moved on to shake Sebastian's hand and hug Alexandra. As I worked my way around him, I ran straight into Robert with a smack that knocked me back a step.

"Hey," I blurted. "Careful."

"Sorry, but you ran into me."

"Whatever."

I tried to work my way around him, too, but he stepped in my way again.

"It's good to see you guys made it."

Was he trying to be nice to me? I looked up to see who he was talking to, since I assumed he must be talking to Alexandra and not me.

No. He was looking at me.

"Oh," I tucked some hair behind my ear. "Yeah, well we should be the ones glad you made it. Since you know, you got separated from us."

"Abducted, actually. Much scarier."

"Mhm."

I could cut the tension with a knife. A very, very dull knife. Maybe even a spoon.

"Ok," I said, trying to take another step forward. "I need to go shower. I've been stuck in a car for days with these people and I could really use a hot shower to relax."

I started to walk away but turned around, just in time to add, "And besides, I had several gallons of dirty water poured on my head. My hair could use a wash."

"It wasn't dirty water."

He didn't even bother to turn around.

"Still. Not my finest moment of the trip. I need the shower therapy."

He grumbled something I couldn't hear.

"What?"

"Nothing." Now he looked at me. His eyes looked guilty, but his lips looked mischievous.

"What? *Tell me.*"

"Aren't you going to thank me for saving your friend?"

He hadn't wanted to say it. When it came out, his eyes grew three sizes. He bit his lip but didn't open his mouth to cover his biting words.

Part of me did want to thank him. He did save Penny, after all. But I wouldn't do it. I didn't want to see my olive branch thrown to the ground and stomped on. Might as well do what Sebastian continues to urge: just keep up the fight.

"Nope," I smirked, tossing my hair over my shoulder. "She would have been fine on her own. She's far more powerful than you."

And with that, I went inside, not even bothering to look back and read his expression.

CHAPTER THIRTY-NINE

Theodore

The gang was finally back together. But with extra members. After the newest arrivals cleaned up a bit, I suggested we go chill at Robert's place, but Jasmine shot me down. Sebastian, shockingly, backed her. He figured that Fadel was staking it out, since it was Robert he really hoped to capture. Stupid, but whatever.

We had divided up the two hotel rooms, one for the ladies and one for us men. I, unfortunately, had been forced to share a bed with Sebastian.

"Can't we just get a third room?" I'd asked, annoyed to have to share a bed at all.

"The hotel got all booked up for a wedding. We're lucky to even have two rooms," Jasmine replied, shockingly without much sass.

"I'm confident in my own masculinity, but it's weird to share a bed. Especially a queen."

"Well put up a pillow wall between you two or something. It's not my problem."

There was the Jasmine sass I missed so much.

So that was how I ended up shoved in a bed next to another man, a lousy line of pillows forming a barrier between us.

"You know the pillows give us even less space, right?" Sebastian asked, peeking over at me.

"Just go to sleep, Caswell. We have stuff to do tomorrow."

Sebastian rolled back over and turned out his lamp. He went silent fairly quickly, likely asleep already. Dang, that was fast.

I tossed and turned for a good thirty minutes before finally giving up on sleep.

I got up and threw on my hoodie. Slipping on my running shoes, I made my way past the bed Eric and Robert were sharing. They were also fast asleep.

I took one of the room keys as well as the car key from the desk and slipped them into my pocket. I'd just go take a stroll around the block until I got tired.

By the time I reached the lobby, it had become clear that someone else had the same idea. And that someone just so happened to be a little blonde cutie.

She stood at the coffee station, making herself a paper cup of hot tea. I snuck up behind her quietly. Lacing my arms around her waist, I whispered in her ear.

"No sleep for you either, huh?"

She jumped.

"My gosh, Theo! I almost spilled boiling water on myself."

She pretended to be annoyed, but I caught a little grin that made my heart sing.

"Good thing you didn't. Come on, get a lid on that thing and come with me."

She took my hand and smiled up at me.

"Where are we going?"

That was a good question. I didn't know. I remembered a place Sebastian used to talk about. Quiet, beautiful. That would be perfect.

"You'll see. Come on."

We ran hand-in-hand out to the van. She buckled in while I plugged the location into my phone. I turned my body away from her so she couldn't see what I was typing.

"You really aren't going to tell me?" She cocked her head and fluttered her lashes.

"Nope," I put the car into gear. "And you better not look at the map."

"I don't think it would make much of a difference. I don't know the area."

I swore she was trying to see the screen, so I angled away even more.

"Still. Just sit back and relax."

Finally relenting, she cozied into her seat and sipped her tea quietly. Her smile made me smile. Until it faded away. Slowly at first, but then she looked quite distraught.

"Hey," I asked, reaching out to hold her hand. "What's wrong? If you're really so upset, I'll tell you where we're going."

She laughed.

"No, it's ok. You're not the problem."

"Well then what is? And don't quote Taylor Swift."

She laughed even harder. Her eyes twinkled when she laughed.

"I can't believe you know that's a Taylor Swift reference. Are you a Swiftie, Theodore Martin?"

"No, not in the slightest. I just don't live under a rock."

"Fair."

She sighed and squeezed my hand, letting that frown settle in place of her smile again.

"I saw my parents. Before I left. Sebastian and Jasmine took me to the farm, and I said goodbye to them."

"You've gotta be kidding," I replied, almost too shocked to comprehend her words.

"Unfortunately, I am not. I really went to see them. It was the right thing to do, since I might not be returning to Victory."

"And how did it go?"

She sat in silence, playing with the zipper on her jacket.

"That well, huh?"

She smiled a little.

"You know, it went just about as well as I expected it would. That is to say it went very, very badly. My mother had a meltdown, and my father raised his voice. Apparently, I'm the worst thing to happen to this family in 100 generations! Or something crazy like that."

She threw her arms in the air for dramatic effect.

"I think it's pretty stupid, all things considered. They wail about how I abandoned them and how I don't really love them all because I decided to be an adult and do things with my life. What was I going to do if I stayed home forever? Just because I'm not under their roof doesn't mean I don't love them or care about them. They want to keep me in a glass box. I can be their pride and joy, but only if I sell my soul to them."

"You make them sound like the devil."

"Ok you're right, that's not fair of me. They're not evil, they just have a different vision of what my life should look like."

"Do they think you're rejecting their lifestyle or something? Do they think you're some big city girl with girl-boss dreams to pursue?"

Penny laughed. "I don't even love the city, really. And it's not like I'm even pursuing a career! No, I'm totally ok with the idea of living on the farm and living a simpler life. I love the tradition that my family has laid out for themselves. The problem I have with their view of my future is that my calling to do something outside their house couldn't possibly be real, since it wasn't them making the decision. So even if I feel compelled to use my powers to protect Victory, and therefore protect them, that's bad because it wasn't in the script they wrote for my life."

CHAPTER THIRTY-NINE

"So, they're controlling?"

Penny nodded.

"Controlling is a good word for it. Territorial. It's not the lifestyle; it's not even the logic behind it. It's that they want me to live my whole life according to their script. Which I could do, but I wouldn't be happy. And even if I did..."

She sniffed back tears again.

"Even if I did, they still wouldn't be happy with me. They still wouldn't treat me well. I still wouldn't be good enough. So why would I subject myself to that? Why wouldn't I just live my life and let them hate me?"

I didn't know how to address that concern. Penny's self-esteem was something I'd helped kindle when we were in high school and early college. She'd come a long way in learning to like who she was as a woman. I didn't want to drag those conversations back into the light of day. So instead, I focused on the problem at hand.

"They shouldn't blame you for living your life, Pen."

"Oh, they don't blame me. They blame you."

I threw my head back laughing.

"Are you for real?"

"Yes! They said that I wasn't an issue until you came into my life. So congrats, they hate you for turning me to the dark side!"

"So do they want you to leave me and go back to them?"

"Essentially, yes."

I rubbed her hand with my thumb.

"And is that something you'd consider?"

"Is *what* something I'd consider? Leaving you?"

"Yeah."

She hesitated for a moment.

"My gosh, Pen, is that something you'd consider?"

"What? No! Of course not!" Penny squeaked.

"But you hesitated."

"Not because I would leave you. Because I'm trying to understand why you think I would."

A wave of relief rushed over me.

"I don't know. I guess it's my own paranoia." I didn't like sharing my feelings. I always thought it was ironic that we encouraged Bianca to channel her emotions since the rest of us were so good at bottling ours up.

"I don't want you to leave me, Pen. I want you to stay with me wherever I go. I don't want to live my life without you— I don't think I could handle it."

She looked up at me again, a misty dampness under her eyes.

My goodness, I'd made the girl cry. That wasn't my intention.

"I'd follow you anywhere, Theo. Those days apart… they were really hard on me. I don't want to be away from you again."

"Good, then it's settled. We'll stay within arm's reach forever. It's like a restraining order but the inverse. I'll only stay more than six feet away while you're in the bathroom."

"Sounds like a plan to me."

Oh, how I loved her laugh.

I took the final turn onto a dirt road, twisting and turning our way up the hill that these Texans considered a "mountain."

When we reached the top, I parked and turned off the car. My spine tingled at the blackness that had shrouded the car, but I knew we'd be fine. We'd be safe. We weren't in danger, at least not tonight.

"I gotta say," I said, helping Penny out. "Sebastian made this place sound much cooler."

Approaching a rock ledge, we looked around at the view. The city below was lit up with hundreds of dazzling, twinkling lights. It was cute, but nothing spectacular.

"Yeah, the city is nice. But I think the main attraction is actually that way," Penny said, turning me slowly by the arms to face away from Durango.

Looking in that direction, all we could see was the sky. And man, it was so much better than the sky in Victory.

Millions of twinkling lights dotted our view. The sky looked so clear, cloudless, like a movie set.

"Oh dang," I whispered as I took a deep breath. "This is amazing."

"Yeah," she replied, taking my hand. "It is."

"You know what's a hundred times more amazing and a million times more beautiful?"

She turned to face me, releasing her hand and moving it onto her hip.

"If you say me, I swear—"

My right hand clutched the back of her hair, my left squeezing her hip as I swiftly pulled her lips to mine. Her hands dropped in surprise, but it only took her a moment to move them to my chest. We moved together, deepening the kiss and the embrace. One of her hands moved from my chest to my back, urging me closer and closer.

We kissed like we were dancing, slowly and passionately, melting into each other with each step.

When we finally broke apart, we breathed heavily in tandem. Her smile lit up the night.

"Aren't we supposed to be looking at the sky?"

"I don't care. I just want to look at you. I love you, Penelope Anderson."

"I love you, too." This time, she kissed me. It almost knocked me backwards. I hugged her tight.

"I just want to hold you forever."

"Please never let me go," she whispered, maybe to me, maybe to the stars.

"I promise you, Penny. You're mine."

We settled onto the dirt, and she curled up in my arms. We sat there for a while in silence, just breathing in each other's company.

"It's getting late," I admitted after a blissful eternity. "We should go."

She let me help her up and we made our way back to the car. As I shut her door and made my way to the driver's side, I took one last look out at the stars, talking to myself.

"Someday, I'm gonna marry that girl."

CHAPTER FORTY

Jasmine

ROBERT: Weird question…

This was unusual. In the two days of text exchanges, I'd always been the one to start the conversation. I'd always ask how they were doing, he'd reply something rude, and I'd snap back. This was our ritual and I was getting used to it. I liked the comfort of it.

But now that we were in Durango, sleeping in two separate hotel rooms, we didn't need to be texting at all. We'd finally made it. What was the point? It's not like our one in-person conversation yesterday went any better than our previous ones.

Still, I couldn't help but let curiosity win.

JASMINE: ???

ROBERT: Your last name is Kahale, right?

Seriously, what was the point of this?

JASMINE: Yeah…

ROBERT: Is your dad John Kahale? The pro surfer?

Oh my gosh. No one knew who my dad was. At least not this far east. He hadn't surfed professionally since the early 2000s.

My dad was my hero. He'd taught me to surf when I was only six. He was the one who made sure I wasn't afraid of water. In fact, he taught me not to be afraid of anything.

"Remember, little flower," he said to me on my first day at my new school in California. "You've ridden the biggest waves and had the hardest crashes. Nothing could be harder than what you've already done. And nothing can bring you more joy and more thrill than facing a fear you think is paralyzing. You are braver than you know."

Thinking of my father brought a certain warmth to my body, like a blanket just out of the dryer. He had always been a comfort to me in difficult times.

Maybe when this war with Fadel ends, I can fly out to California and stay with him and my mom for a while. And maybe I could bring Penny with me. My parents would love her. And she deserved to spend some time with people who would take care of her. I could teach her to surf. We could lay out in the sun for hours, not a care in the world. Not a supervillain in sight. No men to take my friends' attention.

JASMINE: Yes, actually. How do you know him?

ROBERT: Ok don't laugh at me, but Johnny Kahale was my idol growing up!!!

I couldn't help it, but I smiled.

JASMINE: For real? Do you surf?

ROBERT: I grew up surfing but haven't in years. My family is out in California, but I've been in Durango for a few years now because of work. I'd love to go back, honestly.

This was nice. A real conversation. Some humanity under that thick skin of his.

JASMINE: My family is in Cali too! And then I went to college in Oregon. It's technically where I last lived before Victory. But I consider Hawaii my home. That's where I grew up. Mostly, anyway.

ROBERT: That doesn't surprise me at all.

JASMINE: ???

ROBERT: You look Hawaiian.

I frowned. Was this a compliment? An insult? I didn't like that he'd been looking at me enough to determine my genetic makeup.

JASMINE: No, I look like a tan Japanese girl.

ROBERT: No, that's what I look like. You look Hawaiian.

JASMINE: You look like a tan Japanese girl?

I smirked at my own cleverness. I glanced over my phone to make sure Bianca was asleep and couldn't see my grin.

ROBERT: I look Japanese but with a farmer's tan.

JASMINE: Are you? Japanese with a farmer's tan?

ROBERT: I am. And I'm guessing you are too?

JASMINE: Yep. Half and half.

ROBERT: Same but without the cool native part. The other half is actually *from* Cali.

JASMINE: Ah, so the tan is genetic.

ROBERT: Hey now, I also just tan well. I love being out in the sun.

JASMINE: Me too.

Even without a mirror, I knew my cheeks had turned red. Thank goodness he couldn't see me. I'd not been this open about my life back home. Whenever I was asked about my background, I gave the same story. I'm half and half, grew up in Hawaii, moved to California, went to college in Oregon, discovered my powers young, and chose to come out and help the Victory supers. End of story, thank you very much.

But with Robert, I found a certain kinship. The connection was more than just our shared pessimism, snark, and quick wit. He made me relax, like I did at home with my family. Maybe it was our shared heritage or interests. But maybe we were just two people trying to figure out how to be brave. People trying to see how we fit in the larger puzzle.

ROBERT: When you're home, do you still surf?

JASMINE: Yeah, it's been a bit, but when I'm home, I do. I was just thinking I'd love to take Penny home and teach her when this is all over.

ROBERT: Maybe after this is all over, I could go home for a bit too. Maybe we could meet up?

Without meaning to, I raised my hand to my mouth in a silent gasp. This was certainly new.

JASMINE: You just want to meet my dad.

ROBERT: Guilty as charged.

JASMINE: I'd be happy to introduce you. I bet he would love to get out on the water with another surf enthusiast.

ROBERT: Great, it sounds like a plan! Not the meeting your dad part, the part where we go surfing. I guess that might also be with your dad… but maybe we could do dinner afterwards?

I didn't mean to, but I smiled a bit more. This time it spread across my entire face and warmed my body, right down to my toes. I'd spent so much time third wheeling and fifth wheeling for my friends. It was nice to think that a man wanted to spend time with me for once. After all, wasn't I pretty too? I wasn't as sweet as Penny or as personable as Bianca, but I kept in shape and knew how to do my hair and makeup. I just never seemed to have the attention of men like my friends did.

And I never thought I wanted it. For years I'd made excuses saying I preferred to be alone and that it was easier to worry about myself than to worry about someone else. But it still hurt when I'd see Sebastian kissing Bianca when they thought no one was looking. Or when Theo would wink at Penny and she'd melt like a Popsicle on a hot day.

Maybe Robert was just being nice. Maybe he only wanted to take me to dinner as a thank you for my introduction to the famous Johnny Kahale. He did say 'plan' and not 'date.' But nevertheless, I smiled.

JASMINE: I'd like that. A lot actually.

Only Bee's body rolling over and pulling at the sheets shook me out of it. She woke up a bit, groggy but smiling.

"Thank goodness ten days wasn't ten days after all," she whispered. "I missed you, Jas."

I crawled forward and took her hand, squeezing it in both of mine.

"I've missed you too. I've been stuck with your boyfriend for far too long. I'm so glad you can finally take him off my hands."

I smirked a bit as we both rolled over our separate ways. Couldn't let the sappiness win the day.

CHAPTER FORTY-ONE

Alexandra

We sipped our coffee in that early morning "I don't want to be awake" silence.

We found a coffee shop aptly named "Bean There, Done That." The vibes were all over the place. It was as if this shop had experienced and maintained every trend since the 1970s. Each room, nook, and cranny— and there were several— had a different theme.

Coming in the entrance, it looked like a modern urban hipster joint. But rounding the corner, there was a comfy room with plush oversize armchairs, mismatched wood tables and chairs for people to work at, and a brick fireplace. The back had a few other nooks, one with church pews and stained glass, one with rustic farmhouse decor, and even one with groovy 70s paraphernalia.

We sat in the comfy-looking main room, per Penny's "Ohhh! Cozy!"

Penny and Theo shared a love seat, but only occupied a little over half the space, despite Theo's size. Jasmine took an armchair and Robert and Eric sat on wood chairs they'd pulled over from a nearby table. Robert straddled the chair and tapped his foot impatiently.

Sebastian, Bianca, and I shared a couch. Bianca, for some reason, gestured for me to sit between her and Sebastian, acting as though she wasn't trying to create a wall between them. Reluctantly I sat. Across the circle, Eric stared at his coffee like he was concerned it had been poisoned. Bianca wouldn't look at him.

"So do we want to talk about what we're going to do, or not?" Jasmine said, jumping straight to the point.

"Well, I think the prudent thing to do first would be to drive out to Fadel's compound, to see if he's still using it," Sebastian said and clapped his hands together like a football coach on a timeout. He kept his voice hushed, hoping to not be overheard. "Luckily, Eric knows how to get there. He, Bianca, and I can drive that way once we wrap up here— just a bit of surveillance."

Bianca's head whipped over to look at Sebastian. I didn't think much of it, but then I saw her fingers move. Little flames danced around, weaving in and out between her pointer, middle, and ring fingers. I pulled my eyes away and looked over at Theo and Penny. Theo was watching Bianca very closely. He noticed her hands, too.

"We doubt he's returned there, but it would be good to check," Eric agreed with Sebastian.

Bianca snuffed out her flames and leaned back, not looking at either Sebastian or Eric. The pain of having both of them in one room must have been too much for her. Having seen her with both of them firsthand, I knew this couldn't be easy. She really did love them both.

"And what are the rest of us supposed to do? Hole up in this coffee shop all day, pretending like we're useful?" Jasmine asked.

"Well, I think some of you could do a bit of research to see if there are other large properties in the vicinity," Eric replied, cutting Sebastian off before he could answer. "I know Fadel talked about his various assets a lot. I know he had another place in Durango, at least back then. He didn't live at the office or the compound. I would bet anything he still has another residence. I don't think we will find him at the old compound, so our goal should be the house, if he has one."

Sebastian jumped back in, trying to recover control of the conversation.

"And then whoever else can keep Robert moving."

This entire meeting was almost unbearable. Bianca shifted uncomfortably in her seat and suddenly found intense interest reading the label on her coffee cup.

"What do you mean by that?" Robert asked Sebastian, looking annoyed.

"Well," Sebastian crossed his arms and leaned back. "Fadel wants you specifically. And he seems pretty desperate to get you. We don't want him to take you prisoner, and a moving target is harder to hit. I worry that you'd be more easily found if you spent the day sitting on one spot. He's got minions, and they're bound to be hunting for you. If they spread out and you're a sitting duck, odds are you'll be discovered.

"I think you and Jasmine should go out on the town for the day. Keep moving on foot, keep busy. Stay vigilant, though."

Robert opened his mouth, but Jasmine replied first.

"Why me? I want to do research with Penny."

"Because we both know you won't actually do any work," Theo laughed.

Jasmine scowled.

"Ok fair, but Alexandra should come with us," she responded, looking at me.

If I had to be stuck all day with a pair of people, I certainly didn't want it to be Jasmine and Robert, who kept fighting. Even worse would be the trio of Sebastian, Bianca, and Eric…

Penny and Theo were my best bet, even if I would be an awkward third wheel.

"I know the area better than any of you," I chipped in, quickly turning to Sebastian. "Except you, Sebastian. Sorry, I didn't mean to—"

"Don't worry about it," he smiled, a bit painfully. "You're right, you need to do research here."

"And we will also stay here and do research," Theo smirked and squeezed Penny's arm. "We are big fans of research."

"Mhm," Jasmine said, eyeing both of them. Odds were that research would happen, but it would mostly be me doing it.

"Alright, sounds like everyone has their marching orders!" Sebastian said, standing up suddenly, making me jump, almost spilling my coffee.

He put his hand in the middle, between all of us.

"Defenders of Victory on three!"

No one moved. Jasmine looked as though she would either vomit or kill him.

"No."

Sebastian lowered his hand.

"Ok, well, in that case... let's get to work."

CHAPTER FORTY-TWO

Bianca

Before we could get out the door, Theo insisted on talking to me privately. I didn't like the sound of it, but I obliged.

He grabbed my wrist and dragged me around the corner into the empty church pew section of the coffee shop. As we left, he called out to the others, attempting to prevent them from following.

"Just want to recap everything from our trip really quick. Want to make sure I didn't miss any details we could use when doing our *research*," Theo said 'research' in something close to a British accent. It just confirmed for everyone that no real research would be done. "We will just be a moment!"

"Ok," I crossed my arms and stood at the end of a table. "What do you need to recap?"

"Sit," he replied, gesturing to the chair in front of me with an authority I'd rarely seen.

"Theo—"

"No, you're going to listen to me. What the actual heck is going on with you?"

I shook my head.

"I don't know what you're talking about."

"Don't play dumb, Bianca. What is happening between you and

Eric and you and Sebastian? I saw you in Utah. You two couldn't stop smiling and laughing. And then you get back here and go all kissy-kissy with Sebastian like nothing happened out west. Oh, and then you had the nerve to put Alexandra between you two on the couch? I saw the awkward three-way tension. We need to figure this out *before* you get into a car with both of them."

"I—" I didn't know how to respond. I hadn't meant to flirt with Eric. I really didn't want to get close to him again. But also, I really couldn't help it. I cared about him, just like I cared about Sebastian. Maybe that was the problem. I couldn't care about them the same way.

"You think I'm trying to date them both."

"I think," he huffed, sitting down across from me. "You don't want to hurt anyone so you're avoiding making a very serious decision and are therefore hurting two other people."

"I'm not avoiding anything." I knew this was a lie the second it left my mouth. My mind flashed to the couch a few minutes prior.

"It's not my fault that I have to see both of them at the same time," I continued, trying to cover my lie with the truth. "I can't help what's happening."

He put two fingers on the bridge of his nose and closed his eyes. After a deep breath, he continued.

"You're acting like you have no agency in this. You were the one who had the idea to get Eric in the first place. Were you trying to get closure? Has this entire plan been built around your romantic life?"

"You forget that Sebastian was the one who sent you with me in place of himself. I was completely open to having him join me out west."

"That doesn't answer my question. Why are we really involving Eric?"

I threw my hands up, exasperated.

"To help us defeat Fadel! I wasn't lying, I wasn't trying to manipulate anything for my own emotional benefit. I didn't *want* to see Eric like that. I'm happy with Sebastian! I involved Eric for us as a group!"

I swung my arms wildly and slammed my hands down on the table. A spark erupted from each palm and left two charred hand prints on the table. Theo raised his eyebrows in an 'I told you so' manner. I glanced around the room and hoped there were no cameras in the coffee shop.

"I'll leave money on the table to account for the damages," I whispered, reaching into my coat pocket for my wallet.

"Bee," Theo said, ignoring the damage I'd done and grabbing my hand. "Why are you now acting like you're in a nineties rom-com where you can't decide which cute boy to date?"

"This hardly seems fair, Theo," I snatched my hand back.

"Maybe it's unfair, but it's true. You can't stop giggling around Eric. You can't stop talking about how talented Eric is. I know something happened with you two in Utah. That night at the casino, you were acting very differently."

"I thought you were my teammate, Theo," I accused. "I thought you were on my side."

"I *am* on your side, Bianca. I just want you to figure this out because I care about Sebastian and don't want to see him hurt after all this. I care about you, too. You're not yourself lately. Not since we arrived in Crescent Ridge and you saw Eric again."

I tried not to cry. I really, really tried not to. But I failed.

I shivered as little drops of ice clinked off my tapping foot, shattering on the floor. My hands couldn't decide if they wanted to be cold or hot. One second, I thought I would spark a flame and the next, my fingers felt frosted over.

"I can't help it that I used to love Eric. I can't help it that Sebastian entered my life and made me love him, too."

"Bianca," he whispered. "You can literally control the elements.

Look! You're doing it now!"

I opened my mouth to reply, but he continued.

"I've watched you set buildings on fire and freeze bats midair. I've been by your side as you've escaped mercenaries and fought the most evil supervillain ever. Don't tell me you're not capable of controlling your own dating life."

I sniffed and wiped a frozen tear from my cheek.

"I don't know what happened in Utah, but it's not fair to leave Eric and Sebastian hanging, waiting for you to choose between them. Do you know what you want? Because I think you do."

I wasn't going to tell Theo about Eric kissing me. The only person who needed to know was Sebastian. Fear gripped me like an ever-tightening vice each time I imagined telling Sebastian about that kiss.

"I do."

"Can you promise me," he reached out and held my hand again, warming it back up to a stable temperature. "Promise me you'll take care of this? That you'll talk to both of them?"

I nodded.

"I promise."

"And promise me you'll get your head back in the game? I hate seeing you look so weak. You're Bianca freaking Williams, you don't know how powerful you are. Stop letting stupid drama blur your vision."

I smiled at my friend. He was brutal, but he was right.

"Thank you, Theo."

"Now wipe those little icicles," he pulled a tissue from his pocket and handed it to me. "You've got a mission to undertake, and I have research to do."

"Stop saying 'research' with an accent. It makes it way less convincing."

"Never," he smirked, squeezing my hand one last time.

CHAPTER FORTY-THREE

"Research… research…"

"You know just saying 'research' over and over again doesn't actually constitute doing the work, right?"

I looked up to see Alexandra scowling at Theo.

"I'm sorry, I'm just frustrated. I can't find anything," he replied, rubbing his temples with his pointer and middle fingers.

"We've been at it for a solid…" Alexandra checked her phone. "Ten minutes."

"I'm not really a computer guy. I'm more of a punch a villain in the face guy."

Alexandra shook her head and pushed her seat back.

"I'm going to get another coffee. You guys want anything?"

"Yeah, I'll have another…" Theo said, looking at what the barista had written on his cup. "Cowabunga Cappuccino. Seriously, who came up with this place? None of this makes sense."

"I'll have another Extra Groovy Earl Grey with milk," I smiled.

Alexandra nodded silently and disappeared around the corner. The moment she vanished, Theo slammed his laptop shut and groaned.

"Let's get out of here. Why do Jas and the other guy get to have an afternoon on the town? They don't even like each other."

"Maybe if Fadel wanted you instead of Robert, we'd be out and about right now. But unfortunately," I replied, trying my best to keep a straight face, but failing miserably. "He kind of hates you. So now we have to stay here and do whatever Sebastian wants."

"Mmm," he leaned back in his chair and closed his eyes. "As much as I love the thrill of a villain despising me, I cannot wait until he's done and dusted and we can move on with our lives. Maybe go back to fighting bank robbers or something."

I laughed, reaching out to grab his hand, slowly intertwining our fingers and squeezing.

"Actually," his eyes opened with a mischievous glint. "We could shift careers. Picture this: we start finding tax evaders. Better yet, *Sebastian* finds the tax evaders and then I go in and beat them up."

My hand shot up to my mouth as I laughed.

"You've been talking a lot about the future lately. Actually, everyone has. Lots of talk about post-Fadel life."

"Well, this is the closest we've ever been to being free from him, right? I think it's only fair to think about the future and what that will look like."

"But tax-evaders?"

"Hey, just saying'. It sounds a heck of a lot better than what we're doing right now, living in hotel rooms and getting abducted out of moving vehicles. Not to mention fighting creepy dudes who control snakes."

He was right, this trip had been exhausting work. But so had everything leading up to this journey. Our time with Fadel had been a bit of a nightmare since day one. Our lives were completely wrapped up in him. Every thought we had, every action we took, all aimed at stopping this one man. It was a bit infuriating that he took up so much space in our lives.

"Ok," I grinned, reaching for his other hand. We sat holding hands across the table. "Would you rather have a dozen medium-sized villains or one mega villain?"

The corners of Theo's lips curled.

"Depends, by medium-sized do you mean physical size or badness level? Because if we are talking about medium sized men, I'd take a dozen of them, easy."

"Badness level."

"I'd probably keep my same answer. Yep, I want twelve medium-sized baddies who are medium-bad."

I imagined that life. I remembered the life we had before.

We spent years, just the two of us, working together to take down the 'bad guys' in Victory.

I hated to admit; it just wasn't satisfying. I didn't feel truly alive until we found Fadel. Until we were all together. Fadel gave us purpose.

I hated him for it, but also, I guess in a way I owed a lot of my life to his appearance.

"Will we get bored of our lives after Fadel?" I asked, the gears turning in my brain.

Theo must have seen a shift in my expression, since he started rubbing circles into the backs of my hands with his thumbs.

"Hey, hey, no. Don't say that. We could never get bored of our lives. Want to know why?"

He looked completely serious, unwilling to crack a joke and ruin the moment. His eyebrows furrowed, highlighting the chocolate brown of his eyes.

"Why?"

"Because we are all together now. And I know that sounds like I'm trying to be romantic or something, but when I say 'all', I mean *all* of us.

"Even Sebastian?"

That broke him. He smiled.

CHAPTER FORTY-THREE

"Yeah, I guess."

"Even Jas?"

"Unfortunately."

"What about Robert?"

"Ok," he pulled away from me. "Who the heck is Robert anyway? Where did we find him, again? Is he gonna go home at some point, or…"

I burst out laughing again, just in time for Alexandra to round the corner precariously carrying three coffee mugs.

I rushed across the room to help her and she thanked me.

Sitting down again, she looked at Theo's closed laptop.

"So, I'm assuming nothing got accomplished while I was gone."

"Nope," he smiled. "But we did discuss a future of fighting tax evaders."

"Tax evaders?"

"Yep. Easy prey. Medium-sized men. Two punches to the face and they're done for."

Alexandra shook her head.

"Ok, I'm going to do some *actual* work, like Sebastian asked us to."

"Kiss up," Theo said and rolled his eyes. He opened his laptop again.

"Just trying to give these last few days my all."

"Last few days?" I inquired.

"Yeah, once we finish this thing with Fadel, I'm going home. For real this time."

I examined Alexandra's face as she stared at her screen. She didn't look up, her expression remaining unchanged, content.

Alexandra wanted to go back to her life before Fadel, and since she didn't have any sort of powers, that was actually a possibility for her. It didn't matter that I didn't have a real home to return to, my powers gave me purpose. This was the life that I was born to live.

And even if I did have a way out after this, I wouldn't want it.

Because it didn't matter how big or small the villains were or how exhausting it could be at times— I wouldn't want my life to change. It was close to perfect as is.

CHAPTER FORTY-FOUR

Bianca

I thought I knew awkward. I certainly did not. Not until I found myself alone in a car with Eric and Sebastian.

I'd been surprised when both of them agreed to go on this little trip with me, just the three of us. I think Sebastian had been surprised when I also agreed. I hadn't wanted to make it weirder than it already was. And honestly, I wasn't entirely sure how much Eric knew about my relationship with Sebastian.

Sebastian definitely knew about my history with Eric, so if he was cool spending time with him and me, I should be ok with it, too, right?

If he only knew about our kiss back in Utah... then maybe he wouldn't be so cool with things...

What really ended up being awkward was the car situation. Sebastian went for the driver's seat, but Eric held the keys. And to make matters worse, both boys "knew Durango," so they both intended to take the lead. Sebastian looked over at me, hoping for support, while Eric asked, "what does Bianca think?"

I did not want to give an opinion, that's what I thought.

"I think Sebastian should drive and Eric should navigate," I said, mapping it out in my mind. Sebastian liked to be the leader, so he should have the wheel. Eric would like to be seen as knowledgeable about Durango, so it only made sense for him to navigate. They seemed to agree with me, as Eric handed Sebastian the keys and opened the passenger door for himself. I climbed in the back and buckled in.

"Ok, navigator, where to?"

"Same deal as Victory from what it sounds like. Two facilities, one more office and staff-fueling space and then a larger compound outside the city. The office was downtown and the farm property where we trained more extensively, that was off Bucknell Pike. North of the city, I think. It's been a bit since I drove there myself.

"Start off by taking a right out of here and getting up to Marley Street. Do you remember where that is?"

"Yep," Sebastian replied, calmly. If he was bothered by the scenario, he didn't show it.

Notwithstanding Eric's occasional directions, we otherwise made our way out of the downtown area in silence.

"Take a right onto Bucknell Pike and then we should ride that for a solid twenty or so," Eric said, gesturing to a road off to the left.

"Just tell me when I need to turn," Sebastian planned to ride that twenty minutes in silence. And why shouldn't he want that? It was awkward confronting the awkward, so why do it?

Part of me expected one of them to burst the bubble. Initially, I would have sworn it'd be Sebastian. He was by far the more assertive, dominant one. Sebastian wasn't aggressive, but he also wasn't afraid to be bold. He knew what he wanted and he was willing to fight for it. If he wanted to make sure Eric knew that I was his and only his, I could see Sebastian telling him that directly. He was not one to give into passive aggressive behavior, nor one to bottle up issues.

However, as time wore on, Eric seemed ready to initiate that dreaded conversation. This surprised me. I was not used to this newer version of Eric.

The forwardness he'd been showing to me since reuniting was bold, especially for him. Eric had always been more timid, more willing to follow than to lead. That's why he fell for Fadel's schemes in the first place. But he also had a kind heart and a sound mind, which led him out of the villain's clutches and back to his family. I knew Eric as meek and humble.

These two men were similar in so many ways, which may have been what attracted me to both of them. But their differences seemed so clear to me now. Neither one was bad—their virtues and vices wound together to make each a whole person. You couldn't put them on a scale. But they were, in fact, different. And as unfortunate as it was, Eric was different now than he had been back in our days at Fadel's compound.

Not a bad kind of different, just not the man I loved. At least not in that way anymore. Our love had blossomed into a friendship, a kinship, that could only be formed by common experience and mutual suffering. We'd endured something together that we couldn't understand at the time, but coming out on the other side, bonded us for life. We would always be connected. That was why I needed them to be on the same page. Why I couldn't bear the tension. They didn't have to be friends, but I wanted them to have mutual respect for one another.

"You can't force people to like each other," Jasmine had told me as we got into bed the night before. "This isn't Barbie land where everyone is best friends with everyone else. The fact of the matter is that they'll probably dislike each other because they see each other as competition. For you."

I hadn't liked hearing that.

"But I know what I want," I replied.

"But do they know that? Have you been explicit about telling them? Both of them?"

I hadn't had a chance to talk to Eric yet. I didn't want to hurt him, but part of me also was selfish. I feared what he would think of me if I let him down. And I also hadn't yet told Sebastian the truth about what happened back in Utah. I hadn't mentioned the kiss to anyone…

But even without knowing the entire story, Jasmine was still right: I was trying to live in a fantasy world with no animosity.

"You need to talk to them." Jasmine was firm, just like Theo was when he made me promise to be honest with them both.

And yet, I still haven't. The real question was this: who would have a chance to talk to Eric first? Me or Sebastian? If Sebastian, how on earth would that go? And if me, what do you say to a man you used to love when you need to break his heart?

My hands itched from the desire to make a flame. My toes felt cold from the ice trying to form between them.

"You're going to take a right in about a half mile," Eric said, surprising me with the sudden break in the car humming. The anxious realization of tension was thrust upon me once again.

"Right-o," Sebastian replied, not changing his facial expression one bit.

And there we were, back to silence.

CHAPTER FORTY-FIVE

Jasmine

I was stuck with a really hot, six-foot-four man who could control the weather, run a four-minute mile, and surf. It was miserable. Robert said nothing as we walked down 11th Street towards a shop that advertised "Western Gear for the Western Man." I tried to take him in without turning my head. I let my eyes wander up and down his body, from his short, black hair to his scuffed-up Oxfords.

The sleeves of his button down and jacket hugged his biceps tightly enough that I could see every curve. His posture was impeccable, probably from years of perfecting his balance enough to surf.

My gosh, he was so fit. I hated it.

"So," I said, breaking the awkward tension, or at least thinking I was lessening the tension.

"So," he repeated back to me.

"You said you'd love to go back to California."

"Did I?" He looked over at me, but I kept my gaze forward. His lingering stare burned.

"Yeah. When we were texting last night."

I wanted to understand those texts more. Were they just a brief surrender from his ongoing hatred of me? Or was his opinion of me shifting? Not that I would change how I felt about *him* to match. I just wanted to know.

I will continue despising him regardless.

"Oh yeah, the texts. Um, maybe? I would love to, but I don't know how realistic that is."

"Will you go back to your day job after this?"

"Yep."

"Cool, cool."

We kept walking in silence. I looked at the map on my phone. Still .2 miles to the store. Ugh, if only we could be there already so I could slip away into the racks of clothes and disappear for a bit.

"You mentioned dinner," I said. Shoot, maybe that was too bold. I wished I could take it back.

"Oh, in the texts?"

"Yeah," I frowned, concerned that I had to tell him what he already knew. "You wanted to meet my dad and then go to dinner."

"Like a date?"

"I don't know if you meant it to be a date! You're the one who mentioned it to me!"

"Hm. I don't know what I meant by that. I had two drinks last night. I might have been a little off."

My mind went numb, frozen in place. Emptiness was all that remained.

But why did I care? Did I *want* it to be a date? I hated this annoying, handsome, stupid man.

The fact of the matter was that I *did* care. I *did* want it to be a date. No one ever thought about me in a special way. I was never the one asked on dates. I wanted this to be my moment.

I could use my Voice and make him want me.

I almost gasped out loud at the ridiculous thought.

No. Absolutely not.

If I used my Voice, I'd never know if it was real, if it meant anything.

Just because I *could* control my future, didn't mean I should.

I replied in my most not-Voice possible, vulnerable and soft. Very unlike me.

"Oh, well I was excited at the idea."

This was it; I'd put myself out there. All it would take was one no to stab me in the heart. I hated the risk, but I wanted the reward.

"Really?" He turned to look at me. Now I really used my Voice, internally for once.

Do not blush.

"Yes. I thought it sounded really nice. A date, that is."

He just nodded, saying nothing. My gut sank again.

The timing proved terrible. By the time he should have replied, we were at the store. He opened the door for me and followed me inside.

I should have disappeared into the racks of flannel and denim, but I did not. I stupidly followed him to the back wall, where dozens of hats filled the shelves.

He plucked a chocolate-brown leather one off the shelf and plopped it on his head.

"Thoughts?"

"It looks great with the work attire," I laughed. I couldn't decide if the combo of rugged and professional was ridiculous or hot.

"Hey now," he laughed, too. "I was on a work trip. I only have work clothes."

"Have you even washed that shirt? You've been on the go for days."

He pretended to sniff his sleeve.

"Nope," he took off the brown hat and exchanged it for a black one with a chain band around it.

"Absolutely not," my head tipped back as I laughed.

"What's wrong with it?" he teased, but his eyes gave away his disgust.

"It's the chain," I shook my hand side-to-side like I was trying to scare it off. "Try something else."

He took that one off and side-stepped down the wall to the women's hats. He grabbed a pink felt hat with a sparkling ribbon and dropped it on my head. My arms instinctively raised to stop him, but his height gave him a major advantage.

"I look like I belong at a kid's birthday party," I adjusted the hat in the mirror.

"And that's bad because…"

I took it off and replaced it with a light brown one, simple and soft. "How's this?"

"I like it," he reached out and ran his thumb along the edge.

"Now we have to find you one," I shuffled back down to the men's section. He reluctantly followed.

"How about this?" I held up another black hat, simpler than the ugly one with the chain. He tried it on and looked at me with a smolder.

Ok, this look was hot. Absolutely, without a doubt.

"Yep," I said, once again willing myself not to blush. "That's the one."

He pulled it off to check the price tag.

"I guess if I'm living in Texas, I probably should own one of these babies."

Before I could respond, a voice I recognized cut through the silence.

"Have you seen an Asian guy about this tall?"

The voice was coming from the door. I couldn't see who it was over the racks, but I knew it was Fadel's minion, Lawrence. I grabbed Robert's arm and yanked him down to the floor.

"Ow, what was that f—" I slapped my hand over his mouth and whispered.

"Fadel's minion. We gotta go."

We took our hats off and shoved them on the bottom shelf. We slowly made our way towards the door, ducking behind the flannels in each row. I could hear Lawrence's footsteps crossing the wood floor towards the back shelves. My heartbeat was in my ears as we crawled along.

When we reached the exit, Robert looked at me.

"Run on three. One, two…"

But I was already running. He passed me, throwing the door open, causing bells to chime. We bolted through the door and down the road, zigzagging down side streets for three or four minutes.

"I think we're good," he finally slowed down to a stop. I heaved, gasping for air. I was not a runner and that was now extremely obvious. How embarrassing.

"Ok, I said between gasps. "Tomorrow, I say we go back for the hats."

He smiled, breathing a bit heavy himself.

"It's a date."

CHAPTER FORTY-SIX

Sebastian

Bianca knew how to read a room. That's why, when we returned downtown and arrived at the office property, of course finding nothing there, she excused herself and went to get coffee from a local shop.

That left Eric and I alone, which in my opinion, had been a big mistake.

Eric and I stood outside of the high-rise, waiting for Bianca to return. Knowing her, however, it would be a while. She sensed tension and sought to not only avoid it herself, but to push us into it until it was resolved.

I wasn't normally confrontational, not in the way Theo or Jasmine were. But I also wasn't Penny Anderson. I was not afraid to start a conversation, let alone a fight. I believed in what I believed in and I would defend it until the end. That was that.

I didn't want to have a problem with Eric. He seemed like a nice guy. He came across as timid, maybe even emotional, and yet, there was this eager energy about him that made it clear he still saw Bee as his, at least a little.

I knew it was likely he'd still have feelings for Bianca. Who wouldn't? But to see them with my own eyes… to witness their interactions…to actualize something I thought was in her past…it was a bit much. But that wasn't the real issue. I knew that Bianca loved me and if anything could be taken from our last several days together, she had made a conscious decision and chose me.

No, the problem plaguing my mind didn't even reach my consciousness until we arrived in Durango.

"So," I said, breaking the silence. "You were last in Durango, when?"

"Um," Eric awkwardly shoved his hands into his jacket pockets. "A few years ago. Haven't been back since, you know… I was recruited."

I wanted to keep calm. I wanted to be silent—to control my emotions like I'd taught Bianca to control hers. But it proved too much. I was about to be a very bad teacher, an absolute hypocrite.

"So, were you recruited before or after Fadel burned my neighborhood to the ground?"

He looked at me like I'd just punched him in the face. His eyes scoured my face with a speed someone like Margaret Andrews could only dream of.

I kept my expression firm.

Maybe I *should* punch him in the face.

"Hey, man," Eric replied, pulling his hands out of his pockets and raising them between us. "I'm sorry Fadel did that. I'm sorry about what happened to your family. It's an awful tragedy that no one deserved to experience, let alone a good guy like you. But I wasn't a part of that."

"No," I crossed my arms and tapped my fingers impatiently on my sleeve. "You just agreed to join a murderer after what he'd done."

"You could say the same about Bianca, right?" Eric didn't hold back. I never took him as a confrontational guy, but this was a clear declaration of war.

I took a step forward, clenching my hand into a fist. He was one wrong move away from a broken nose.

"Don't you dare drag her into this," I said as I approached.

"It's true. Bianca also joined Fadel after the incident in Durango. If you consider me bad, you have to consider her bad, too," he expressed, a new fire in his voice. He pushed up his glasses and stared at me with renewed intensity.

"Bianca didn't know about Durango," I practically spat back. "She came to Victory with no knowledge of what happened. It wasn't national news, man; it was covered up. But you lived there. You must have known."

I thought I was going to punch him, I really did. But before I could even lift my arm, his expression changed. The anger I expected washed away and instead resembled sadness or embarrassment. Maybe it was guilt. He took a deep breath before speaking, his response spilling out with a contrite vulnerability that prevented me from speaking. He raised his hands between us again, like a peace offering or at least a wall of self-protection.

"We all—Fadel's minions, as you call them—had been given the same narrative. We were the ones protecting the city. Those nine people were working against us. They wanted to take over the city through force and rule it as a higher class of beings. We represented the common man and helped preserve his ability to rule. We were the ones who stood for equality and justice.

"Obviously, that was not true. But when you're twenty-something and have the ability to make major change in the world, you look for opportunities to do so. Fadel offered me the chance to be a hero. He spun a tale so believable that my ego couldn't help but join him. But clearly, I was wrong.

"I spent too much time being the exact villain I was trying to stop, and I hate myself for that. I hate myself for being blind, for letting my own narcissism take control of my life. I hate myself for supporting destruction and violence, even though it wasn't my intention. And then to make matters worse, I ran from my sins. I thought fleeing would fix things. I thought that I could reform my life and it would make up for everything I'd done. I wanted redemption, but I didn't go about it in the right way."

I stood in silence, unsure how to respond.

"You've still insulted Bianca," I managed to say at last. "She's not a villain."

"I know," he nodded. "But I'm not either. I'm sorry I didn't mean to insult her character, I'm just trying to say that if you believe her story, you need to believe mine, too. We were in it together. We suffered through it together."

He sighed.

"Bee," he muttered, as if she was standing right there with us. "I'm sorry I ran. And I'm also sorry I didn't want to come when I was offered the chance to change. I'm sorry that it took Charles to convince me. I was a coward."

I let his admission hang in the air for a moment. Even if I was to forgive him, I wasn't going to brush his cowardice and betrayal under the rug. I couldn't let him do what he did to Bianca, or to anyone else, again.

"I don't like that you joined him after the terror he instigated. I don't like that you fell into his trap, whether it was intentional or not. I don't appreciate your participation, no matter how passive. I don't care that it happened to Bee, too. I can still be mad at you. I'm allowed to not trust you."

He looked like a beaten puppy. All the fight had been drained from him. I continued.

"But you're right: Fadel is a master manipulator. What matters is that you're here now and willing to fight. But I need to know, will you actually stay this time, or will you go back to being a coward? How do we know you'll be loyal until the end? I don't want any of my friends, especially not Bianca, to get hurt because you weren't willing to stay.

"I don't just want words anymore. I want action. That's what makes you and Bianca different. Bianca proved to us that she was reformed, that she was willing to do what was right. Honestly, it sounds like you've just been a coward. Show me why we should trust you, why I shouldn't just pound your face in and leave you here on the sidewalk. I don't play games with cowards."

Surprisingly, he didn't have to think long before answering.

"I will stay with your cause for life," Eric said and moved his hand over his heart. "You have my word."

"Your word doesn't mean much," I said, my fingers itching to clench back into a fist.

"I know I originally told Bianca I'd only stay for the first leg of the journey, but if Fadel gets away again, I will stay with you all physically until he is defeated. I will not run again. I'm with you through it all, from this point on."

"Does that mean you intend to return to Victory with us?" I asked, astonished at how this conversation had turned. First of all, I anticipated a bit of a brawl. But that aside, I expected Eric to do his thing and leave, just as he once said he would. I wanted him to serve one last mission and then return to his life before Fadel, casting off any prior allegiance to the man with the staff. That's all I really needed from him. But the prospect of gaining another ally proved more valuable in my mind.

"No," he replied. My gut lurched, worrying that I'd jumped the gun a bit too soon. However, Eric had something bigger in mind: something grander than even my best-case-scenario could conjure.

"I know what my role is. It's what Charles and I talked about when we went off to speak privately. That night at the casino, he and I took time away from Theo and Bianca, and that's where he convinced me to come out and help. He talked me into coming along to help you all. But he also convinced me to assist him in a master plan. When this is over, I'm going to return to Utah and help Charles with his mission."

He looked at me and smiled.

"Charles is actually going to accomplish what Fadel once tricked us into thinking we were joining. He's going to collect supers. He's going to offer them protection at a facility he's building in the desert. And then he's going to help them train so they can go back to their communities, or to other places in need, and become the real heroes. We're going to build a network of heroes, one at a time, who can actually make the world a better place. Charles wants my help with that."

"He's doing a large-scale version of what we've built in Victory."

"Precisely," Eric replied.

"That's a noble mission."

"I won't pretend it's not entirely selfless," Eric closed his eyes and leaned his head back against the wall. "He offered protection for Sophia, my niece. And my whole family, really. But I thought about Soph and what she represented and I knew I had to do it. I promised Charles I would come with you and that when I was finished, I would return and help him with his project."

"I commend you," I said at last. "And I apologize for being so confrontational. It's hard when it involves—"

"Your family. I know. And I'm sorry, too. For real. I don't know what I'd do with myself if my parents had been killed by Fadel. I think it's pretty impressive that you packed up your life and now are working hard to avenge them. They would be proud."

I just nodded in return.

Gosh, I hope so.

"Thank you for not punching me," he said. "I know you wanted to."

"I didn't necessarily want to, but I was close. Be careful with how you talk about my friends. I don't care how nice you are or how pure your intentions may be, I will do whatever it takes to defend my friends."

"Understood."

We stood in silence again, unsure of where to take the conversation, since Bianca still wasn't back.

"Hey, since we're in the spirit of apologizing, I'm also sorry for what happened in Utah," Eric said, eyes locked on the pavement. "I had no idea, really."

I was confused.

"What happened in Utah that's worth apologizing over?" I asked, beginning to worry again.

Before Eric could respond, Bianca rounded the corner. She looked between the two of us and must have sensed the shift in tension.

"Ready to go?" she asked, holding out the tray of drinks to us. We took our coffees and Eric took the tray, tossing it in the trashcan.

I wanted to pull her aside now. I wanted to confront whatever was going on. I wanted to get all of this mess over with.

But I had to keep the mission in mind first.

"Yep, ready to go. Let's hope the others actually found something," I said, not confident that Theo and Penny had succeeded in their task. We knew how hard it was to find Fadel—we'd been through this before.

"Yeah, I don't want today to be a complete bust," Bianca agreed. But I shook my head and grabbed her free hand.

"It wasn't a complete bust."

CHAPTER FORTY-SEVEN

Alexandra

Theo and Penny were of no help. But it's not like I was doing all that great, either. I knew the area well, of course, so it made sense for me to be assigned this task. But none of the properties I found in my search made sense for Fadel. Most were too close to other houses or too close to the compound property he used to train his minions on.

I recalled that he would commute, complaining about driving over thirty minutes to get to the office. I knew the property for training was about an hour from the office, so this would logically fall somewhere in between.

If I didn't know where Fadel owned a second home, who did?

Well for one, Zeke might…

Was it a risk to text him? The last time I saw him, he helped us escape. He had been tracking our location while we were driving to Durango, but after Lawrence took Robert and Penny from us, I stopped sharing it. It felt far too risky to have him track us.

Whether I wanted to admit it or not, I couldn't fully trust him. He still worked for Fadel, even if he helped us here and there. He would always choose himself and his family over me.

"What are you thinking?" Theo asked, eyeing me across the table.

237

"Nothing," I pretended to be typing into Maps.

"Obviously it's something. What do you have in mind?"

Reluctantly, I sighed and leaned back in my chair.

"I was thinking about Zeke. I wonder if he could help us again."

"I don't really trust him, but I feel like there could be a way for us to ask for help without putting our own location at risk. We could get information out of him without showing our own hand too much."

"How could we do that?" Penny asked between sips of tea.

"We could ask him directly and see how he responds to it? If he says no, we change gears. But maybe he can give us something." I didn't like the idea of asking, but I was fresh out of other ideas.

"Can you text him?" Theo asked.

"If I'm being honest, I'm a bit scared to."

"Do it. There's no harm in trying."

"How do we know we won't walk into another trap? This guy can't be trusted," Penny threw out. I must have looked bothered because she quickly continued. "I'm sorry, I don't mean to offend, but his track record is really shady."

"No, it's a fair point. I think I'll be able to tell based on the location. If he's going to lie, he'll have to be smart about it. I know the area better than him."

I bravely pulled out my phone and drafted the message.

ALEXANDRA: I need your location. Or the location of F's latest hideout.

To my surprise, he began typing back immediately. My hands perspired and my heart thumped.

ZEKE: I can't give you that.

I sighed, frustrated. But I pushed on anyway.

ALEXANDRA: Are you serious? You're not still working for him, are you???

I couldn't believe it. Why did he bother helping us if he was just going to turn around and deny us when we really needed the help. He was untrustworthy, only looking out for himself. I started angrily typing a response when his reply popped up.

ZEKE: I can't tell you where he is, but I can tell you where M&L are going to pick up dinner in 20 minutes. They placed an order online and will bring it back to F's hideout.

"Guys, I think I've got something," I said, partially to the others and partially to myself.

Zeke sent the website of a pizza place not far from here named *Pizza Paparazzi*. I sprang up.

"Theo, get the car keys."

* * *

The sunglasses and baseball cap were a stupid disguise, especially with all three of us doing it. But from the safety of the car, I didn't feel as nervous about getting caught.

I kept low in my seat, peeking out over the dash as Maggie and Lawrence exited the pizza shop and climbed into their car. I jotted down the license plate number into my notes app.

As they took off, Theo followed from a safe distance.

We drove for fifteen minutes, winding through downtown and then out into the country. I expected we would be heading somewhere even more remote, that is until they slowed down and took a turn down an unmarked dirt road. It looked like a long driveway, wrapping around an orchard.

It was a big property, remote enough to be hidden.

"That's it," Theo smiled. I dropped a pin on my map so we would be able to find our way back here later.

"We're good, I got the pin. Let's go," I said, urging Theo to step on the gas before the others realized they were being followed.

"Sebastian will be pleased," Penny replied. "Just a shame that their trip was probably a waste of time."

CHAPTER FORTY-EIGHT

Bianca

The tension I'd been observing all day between Eric and Sebastian had vanished. Unfortunately, new tension took its place, and I feared that it was now between Sebastian and me. He was being overly peppy towards Eric.

Overly peppy wasn't like Sebastian. Clever, yes. Sweet and funny, of course. But acting like Penny? Forget about it.

The two obviously cleared the air between them, but at what cost? What had Sebastian told Eric? Or worse, what had Eric told Sebastian? I'd planned to talk to both of them. Today. But they beat me to it and talked to each other first.

Sebastian pointed out landmarks as he drove, telling us stories of his boyhood.

"And that road takes you to Switchback Hill. My cross-country coach in middle school used to drag us there to work on running hills. Kind of stupid, since all our races were on flat ground. This being Texas and all."

"You see that mall? That's where my dad took me to the theater when every new Marvel movie came out."

"My best friend growing up lived in that subdivision. They had the best trick-or-treating on Halloween."

That was the most positive I'd seen Sebastian when discussing his hometown. Normally, it was not a topic of conversation I was comfortable broaching.

I had to admit, despite the awkwardness I knew hid underneath, I liked seeing this passion. I always loved the way he spoke of his parents, but this brought those stories to life in a new way. It could have been a really special, really intimate ride had it not been for Eric in the passenger seat.

"I've run that trail over there so many times," Eric chipped in. "Do not recommend running in July here, it's brutal."

Sebastian had made the first move, talking to Eric. He wanted to fix things before they were ever really broken.

Theo was right: I needed to follow up on his good will and set things in stone, once and for all. With both of them.

Theo was also right in saying that if I didn't have this conversation soon, it would continue to affect my ability to perform in battle. I couldn't risk any of my friends getting hurt because of my weakness.

I needed to talk to them, and I needed to talk to them as soon as possible. Preferably, now.

We pulled up to the hotel and Sebastian let the two of us out by the front door so he could go park across the street.

Now was the moment to talk to Eric, a gift given to us by Sebastian himself. I just needed to build the courage.

I'd faced a literal supervillain, saved people from burning buildings, rescued children from a threat to their school, and traveled across the country with only Theo. If I could brave those fears, I could have one conversation with my ex, right?

Eric looked at me expectantly. He knew what I was thinking. He wanted me to say it, to put him out of his misery. He wanted me to just admit that what we had was gone.

"Eric," I started. "I…"

But I couldn't find the words. I just looked at him, my eyes glazing over with frosted tears. My hands were cold as the sadness poured into them.

"I…" I kept trying. I refused to let the tears fall. "I'll see you tonight. I need to go lie down for a bit. Long day, you know?"

Cowardice won. Again.

He agreed and we parted ways. He went to get more coffee from the table in the lobby, and I made my way to the elevator.

As the doors closed, I looked to where he stood alone, not at the coffee station, but staring out the window, like he was wondering what all this was for if not for me.

* * *

Before

Eric had been gone for two weeks, and I hadn't received a single text or call. He just left me there alone, not even sure where he'd gone. I knew he went west, but that was all.

It just seemed so unfair that he couldn't even tell me where he was going. I promised him not to follow him, at least not yet. But he acted as though he wanted me to find him.

How?

How on earth did he expect me to find him?

I'd never seriously dated before—my track record wasn't great when it came to relationships, at least when I was young. I did date a guy for five months my freshman year of college. It was short and awkward, not really something I thought would last. Yet I was still surprised when he broke up with me. He came over to my house one night and told me he didn't love me and wasn't sure he could "get there." I told him I didn't need my boyfriend of five months to love me. But he was sure in his decision. He was dating Lacie Buckwiler three weeks later. I'd cried for a week over James Parker.

That had been my worst breakup until now. It was 90's movie quality: a sad girl, a self-assured boy, pints of ice cream sprinkled with salty tears, and Taylor Swift on repeat. But this breakup with Eric. It wasn't even a formal breakup. He just up and left, didn't even say we should end our relationship. Did he even technically break up with me? Or was this so tragic it didn't need to be explicitly stated?

I thought my high school boyfriend broke my heart, but I didn't know the true pain of heartbreak. Heartbreak was shattered glass stabbing into your chest. It was hot and cold, fire and ice, flowing through your veins. It was feeling so heavy you could barely lift your head in the morning but also feeling so lightheaded that you worry you'll float away. That's what it felt like missing Eric.

BIANCA: Eric, please tell me where you went

BIANCA: Eric, where are you?

BIANCA: I still love you

Alexandra combed through my hair with her fingers as my head rested on her lap.

"I just don't understand why he'd leave," Maggie tucked into the fleece blanket on her lap and gingerly sipped her cocoa.

"He said he just didn't belong here anymore," I cried. I hadn't told my friends the details. All they knew was that Eric was gone. That he kissed me goodbye and disappeared.

"Why would anyone want to leave? We have amazing jobs, the best of friends, and you are such a good girlfriend! I just don't get it!" Alexandra exclaimed.

"Was. I was a good girlfriend. But we aren't together now."

"Maybe it's just a break," Maggie gently suggested. "Maybe he just needs some time to work through some personal things."

"No," I shook my head a bit, causing my hair to fall in my eyes. Alexandra

brushed it back out of my face and tucked it behind my ear. "He left. He's gone. We aren't together if I don't even know where he is."

My friends didn't respond to this. They knew I was right.

"He wasn't the one," Maggie said. "And that's ok. You're amazing and you'll find someone just as amazing."

"Eric was amazing."

"That's true," Alexandra weighed in. "But it doesn't mean you need to end up together."

I didn't disagree. We didn't need to end up together, married with babies. Maybe that's what I wanted, but it wasn't reality.

Regardless, when I woke up from Fadel's spell and decided to leave Victory, it was towards him that I'd be running, whether he wanted me to or not.

CHAPTER FORTY-NINE

Jasmine

"Hey," I said nervously when Robert opened the door.

"What's up?" he asked, looking just as confused as I expected him to be.

"I thought we could go on a walk," I rocked a bit on the balls of my feet. Was the lipstick too bold?

"Haven't we already walked enough today?"

The stubbornness… I hated it. I also loved it.

"We should go for a walk. Bee wants alone time, so I need to get out, and I don't want to go alone."

"I could grab Sebas—"

"Yuck, no. I don't want to spend more time with Sebastian than I need to. Come on, it'll be fun."

He finally agreed to accompany me and went to grab his coat and shoes. We didn't say much in the elevator or on our way out the front door of the lobby.

Why was I so nervous?

"So," I said.

"So," he replied.

Dang, why was this so hard?

"I feel like we should talk about what's been going on. Between the two of us…"

"Oh?"

My gosh he was so tall and looked so nice in that jacket.

"I think we both know there's something here and we need to acknowledge it."

"I agree."

He agreed. Oh my gosh. What now?

"You start," I blurted out.

"You want me to start? You literally brought up the conversation. Seems a little unfair, don't you think?"

"Ok, fine!" I threw my arms in the air for emphasis. "I think you're great! I keep trying to hate you and I'm failing."

He smiled but not in a sweet, kind way. No. He smiled in a 'I win' sort of way.

"What?" I practically yelled. "You're going to laugh at me now and make me regret everything I just said?"

He laughed.

"No, but it is fun to hear you admit it."

"So, what now? What do you have to say?"

I'd never been so scared of the truth. Either he hated me for real, which would break my heart, or he liked me, too, which would change everything. Either way, I was completely and utterly doomed.

"I also think you're awesome."

"You do?"

"Yeah," he smirked. "You're amazing. And I haven't been able to take my eyes off you since we first met."

I thought I may have blushed. I'd never blushed before.

"So, what do we do now?" I asked, stupidly.

"What do you mean?" He laughed.

"Do we like kiss or something?"

"Well," he reached for my hand and pulled me to a stop. His left hand slid around my waist; fingers hooked through my belt loops. His right hand moved up to the side of my face and tucked a strand of hair behind my ear.

"Well," I replied nervously.

"This is definitely a lot more romantic than an airport kiss to mask our identities," he whispered, smiling.

"What do you mean?" I asked, definitely not whispering.

"Alexandra and I," he replied. "When we were running from Fadel's helpers. You knew about this, right? Alexandra must have told you."

I pulled away from him.

"No," I scoffed. "She didn't. We don't exactly talk. What do you mean you kissed Alexandra in the airport? Like the day you met her?"

"Yeah," he looked nervous now. "We were running from the fast girl and the teleporting guy and then we kissed so they wouldn't see us. It didn't mean anything. It was just kind of spur of the moment."

"Who kissed who?" I asked, knowing the answer but not wanting to accept it.

"Does it matter?"

"Yes!" I yelled. "It does!"

"But it didn't mean anything so it shouldn't matter."

"You kissed her, then. Obviously," I couldn't believe what was happening. My perfect moment— a moment I waited so long for, ruined.

"I'm sorry," he said. "I didn't realize this was such a big deal. We didn't even know each other yet."

"But why didn't you tell me sooner?" I wanted to cry now. I know I was being unfair, but I couldn't help it. I was hurting.

"Because we weren't a thing! I thought you hated me!" He was yelling now, too. "What was I going to do? Walk up to you and be like 'hey Jasmine, I kissed another girl like a week ago, but don't worry, it meant nothing and you shouldn't worry about it'? That's weird,

Jasmine!"

"I don't know!" The uncertainty fell from my lips. "I just hoped you'd be honest with me!"

"Well, I am now! Doesn't that mean anything to you?"

I couldn't take it anymore. I turned on my heels and took off running towards the hotel.

"Jasmine!" I heard him call after me. But he didn't follow. He got the message: I wanted to be alone. I didn't want him to see me cry.

I was wrong.

Having adult conversations with men about your feelings was never worth it. Better to just avoid the awkwardness altogether and accept being alone.

CHAPTER FIFTY

Theodore

"Get ready to thank me," I announced, throwing the door open to our hotel room. Sebastian looked up at me from where he sat on the bed. Robert lounged on the couch, eyes on his phone, looking sad. Eric was MIA.

"You found Fadel's location?" Sebastian asked.

"I did indeed," I replied, flopping down next to him with a pillow. "All that research finally paid off."

"How'd you do it?" Sebastian was obviously trying to flatter me, and despite my awareness of this fact, I didn't care. Flatter away, math boy.

"Well, if you really want to know," I flashed him an award-winning smile. "I risked life and limb to get you that information. That *classified* information."

"Please tell me you didn't do something illegal."

"No," I rolled my eyes. "I just harassed Alexandra to talk to Zeke. And then we followed that speedy chick to the property. Or at least to the last turn. Then we sped off."

"I'm confused," Sebastian wrinkled his eyebrows.

"Nothing to be confused about. We got it all worked out. Here's the address."

I pulled a crumpled receipt out of my pocket with the address scrawled across the back.

"This is in the foothills," Sebastian said, reading it a few times. "I know the general area. Those are some big properties, very remote."

He sat up and started searching maps on his phone. Pushing off the bed, he kept his eyes on the phone and began pacing.

"So, thanks to yours truly, this could be over sooner than we anticipated. We could be home by Monday."

This got him to look up.

"By home, do you mean Victory? I've been thinking a lot about that lately."

"I think everybody has. And yeah, I mean it can be Victory. I'm going wherever you're going, brother," I stuck my hand out and he grasped it. We pulled together for a very manly hug, complete with pats on the back and nods of the head.

"Can you go knock on the girls' door and tell them to come over here? I'll give Eric a call and tell him to get back as soon as possible," he asked, dialing.

"You're gonna call Eric? You?"

He didn't look puzzled, he looked content.

"Yeah, we're cool."

"Thank goodness," I responded. "I was tired of pretending to hate him. That guy is really freaking cool."

CHAPTER FIFTY-ONE

I knocked on the door a second time.

She was hiding from me. I knew she was.

When the door finally opened and I saw her face, I knew something was really wrong.

"Hi," she squeaked out. "Do you want to come in?"

"Yeah. I think we need to talk."

She opened the door and gestured for me to follow her inside. We sat on the edge of the beds, me on one and her on the other. Our knees were about a foot apart. I could hear her breathing.

"Eric and I talked earlier."

"Oh?"

"Bianca, I—"

But I couldn't go any further. A sheet of ice erupted under her, freezing her to the bed and securing her feet to the floor.

She looked around herself in shock. Her eyes filled with tears as she took in the manifestation of her emotional overload.

"Well," I smirked. "I guess you can't run away from your emotions now."

"Or this conversation, apparently."

"Bianca, I don't want you to run away from your emotions, or hard conversations, or the people who love you. Hasn't that been the root of all your problems? Running away has never helped anyone, especially not you."

"I've been trying to control my emotions, Sebastian. I feel like my life is spiraling a bit out of control. My powers aren't cooperating because I keep having these emotional mood swings. You taught me how to accept my emotions, which let my powers flourish. But I still don't know how to control them. I've just been bottling them up and pushing them aside. And all this between you and Eric… it's been too much."

I watched as the ice continued to harden. Frost now inched up her legs.

She was right about not being able to control her powers when the emotions overwhelmed her. But still, it took a truly intense sadness to create ice like this. Bianca wasn't just sad or stressed, she was in pain.

The ice was a cry for help.

"Bee…"

"I don't love Eric anymore. Not the way I used to. But I was scared I did. It took seeing him again to see that. It took seeing *you* again to know for sure."

"I know," I reached for her hand, but she pulled away. I settled my hands on her icy knees instead. A thin layer sat between my skin and her jeans. But my body heat slowly melted the ice, allowing me to touch her, to give her reassurance.

"Bee, I know you don't love him anymore. I see the way you are with him, and I see how you are with me. I'm not worried about him as competition."

"Then why did you two need to have a talk earlier? Were you not trying to find out where he stood with me?"

"I wasn't concerned about him as competition; I was concerned about his loyalty to you and to us. But that doesn't matter now. He and I worked that out. What hasn't been worked out is what's happening now, between you and me."

She buried her face in her hands. I sat in silence, waiting for her to finally tell me the icy secret that had been holding us back, holding her in place.

"Eric kissed me in Utah."

That was it. Just five words and her tears started to flow again.

"I didn't want it, believe me. I'd been trying to figure out how I felt about him, that's true. But I didn't want to kiss him, I promise."

The image stung. My girlfriend… her ex…

Maybe I was too soft. Maybe I was letting her slide too easily. But if the ice covering her body meant anything, I needed to trust her.

"I believe you," I said, truthfully. "I gathered as much from my talk with Eric. He didn't tell me directly, but he apologized for what happened in Utah. I didn't know what he meant."

"And I'm sorry, too. I really didn't want that to happen."

To show her I believed her, I reached for her hand again. This time, she let me take it. I massaged warmth into her fingers.

"I don't want to kiss anyone else, ever again. I just want you."

I smiled.

"That's all I want, too."

She wiped away her tears.

"Does this mean we're ok? That we're still together?"

"Of course," I said, and I meant it. "I could never leave you."

"You summed it up perfectly," she sighed. "Eric's a great guy, but you're the one for me."

I pulled her into a hug, breaking the remaining ice from around her ankles.

"I love you, Bianca. But if we're going to be ok, please promise me two things."

She looked up at me with her blue eyes, still wet from crying.

"Anything."

"Promise you'll talk to Eric. He needs to hear from you himself. We can't keep dragging this out if we're going to work as a team to take down Fadel."

"I promise," she nodded. "No more cowardice."

"No more cowardice."

"And the other thing?"

I brushed her hair behind her ears and planted a kiss on her forehead.

"You let me help you more. We learn how to balance the strength of your powers with the control you need to wield them effectively. I don't want to see you swing between these extremes anymore. You're powerful now, really really powerful. But think about how much better you'll be if you truly know how to use them. I think your mental state will thank you for it, too."

"I'd like that," she snuggled into me.

"I need you to trust me, Bee. You need to let me help you."

"I do trust you."

And we both meant it. This wasn't how I wanted our story to go. I never wanted my girlfriend to kiss her ex on a road trip with my best friend. But all of this—every last detail, good and bad—it was all leading to something bigger than all of us. This wasn't just a story of Bianca and my love. This was two people trusting each other enough to accept each other's weaknesses and build up each other's strengths. This was a group of people uniting to accomplish the same goal. This was good conquering evil.

"Good," I said. "Now let's get back to business and annihilate your old boss, shall we?"

CHAPTER FIFTY-TWO

Robert

"You're staring again."

Startled, I focused my gaze onto Eric, who sipped his coffee while kicked back in one of the plush lobby armchairs. We had been waiting for Sebastian, Theo, and Bianca to get back downstairs with the keys so we could head out to the bad guy's hideout for at least fifteen minutes.

Jasmine, Alexandra, and Penny sat on a couch across the room, talking about who knows what. Actually, I knew what. They were talking about me.

I couldn't help but stare. I couldn't help but think about what horrible things she had to say about me.

Had I really deserved this level of coldness?

"It was one kiss, man," I said aloud. Maybe to myself, but also probably to Eric.

"You kissed Jasmine once?" he asked earnestly.

"No, I kissed Alexandra. Back the day I met her at the airport."

"And you care about that, why?"

"Because I told Jasmine about it, trying to be transparent, and she flipped."

"And you care, why?"

"Because I thought we might have had a little something."

He laughed.

"I thought you guys were like mortal enemies?"

"We've kind of swung back and forth on that. Most recently, we've been getting to know one another more. Well, I guess not *most recently*, since now she won't even look at me."

"Did you explain that the kiss with Alexandra meant nothing?"

I ran my hand through my hair and sighed.

"I did, but it doesn't seem to matter. I think she feels like the second choice. Like the default option."

"I know how that feels." Eric replied, catching me off guard. "One kiss seems to cause a world of hurt, lemme tell you."

"And what would you want the other person to do, if you were feeling like a backup option?"

He thought for a moment.

"I think I'd want her to let me go. To stop playing both sides and try to make me feel better. Just be honest, say it out loud, and move on."

"And that's if you are the second-choice option?"

"That's if you're anything but the first. If you're not the first, it's not worth the effort because it's not really what's meant to be."

I thought about that. How did I know if Jasmine was what I really wanted? How did I know she was worth the effort? Was she? I barely knew the girl and most of the time we had known one another we were enemies. But something in my gut told me that this was good, that it was worth pursuing.

"Maybe we need to let these girls go," Eric said. I know he was intending for this comment to be advice for me, but I think it was meant even more for him.

"I haven't known you long," I told him, leaning forward and patting his shoulder. "But I think you're a great guy. I'm sorry things aren't working out for you."

"That's ok. I hope things can work out for you. Or that you can at least find some peace."

I looked up at Jasmine again. As if my gaze pierced her soul, her head snapped up and our eyes locked. She glared at me and went back to talking to Penny.

Maybe Eric was right. Maybe I just needed to walk away.

CHAPTER FIFTY-THREE

Bianca

Only Fadel could make such a beautiful place feel so unwelcoming.

As we pulled down the winding, wooded drive, I'd been transported to another time. The little gate houses, the orchard and vineyard, the store houses. And the mansion, my goodness. It wasn't just a mansion; it was a Mansion.

The three-story plantation-style home had a crisp white exterior with cream clapboard siding. A wide wraparound porch stood supported by stately columns. The porch was adorned with ceiling fans and lined with rocking chairs and a swing, inviting lazy afternoons with a glass of sweet tea and biscuits. Both the second and third stories had generous balconies. It was the kind of home, the kind of property, I would settle into and never want to leave.

I imagined a stone fireplace, rocking chairs, and hot tea. I saw myself cozied up to Sebastian after a long day of exploring the property. I imagined quiet moments in the orchard and late-night strolls through the woods.

I often thought about life after Victory and my mind always seemed to drift to Durango, to where Sebastian grew up. I knew my dreams were foolish, there'd be no way he'd want to come back here long term, but I let myself imagine. Seeing this estate really brought those images to life.

But this Mansion wasn't Sebastian's. It was Fadel's. Or at least temporarily so. The Fadel family home was in Colorado, according to Charles. And that home was abandoned when Charles moved west. I wasn't sure what the elder Fadel's connection was with Texas, Durango, or this house.

Why had he chosen this location? Maybe because it made him feel rich. Maybe it made him feel more like Charles. It was distinctly American in architecture and adornment. Maybe it made him feel like he was living in his own dreams.

We had this in common.

"This property is massive. It's gotta be hundreds of acres," Penny said, her mouth hanging open as she looked from window to window.

"How are we going to find Fadel, or literally anything?" Jasmine asked.

"That's not your job, or your problem," Robert replied to her, causing her to snap her head and lock her glare in his direction.

"It's not yours either," she huffed.

"It's *my* problem," Eric said, attempting to smooth over the unnecessary tension. "I'm supposed to be the Fadel expert, since I worked with him in Durango."

"But you didn't work *here*," Sebastian said. "You worked at the compound. You weren't even sure this place existed. Take it easy on yourself."

Sebastian put his hand on Eric's shoulder and gave him an encouraging pat.

"There are a few outbuildings around. Maybe he stores the staff in one of those?" Penny asked, hopefully.

"He likely has the staff on him. If not, he keeps it in the house. He has a vault somewhere in the mansion; I'm positive about that. He would want to keep it close by but stored for safe keeping. If it's not on him, it's locked up tight."

"Maybe there's an attic. Or maybe it's in the cellar," Penny said, pointing to the lower level of the house and a small, slanted cellar door. It looks like this house has one."

"That would make sense. He did store his staff in a sub-level of the compound." Eric closed his eyes and massaged his forehead and temples, as if easing a tension headache.

"Are you ok?" I asked, moving my hand towards his, but pulling back at the last moment. I couldn't do that. I needed to set boundaries.

He seemed to notice this move and cleared his throat uncomfortably.

"I'm fine, just a bit hard knowing we are about to see Fadel again."

"Understood. I'm sorry we put you in this situation. But I'm happy you're here. Your insight is invaluable."

"I hope so. Otherwise, there's no point in being here."

"Harsh, but fair," Penny said, reminding me that Eric and I were not alone.

"Ok, I texted Sebastian to park over on the side of the road up here. We don't want to get too close to the house. We can walk up the drive and spread out from there."

As we all jumped out of the vehicles and assembled by the roadside, we divided quickly into groups.

Theo and Alexandra would meet up with Zeke and find Lawrence and Maggie. The goal would be to get them away from the house in any way they could manage. Robert and Jasmine would search the basement for the staff and use their powers to destroy it, if that was even possible. I would go with Sebastian, Penny, and Eric to the Mansion to find Fadel.

"This is some Scooby Doo nonsense if you ask me," Theo said.

"You're just mad you're not with Penny," Jasmine scowled.

"Yes, and what about it? Fred and Daphne always got paired together."

"You think you're Fred?" Jasmine laughed. "That's cute."

"Who else would I be, the dog?"

Jasmine didn't bother replying but instead raised her hand like a kid in a classroom. Sebastian looked up from his notepad and sighed.

"Yes, Jas?"

"I don't think I should be with Robert."

Robert perked up but said nothing.

"Why is that, Jas?" Sebastian's irritation was palpable.

"I need someone better to protect me."

"Dang, that's cold," Theo laughed.

"Robert can protect you," Sebastian replied. "I've seen him in action. You'll be fine."

Before she could object, Sebastian clapped his hand against the notepad.

"Ok team, you have your assignments. If all goes well, this will all be over soon. We could be free by bedtime. Just protect each other and leave nothing on the table."

"We've got this, guys," I added.

"You're Victory's defenders. You've saved countless lives. You've rescued children, turned villains into heroes, and driven a supervillain out of a major city. He has less minions now, he's tired. In fact, he's weaker than ever. Now is our opportunity to seize the moment. If we all work together, we can find the staff, destroy it, and end him once and for all. I know this sounds daunting, but we can do it if we all work together. Are you with me?"

I looked up at my boyfriend and gushed with immense pride. Knowing him was a blessing but loving him was certainly a gift. Especially after our last conversation, I knew for sure that he was the man I wanted to spend the rest of my life with.

I would follow him into battle anywhere he asked me to go. I wasn't scared of this war because he was leading our troops and because I was facing the fire with the best of friends by my side.

I'd never been more ready.

CHAPTER FIFTY-FOUR

Theodore

"Meet up with the guy who betrayed you," I muttered to myself. "It'll be fine, it's not like he'll betray you again! 'Lure the goons away from the mansion,' he said. Maybe Sebastian should try and be bait for once, see how he likes it."

We each carried a flashlight as we slowly made our way into the orchard. It was creepy like a corn maze, but without the corn. Or the cider and donuts at the finish. Rows of apple trees seemed to stretch endlessly from the road to the horizon. The canopies blocked the sky in places, plunging our steps into darkness. I hated every step we took. I felt weaker in the dark, and that wasn't good, since we were mere minutes away from combat with supervillains.

We moved cautiously. The beam of light from Alexandra's flashlight wobbled as her hand shook. I took a deep breath, reminding myself that I needed to be the rock here.

I offered her an arm to guide her and she took it, holding on at my elbow with her free hand.

"Hey," she replied, an edge in her voice I didn't often hear. "He's not going to betray us again. And you have to remember; he helped us escape at the boathouse."

"I wasn't there, Allie," I said, rolling my eyes. "I was in hell's outhouse, also known as Falcon Creek."

"You were out of Falcon's Creek by that point. And don't call me Allie."

"I literally could care less when I was in that stupid town. I was there and that's all that matters."

"And Zeke helped us escape, so that's all that matters to me."

"You're defending him too much. I'd say you're coping."

"I am not! He only betrayed us to protect his sister."

"Which was some Fadel trickery anyway. Literally a bluff that caused him to bluff you. A double bluff!"

"It doesn't matter. The motive is what really counts. He was trying to show loyalty to Fadel to protect his sister, whom he thought Fadel had captured. Now that he knows Fadel was lying, he won't do the same thing again. He's on our side, Theo, I know it."

"Well, I hope you're right," I said, looking around. Chills ran down my spine. The darkness was spooky as sin, much worse than in Scooby Doo.

"It's so dark," she whispered as if reading my mind. "I'm really scared, Theo. I feel like we're being watched."

"Just like I felt in—-"

"If you say Falcon's Creek one more time, I'm going to kill you."

"Ouch."

We came to a stop, completely surrounded by trees. The silence was deafening.

"How will he know where to find us?" Alexandra asked, tightening her grip on my arm.

"I don't think we need to worry about that," I pointed my flashlight behind her. "I think he already has."

Alexandra whipped around to see Zeke approaching at a jog.

"Zeke, are they coming?"

"They're not far behind me. I broke away and have been evading them for about twenty minutes or so. They've gotta be catching up by now."

Zeke's arms were bruised up, and his left eye was black and blue. A long cut ran from the corner of his mouth down his chin.

Alexandra noticed this, too, which wasn't surprising, since it was horrifyingly obvious, even in the darkness of the orchard.

"Zeke, my goodness! What did they do to you?"

"Oh, the bruises?" He smiled a little.

"And the black eye! And the cut!" Alexandra whisper-yelled with both shock and fury.

"They'll heal, don't worry. Fadel just roughed me up a bit."

"Well, you don't have to deal with him anymore," I cut in. "You're with us now. We will stop Fadel tonight and then tomorrow, we will all go home."

"Sounds like a plan to me, brother," he said, shaking my hand and looking me in the eyes. Alexandra might have been coping a bit by defending his past so strongly. But I had to agree, he would stand by his word this time.

"Once they get here, we split up. You two run that way," I said, pointing off into the distance, away from the direction we came. "You'll circle around to the left and loop back to the road over that direction. I'll run back towards the car and drive to the main road to meet you. We can then drive back towards town, where I can drop you two off at the safe spot."

"Got it," Zeke nodded.

"The most important thing is that you two stay together. Alexandra can't defend herself, so you need to keep her in your sight at all times."

"I'll stick close to him, don't worry, Theo."

"Ok, let's get—-" The sound of cracking leaves stopped me in my tracks.

"They're here."

The words spilled out of Alexandra's mouth, no louder than a breath. A crack made us jump and suddenly, Lawrence stood ten feet from us.

"There they are!" he yelled.

"Run!" I screamed, and we all took off, with two villains on our tail.

* * *

I wished I'd done more cardio back in Victory. I spent so much time working on combat and lifting but spent little to no time running. That neglect was really coming back to haunt me now.

Typically, I'd use my powers to at least get a boost from the wind. But amongst the trees, the air was still. I had nothing but my two legs to protect me now.

As Lawrence continued to chase me, I prayed that Alexandra and Zeke were in better shape than me. Especially since the villain following them literally had super-speed.

"I'm going to get you, you bastard!" Lawrence yelled after me.

"In your wildest dreams, you… you… bastard!" I yelled back, unable to come up with a more clever response.

My throat was desert dry. The huffing and puffing were embarrassing. Thank goodness Penny wasn't here to see this. I didn't care about the darkness anymore; I just cared about running for my life.

I could see the car up ahead.

Come on, come on, come on.

I just needed to get to the car and drive it to the meet-up spot: easy. That would get the minions far enough away from the house that we could escape. I wouldn't fail this time. I would complete this mission, and we would all go home safe and sound.

I pulled the key out of my pocket as I ran and hit 'unlock' about a dozen times.

The final push...

CHAPTER FIFTY-FIVE

"When Eric said 'cellar,' I was picturing a lovely old wine cellar with oak barrels and little tables we could sit at while we pop open a bottle and eat fancy cheese."

What Eric had apparently meant by 'cellar' was more of the storm shelter type cellar from *Twister*. It had the same little outdoor 45 degree angled wooden flap door and everything. In fact, there was no entrance into the house from this particular basement, just the one outside.

"Hey, no need for the cellar slander. There's wine in here, it's just old and dusty," Robert said, pulling an ancient-looking bottle of Merlot off one of the creaky metal racks.

When we'd arrived at the house, Eric told us that the cellar was one of the places Fadel used to store important things. Fadel apparently appreciated the single entrance and exit. It meant extra security. It also ensured that he could remain close to anything that mattered. Like his staff, hopefully.

"There's no way the staff is here," I muttered to myself.

"Yeah, what did Sebastian expect us to find down here? A glowing staff plugged into a mighty staff-stand? Gold embellishments? Or maybe a big sign that reads, 'Hey! Here's the Bad Guy's Staff!'"

"Yeah, for real," I absentmindedly replied as I dug through an old desk in the corner.

The cellar was quite eclectic. There were racks of wine bottles and even a few whiskey barrels. There was also a desk with two big file cabinets off on the side. Otherwise, the place was empty, dusty, and staff-less.

"You know," Robert said, hovering over my shoulder. "The staff is a bit too big to fit in those drawers."

"Shut up," I replied, not even bothering to look at him. "I'm not looking for the staff right now."

I kept flipping through the drawers, rifling through the papers.

I found dozens of receipts dated within the last five years. All of them were for construction equipment, particularly metal sheets, various rods, and electrical gear. I also found a few power company bills.

"Look," Robert said, pushing papers aside and pointing to a folded paper underneath an opal paperweight. "That looks like a map."

I took the paper and unfolded it while Robert moved on to search the drawers of the file cabinet.

"They're all empty besides the bottom one," he said. But I wasn't listening, I was looking at the map.

It was a basic map of the United States, with a few cities circled and a few starred. Colorado Springs had an 'X' through it. Salt Lake City had a question mark. That little town near Baton Rouge was circled. So was Victory. Victory also had a star. Several more cities were circled or starred, including a place near Boston, a place in Southern California, near my hometown, and a town in North Carolina. On the back, there was a list of names.

Bianca Williams - Indiana (northern?) was scribbled out. Underneath, he'd written *Bianca Williams - Victory, Virginia.*

He'd also written:

Molly Meadows - Victory, Virginia

Robert Arashi - near Durango, traveling often, location unknown at this time

The list went on and on. These were identified supers. He'd been tracking people for years now. He'd been tracking *Robert* for years now.

"Can you command this safe to open?" Robert asked, snapping me out of this hypnotized daze.

I folded the map up and put it in my pocket, feeling a little lightheaded.

"What safe?"

"There was a small travel safe in the bottom drawer of the file cabinet." There was, indeed. Robert held it on his lap, fiddling with the lock.

"*Open,*" I said, focusing on the keyhole. It took three tries, each more aggressive than the last. It hesitated at first, but eventually, it clicked open.

Shaking off my frustration, I went through the safe. Inside were only three documents. Three signed, dated, and notarized documents.

"Geez," I scanned the numbers on the top page. "This is the deed to the property. It's worth $70 million. Or at least it was a few years ago. And get this, it's not in his name."

I couldn't believe my eyes. They were all legal documents, each with the same names listed somewhere. The first was the purchase of the property in 1983 by a man named Maximilian Chester. And then, five years ago, a transfer of ownership to C. Fadel via an estate gift. Chester had died and left the entire estate to Fadel. It was there in black and white: C. Fadel.

Who was Maximilian Chester and why was he leaving such a big gift to Fadel?

I pulled out my phone and began snapping pictures of each page.

Hitting the final document, a single leaf of paper, I stopped dead in my tracks.

It was dated just before the time he left Durango. It was a transfer of ownership, signed and notarized. From C. Fadel to…

My. Goodness.

Instead of taking a picture this time, I folded the page up and tucked it into my pocket with the map. My pocket was bursting but this one needed to come with us.

"Robert," I whispered. "This house belongs to Alexandra."

CHAPTER FIFTY-SIX

Sebastian

Getting inside the house was the easy part. Finding Fadel proved much more difficult.

Eric picked the lock and we slipped inside. I'd secretly hoped that Fadel's whereabouts would be obvious, maybe a light on or sound coming from a particular part of the house. The problem with this hope was that the house wasn't an ordinary two-story suburban home.

No, this was a full-blown mansion. Inside the door stood a grand staircase, leading up into what appeared to be two halls. To each side of the stairs, large double doors stood like soldiers on each side of the staircase, presumably opening to the two major lower wings of the house, which were visible from the outside as well.

"The windows were all dark on the lower level, at least it appeared so when we approached. I think it's safe to move through one of these wings, but we should do so quietly and cautiously," I said, waving the others along towards the set of doors on the right.

"I'll lead with Bianca right behind," I continued. "Bianca, can you give us some light?"

"I can try," she replied, focusing on a slightly shaky hand. "I'm not even that nervous, so I don't know why it's not working as quickly as normal. I shouldn't be having an issue."

It was almost the exact opposite of the conversation we'd had earlier. Recently, the fire came a bit too easily.

Finally, a small flame appeared in the center of her palm and she twisted her wrist, letting the flame dance between her fingers.

"Ok, got it," she said, taking her post by me.

"Eric, can you check the next room and make sure it's clear?"

He silently saluted and disappeared, reappearing only a moment later.

"I was only able to check the next two rooms. I'm feeling a bit slow. Not sure what's up. But the good news is they're all clear."

"Excellent," I said. "Thank you. Now if you and Penny take up the rear, we can start moving."

We slowly inched our way across the first room—the formal dining room—and continued down a back hallway to a sitting room. As I walked, each step was like walking on glass. I tried to stay on my toes, making no noise. The last thing we wanted was for Fadel to hear us and appear. We needed him to play defense tonight.

"Do you hear that?" Penny whispered. We all listened. Muffled noise leaked through the ceiling from the room above us.

"It sounds like music," Bianca whispered back.

"Truly creepy," Eric added, and I agreed.

"Let's find a way up," I said, leading my friends through the room to the far door.

"I can go on ahead and see if I can find a staircase," Eric said.

"Please do."

He disappeared and reappeared a few times. He looked increasingly more frustrated with each reappearance. When he finally stopped, he let us know of his findings.

"Ok, through this door is a solarium. Around one side of the solarium is the kitchen. In the back of the kitchen is a servant's staircase. I don't know where it leads."

"Well," Penny said. "It sounds like we're about to find out."

We followed Eric's instructions and made our way up the servant's stairs, one at a time. The walls were tight, my arms brushing them as I ascended. The darkness ahead of me was eerily palpable. Bianca's flame had disappeared, shrouding us in total mystery.

Reaching the top, I found a wooden door with a large brass knob with an old-fashioned keyhole. I leaned down to peek through it, sensing a bit of light on the other side.

While it was dimly lit, the adjacent room was bright enough for us to see that it was empty. I twisted the handle and let us in.

We stood in a tiny bedroom, no bigger than Harry Potter's cupboard under the stairs. The door to the hallway stood open and music drifted down the hall, beckoning us to follow.

Für Elise played, crackling as it went. I could visualize the turntable and the record going round and round and round.

"So freaking creepy," Eric whispered, rubbing his arms.

"Plan?" Bianca asked me as we approached our final destination.

Sometimes being a leader was great. I loved making the plans, calling the shots. It reminded me why I came out to Victory in the first place. I knew I didn't have actual powers like the others, so moments of heroic leadership gave my pretend powers life and purpose. Moments like this were what fueled my ambitions and satiated my thirst for adventure.

But moments like this also terrified me.

Being the leader meant that it was my call—and mine alone—what dangerous, possibly life-threatening action my friends would take. And because my friends were loyal, they would trust me, even if it meant risking their lives.

Should they be so trusting? Should they follow me blindly without question?

A great leader would say yes, because a great leader would know with full confidence that his plan was perfect. They would know the risks and still be willing to take them because they know that their plan is the best possible option, despite those aforementioned risks.

Normally, I didn't question my plans. Normally, I tried to channel that great leader and therefore, I found it appropriate for my friends to follow me without question. But tonight was different. Tonight felt off. Something in my gut pulled me away from the door. A part of me wanted to turn around, go back down the stairs, and tell my friends that we'd try again tomorrow with a less insane plan.

But there stood Bianca, trying to light another flame, despite her shaky hand and furrowed eyebrows. Penny bounced between the balls of her feet, as if warming up for a five-mile run or a dance marathon. Eric looked around the room, as if soaking up every little detail to preserve the memory for some later time. Perhaps he'd already crafted the narrative: "Hey, remember that time we all broke into an old mansion in Texas and defeated a supervillain? There was that creepy staircase that led into a very beige, very compact room. Smelled like cedar and old books."

I couldn't let these people down. They looked up to me and needed me to decide for the collective.

A good leader might be confident in their own plan and use it to inspire others to action. But oftentimes, the leader was considered good because their followers were inspired by the plan, whether it was good or not. The followers deemed the motivations as good and therefore, the leader could be trusted.

My friends trusted me, so whether the plan was good or not, it was my duty to follow it through till the end.

"Be ready," I whispered. "He's not going to see us coming, so we need to use every second to our advantage. Act fast. If he has the staff, the goal is to get it away from him. If he doesn't, the goal is to apprehend him. I'll lead the charge."

Everyone nodded their heads in unison.

"It's four on one, thanks to Theo and Alexandra. This should be a piece of cake. Just keep moving and keep alert. That staff has some crazy powers, so be careful."

"Whatever you do, don't grab it while he's holding it," Penny said. "Try to knock it out of his hand first."

Penny would know. She'd experienced the sting of its power firsthand, when he first started using the electrical currents he'd stolen from Molly Meadows. I dreaded something like that happening again. But there was no time to worry. Theo and Alexandra could only lure away the minions for so long.

"Ok team," I said. "We've got this. Let's go."

* * *

We followed the music to a large wooden door, which stood partially open. A quick glimpse told me that we stood in front of the library.

I counted to three in my head.

One. You've got this.

Two. Lead them into battle.

Three. Please let this work.

We burst through the door to find Fadel at a large mahogany desk. He looked up, unbothered.

"Oh, hello there. I wasn't expecting visitors tonight." Despite his claim, he didn't look surprised in the slightest. He simply smiled and picked up the staff leaning on the desk next to him.

His eyes scanned over us, one at a time. His gaze stopped on Eric.

"I should have known," he muttered, frowning. Eric was the surprise he truly didn't expect.

"Welcome back, Mr. Vardoger. Must be wonderful reuniting with your little girlfriend. You two do love playing superheroes together, don't you?"

"It's over, Fadel. We have you cornered," Eric snarled.

Fadel smiled again, sending a chill down my spine.

Bianca tried lighting a flame to no avail, only producing smoke.

It wasn't like her to be scared like this—scared enough that her powers wouldn't work. But her face didn't scream fear. It read as confused and frustrated.

"Oh, that's not going to work, Miss Williams."

He grinned mischievously.

Any intentions we had of attacking swiftly were tossed out the window the second Fadel smiled.

"You see this?" He patted the side of a record player on the corner of his desk. "My latest invention. You thought the staff was impressive? This here does the opposite."

He laughed.

"Meet 'The Dampener.'"

CHAPTER FIFTY-SEVEN

Before I could comprehend what Fadel had just said, Sebastian charged forward and snatched a fountain pen with one hand and a metal clipboard with the other.

I followed him towards the villain, dodging his staff as he swung in my direction.

Sebastian sliced at his neck with the pen at an awkward angle, but Fadel ducked and thrust with his staff, which knocked Sebastian back. The pen flew out of his hand. He clutched the clipboard and swiped Fadel's ankles, knocking him off-balance.

Bianca and Eric, meanwhile, had come around to the back of the desk, intending to surround our prey. Eric suddenly disappeared. When he reappeared, he looked confused.

"It's not working right," he said to himself, exasperated.

"I can't get fire," Bianca added, opening and closing her hands like she was trying to get feeling back in her fingers. She became angrier each time she opened and found nothing inside.

I didn't like what this meant for me, but I stumbled forward anyway.

I sashayed over and executed a roundhouse kick, aiming for Fadel's chest. Normally, this would knock him over, no problem. But today, my foot landed with the force of a toddler whacking another with a teddy bear. He didn't even flinch.

Fadel smiled down at me and grabbed me by my shirt, tossing me aside. He took his staff and threw two balls of fire at my feet. I quickly stomped them out, terrified at our inability to keep up.

As Sebastian and Fadel grappled, Eric joining in on the back, Bianca scurried over to me.

"The record player is dampening our powers," she said. "It's not stopping us from using them completely, but it's not allowing us to work at full capacity."

I watched as the boys struggled with Fadel. Eric looked more and more tired with each teleport. Each time he disappeared, it took several seconds for him to return.

Sebastian, however, was working at full speed; the cogs in his mind turned to calculate each precise angle and velocity. Not only that, but his body kept up perfectly with his mind; each equation followed through to its real-life conclusion.

"Bee," I asked, a bit flustered. "Why aren't Sebastian's powers dampened?"

She flashed me a look I'd never seen before. It wasn't quite fear. It looked instead like concern mixed with grief. Maybe even guilt.

She opened her mouth to reply but quickly shut it as Eric flew across the room and landed at our feet.

"Eric!" She cried out, reaching for him to make sure he was ok.

"It's no use," he yelled. "We aren't going to be able to take him when he has both his staff and the Dampener. Bee, you help Sebastian, Penny and I will get the music box."

Bianca pushed off the ground and ran at Fadel from behind, kicking him hard in the back of his knee. He fell to the ground, still clutching his most prized possession. Sebastian came in with a lamp, wielding it over his head like a sword.

Before I could see the impact, Eric grabbed my hand and yanked me towards the desk. The Dampener continued to turn the record, playing a crooner song I'd never heard before.

This is a lovely way, to spend an evening,
Can't think of anything, I'd rather do,
This is a lovely way, to spend an evening,
Can't think of anyone as lovely as you.

"Can we just turn it off?" I asked aloud, reaching for the arm. As my fingers touched the metal, an electric shock shot up my arm.

I flashed back to the day I grabbed his staff and electricity filled my body. I remembered the way Theo rushed to me and collapsed by my side, clutching me. I remembered the world going dark.

I screamed out in pain and fell to my knees. The shock wasn't as bad as before, but it still came at an unexpected cost. My hands went numb and I bit my lip to fight back tears.

Eric tried kicking it off the desk, but it didn't budge. He yelped in pain but held strong.

"I think he has it secured to the desk, and it's clearly booby-trapped. We're just going to have to keep trying for the staff," he said, pulling me up.

How were we supposed to take him down without our powers?

I followed Eric back into the battle, just in time to see Bianca kick Fadel in the chest.

Sebastian had taught her so much about self-defense, even I was impressed. I just hoped I could keep up, since there was nothing special about me to help us now...

CHAPTER FIFTY-EIGHT

Theodore

I had to be going at least 70 as I sped down that dirt road. I whipped around the last turn and eased on the brakes, coming to a stop right along the edge of the orchard. No sign of Alexandra or Zeke yet.

Come on, come on, come on.

The trees loomed next to the car, casting a long, dark shadow over the road. My eyes tried to adjust to the darkness between the branches, but I couldn't see anything. I envisioned Fadel or one of his goonies running out of the woods. That would be a jump scare for sure. If anyone was going to run out from those trees, it better be a guy built like a fridge and a former receptionist.

Everyone had been talking a lot about what the "after" looked like. After this battle… after tonight… after Fadel…

There was a good chance that tonight would be the last battle with Fadel. After this, we might not have to deal with him anymore. It would be over and we could go live normal lives. But what did normal look like for someone like me?

I'd been using my powers since I was a kid. Yeah, I wasn't using them to fight bad guys or anything, but I've always known I was different. And when I met Penny… Penny changed my life. She changed the way

I looked at myself. I was no longer the kid who could float around the house or do neat tricks to impress my friends. Penny showed me my potential.

We had been watching late night TV in my parent's basement back in high school when a news story appeared: "Mystery Robber Cracks Another Vault." I'd never forget that headline.

She turned to me without missing a beat.

"What if we stopped him?"

"What if we stopped who? Jeff Bridgeman? He's not a great anchorman but I don't think he's worth protesting or anything."

She unfolded her legs and angled my direction. Her tank top hugged her ribs, and her shorts clearly defined those delicate hips of hers. She began pulling her short, blonde hair back into a small ponytail. She always started messing with her hair when she got stressed or antsy.

"No, I mean the robber. What if we stopped the robber?"

"Like right now?"

She bit her lip and nodded. A small smile spread across her face.

"Who do you think we are? Spiderman? We aren't heroes, Pen. We're weirdos. Freaks, if you will."

"Your friendly neighborhood Spiderman. But before he got the cool outfit. I think that could perfectly describe what we are capable of."

I laughed at her moxy.

"Pen, I literally float like a piece of trash on a windy day, and you kick things really hard. How on earth do you expect us to stop a bank robber?"

"We'd figure it out. And you are much more than a piece of trash. You're strong and brave. You literally take kickboxing and that other form of martial arts I can't pronounce."

"So we'd just go beat this guy up? Is that your plan?"

"I say we at least go stake it out and see what's up."

She pushed herself off the couch and giggled, reaching her hands out to pull me up. She wouldn't be able to lift me, but it was a cute gesture anyway.

"Please? It would infuriate my parents if they knew, so I think that's extra motivation to do it," she grinned. Her rosy cheeks shone at that moment. She just had so much life in her. She was radiant.

"How can I say no to that goofy smile," I said, letting her attempt to pull me up, helping her with a bit of momentum.

"Hey, you like the goofy smile," she replied, blushing. She was right, I did. I still saw that smile every time I closed my eyes. Every time I smelled roses.

When I finally saw a shadowed figure coming out from the trees, my heart leapt, thinking maybe it was her.

No, you idiot. She's back at the house. It must be Allie.

But it wasn't Allie. It was Zeke, and only Zeke.

I rolled down the window and unlocked the passenger door. He flung it open and jumped in.

"How far is she behind you? Alexandra. Where is she?"

I'd expected her back first, since she seemed quite nimble, especially compared to Zeke. But regardless, they were supposed to arrive together.

"I don't know. Shortly after we started running, she got spooked. She turned the wrong way, and I lost track of her. Maggie followed her. I think they might have circled back towards the house."

"You've gotta be kidding me!" I yelled, punching the steering wheel. The horn gave a pathetic honk. "We need to go."

I threw the car into drive and slammed my foot on the gas.

"Aren't we supposed to be going downtown?" Zeke asked, as I sped towards the house.

"Weren't you supposed to protect Alexandra?" This could not be happening. "Nope, you're coming with me back to the house. We've gotta find her. And the goons. We were supposed to drag them *away* from the house, not towards it."

"I didn't mean to lose her, man," he replied. "I want to leave. This isn't my problem anymore."

"But you did," I replied, taking a sharp left. Zeke reached for the overhead handle. "It doesn't matter; we're going back regardless. If you want to leave, you can, but I'm going in and I'm not going to waste a single minute taking you elsewhere so you can be a coward."

He opened his mouth to reply, but I'd already stopped the car and took off running towards the estate. I kept the car keys in my pocket. If he wanted to run away from his problems, he'd have to do it on foot.

CHAPTER FIFTY-NINE

Alexandra

One second, I was running next to Zeke. The next, he was gone.

To be fair, I was running slightly ahead of Zeke, and doing so at a much slower speed than I'd wanted, since he was so dang slow. And maybe that was how I lost him. Maggie zipped right up next to me and snatched at my hair. I screamed and took a sharp right turn. She miscalculated and got ahead of where I was initially running.

I didn't even bother waiting for Zeke anymore; I bolted. I took off so fast I couldn't even hear him behind me. I dodged trees and jumped over fallen branches. I was a deer running from the hunter. I was in the freaking Hunger Games. And I was terrified of getting caught.

My breathing started getting heavier. My throat burned from the cool air drying out my nostrils. I tried to swallow, but it stuck. I glanced over my shoulder to see if anyone was behind me.

No one.

I slowed to a stop, panting and coughing. The silence was deafening. A ringing sound battled the hollow thud of my heart as I tried to listen around me.

A crunch of dry leaves from a few yards away caused me to jump. I jogged a little again, weaving between trees, trying to lose my pursuer.

The moonlight did little to help me. I was running through inky blackness.

I stopped behind a large, fat-bottomed apple tree and crouched down, my back pressed up against it.

I listened hard but only heard the wind.

Where did they go?

A crack and a breeze on my right gave me chills and made me jump again. Lawrence must have been close. But it was Maggie I heard first.

"Where is she?"

"I don't know," Lawrence replied.

I tried to calm my breath, scared that my panting could be heard.

"Where did Z go?"

"He was running towards the main drag. I think he's trying to get back to the road. I bet he's meeting up with the dude in the car."

"Why did Alexandra run the other way then?"

The other way… oh my gosh, I'd gotten turned around. When I turned, I tried to correct my steps to face the road again. I must have over-corrected, and quite badly, too. I was leading them straight towards the house. I had one, singular job, and it was to take them *away* from the house.

What had I done?

A loud boom sounded from the manor. A scream that sounded a lot like Bee's rang out.

"The doctor! They've attacked!" Lawrence yelled. "Come on!"

"We need to find Alexandra!" Maggie replied, her voice shaking. She was scared of going to the house, but she might have been even more scared of losing me. The doctor didn't like when people got away.

"Screw her. She doesn't have anything he wants anyway. He still wants Arashi. Oliver is nothing to him now. We need to go help him. Otherwise, he'll try to kill us like he's trying to kill Williams and the others. You know that, right? I know you heard him last night! If we don't help him now, he doesn't want us anymore. If we don't go back to the house right now, we're next."

He didn't sound like an underling worshiping his master, he sounded like a prisoner scared of his jailer. Maggie must have agreed because the sound of their steps faded away, crunching and cracking as they ran.

I waited another minute or two, petrified to move in case they were still present. When I decided to keep going, they were definitely gone. They'd run back to the house. I'd failed at my one task.

I wanted to cry. I had been inadequate once again. I wasn't like them and I would never be. When this battle was over, I would go home. For real this time. I'd put the last several years in the past. I'd start over and live the normal life I was born into.

I took off running in the direction of the noise, scared of what I'd find there, but still hoping I could make up for the major mistake I'd just made.

CHAPTER SIXTY

Bianca

I kicked him in the chest again, for good measure. Sebastian had taught me that move a few weeks before we left, and I'd been practicing it on my own ever since.

Fadel stumbled backwards, but his hands still gripped the staff.

He swung it at my head and I ducked, a small buzzing noise whooshing over me as it went by. He was using the electric charge again. While I was down, he seized the opportunity to knock me off balance and kicked me in return, knocking me off my feet and onto my back.

"Bee!" Penny yelled as Fadel slammed his staff down next to me. I rolled to dodge it as he brought it down a second time. Sebastian jumped in between my body and Fadel, wielding what appeared to be a metal bookend.

I scrambled to my feet and retreated towards the doorway, just in time to see Fadel crash into one of the bookshelves.

He swung his staff around his head, throwing flames in every direction. A few caught, burning into the books on the shelves.

"No! Not the books!" Penny squealed.

"Penny, not the priority," I replied as I blasted a beam of ice at the burning books.

"Sorry," she yelped and began to chassé straight towards Fadel, ending with a nice kick to his throat.

That one got him down, even without her powers working to their full effect. But before we could make another move, he disappeared with a *crack*.

"Find him!" Sebastian bolted towards the door. Eric disappeared with a small *crack* like Fadel's.

We ran down the hallway, looking for signs of him. I ran into a bedroom, opening the bathroom door. Nothing. I ran to the window, hoping to see if he was outside, trying to escape.

"He can't be far," Eric yelled down the hall. "If he's anything like me, he can only get so far with each teleport. He's still in the house somewhere."

I couldn't see him out the window, but I could smell something.

"Guys, it smells like smoke," I yelled to my friends.

And then I saw it. Smoke drifted from the house, coming from the roof.

"Guys," I yelled. "I think he's on the roof. And I think he's trying to set the house on fire."

"He's trying to trap us!" Penny shrieked.

"Start looking for an entrance to the attic! This place has to have one!" Sebastian called out instructions as we ran from room to room.

"In here!" Penny cried out. Sebastian and I came tumbling down the hall and into another bedroom. Eric suddenly appeared to my left.

Penny pulled the trap door downwards with all her might and jumped out of the way as a rickety ladder spilled out of the dark hole.

Sebastian jumped onto the ladder, climbing every other step. I followed him, with Eric and then Penny bringing up the rear.

When we entered the attic, Sebastian identified a window large enough to fit through and kicked the glass out. Quickly, and not-so-carefully, he pulled himself through, up, and out.

"I'm scared," Penny said, looking at the window.

"I'll go first, and I can pull you out," I replied, as if I wasn't just as scared. If I tried to make a fire right now, I'd definitely fail.

"I can hold you from down here. I won't let you fall," Eric told me.

Penny stepped back so that Eric could help me position myself back-first out the window. Bracing my hip on the windowsill, I reached up and grabbed a ledge. Eric kept his hands firm on my thighs. A shiver ran down my spine, and I tried to push my focus elsewhere.

Outside the window, cold air mixed with black smoke, obscuring my vision and causing my hands to shake.

"Eric, I'm scared," I said, hoping he would pull me back inside to safety.

"You've got it, Bianca. Just pull yourself up. I won't drop you," he replied as calmly as ever.

This was a really stupid idea.

The wind whipped my hair in my face. I needed to go back in and find another way. I couldn't get up.

But before I could turn back, two familiar hands gripped my wrists and yanked me upwards. I screamed as my body flew into the sky. A strong arm seized my waist and pulled me onto the roof ledge, releasing me onto my stomach.

I brushed my hair out of my face and stood up next to Sebastian.

"Grab Penny," I instructed him as I began making my way across the roof.

Fadel was up ahead. He tapped his staff on the shingles and caught them on fire, one by one. He hadn't seen me yet.

He was so precariously close to the edge. All I had to do was push. *Could I really do that? Could I kill him?*

He had killed so many people, including Sebastian's parents. This would be justice. This would be what he deserved, and it would be so easy.

I crept closer and closer. Glancing over my shoulder, I observed my friends following me. Sebastian nodded in my direction. He was giving me permission. He was urging me to do it.

I didn't mean to, but I looked at Eric, too. He gave me the smallest bob of the head. He was also telling me yes.

I was three yards away. Two. One.

I slowly reached out my arms, ready to end it for all time. Ready to take my revenge.

I was going to do it.

I was going to take down Chakir Fadel.

"Dr. Fadel!" Someone cried out behind me.

Fadel whipped around, shock written all over his face as he turned towards me. He suddenly seized me by my sweatshirt and pulled me off the ground. My legs kicked and swung around, terrified. My hands grasped blindly for his, trying to secure myself. I wanted to burn him. I wanted him to put me down. But I couldn't conjure the courage or the spark I needed.

"Sebastian!" I yelped.

I turned to look at my boyfriend but was surprised to see Maggie Andrews approaching us. It was her. She had yelled to Fadel.

But she wasn't supposed to be here. She was supposed to be with…

Alexandra suddenly appeared at the window ledge, pulling herself up.

What were they doing? Why were they here?

"Sebastian!" I yelled again, my voice weak as the fabric of my shirt tightened around my throat. Fadel swung his arm out, holding me up on the edge of the roof. My feet desperately scraped the tiles and tried to find their footing.

"No!" Maggie cried out again. "Stop, don't do that!"

"What did you say, girl?" Fadel growled, holding fast to his plan and refusing to release me.

"Please don't kill her!" Maggie's voice cracked. I didn't expect empathy from someone I'd branded a villain, but maybe there was part of her that remembered we used to be friends. We used to be so close. Maybe that meant something to her, too.

I tried to turn my head and look at her, but my angle made it impossible to get a clear view. Fadel, however, had her locked in his sights. The fury in his eyes spread like a match dropped in gasoline.

"Dr. Fadel, you can't kill her. Please!" Maggie begged.

"Choose a side, girl!" He screamed and gripped me tighter.

Smoke filled my lungs, but I couldn't cough. My shirt was too tight around my throat.

"Please!" Maggie cried.

Fadel released my shirt and I closed my eyes, ready to fall. But instead of tumbling down towards the garden below, I was struck hard by a heavy object, flung backwards, and landed on my stomach on the roof.

I rolled over to see Sebastian laying next to me, sighing. The wind had been knocked out of him. He must have run and tackled me. I wanted to thank him, to squeeze his hand and let him know we were both ok. That he had saved me. But instead, I looked up at Fadel, expecting him to come for us.

But he wasn't coming for us; he was moving towards Maggie.

I started blasting ice at the flames, snuffing them out as quickly as possible. But I could barely focus as he strode towards my former friend. I was scared for her.

"I am sick of all these disgusting traitors. You're worse than the brats trying to kill me."

Maggie stepped backwards as Fadel approached. I scanned the roof-line, hoping someone would move to protect her, but no one did. No one except Lawrence, who had pulled himself onto the roof behind Alexandra.

"Dr. Fadel, she will obey you," Lawrence said. "She's just scared."

"I'm tired of you fools being scared. Scared sent Mr. Vardoger to Utah. Scared turned Ms. Williams over to the enemy. Scared made a traitor of Ms. Oliver. That's three strikes."

"We're loyal," Lawrence said. "We are, right, Maggie? We won't leave you, sir."

Maggie didn't move. She didn't nod. She didn't agree. She stood frozen in place.

"I'm not worried about you leaving, you idiot disgrace of a boy. No, Ms. Andrews has demonstrated what I've known all along: any friend of Bianca Williams, past, present, or future, cannot be loyal to me."

Lawrence opened his mouth to reply, but it was too late. Fadel stood only feet from Maggie now. Maggie hovered precariously close to the edge of the roof. At first, I thought I saw tears on her face, but in reality, the shock had just frozen her face in fear. She trembled, holding her shaking hands up between her and the man approaching.

She could run; she could use her powers to move around him and escape. But the fear paralyzed her.

The biggest enemy was always fear.

"Please," she whispered, so gently we could barely hear her. I was no longer looking at Fadel's minion. I was looking at every person he'd ever despised, everyone who had ever betrayed him. I was looking at Alexandra Oliver. I was looking at myself.

"I'm going to make you an example so that next time, my followers know not to stand in my way."

This time I was the one who yelled.

"Fadel! No!"

But it was too late. Fadel swung his staff and slammed it into the roof by his feet. Out of the glowing orb blasted a bolt of lightning, striking Maggie square in the chest. She screamed as she collapsed. A deafening thud rang out as her body hit the roof.

"No!" I ran forward to fight him, hands outstretched with fire in my veins. My entire body pulsed with rage.

Fadel's head whipped around and he lifted his staff and struck it against my calves. I tumbled over backwards, my flames snuffed out. He made his move, approaching his other minion with determination in his stride.

Lawrence backpedaled, just like Maggie had. His face said it all: he knew he was next.

I worried that the fear would take him down, too, but somehow, he managed to teleport away, leaving Fadel staring at an empty corner of the roof.

Fadel cursed and turned back towards Maggie, who still hadn't moved.

"Disgusting traitor," he spoke into the wind. And then swinging his staff over his head, he disappeared with another loud crack. A large ring of char encircled where he once stood.

I screamed but couldn't hear it. My heartbeat drowned out all the noise.

He was gone. Again. He'd escaped. *Again.* But this time, he'd left more than just destruction in his wake.

Maggie lay unmoving several feet away. I couldn't see her face, but I knew.

The house shook like an earthquake, knocking us all off balance. Sebastian fell to a knee and Penny gripped his arm, steadying herself. Eric had fallen down to all fours.

Alexandra swayed in place; eyes locked on Maggie. I rushed forward to grab her and support her weight. My hands froze onto her wrists, but she didn't notice. I let anger wash over the cold again and my hands relaxed their grip, the ice melting away and leaving a puddle at our feet.

"Bee, Bee," she muttered. "Maggie…"

I stabilized her as she took two steps towards where Maggie laid. I let go and allowed her to move closer. She was still several feet away but stopped suddenly at the sight of her limp friend. Her lips opened slightly. No sound came out of her mouth, but her eyes screamed in terror.

Her best friend had been murdered in front of her, and there was nothing she could have done to stop it.

* * *

Before

We lay on the floor of Alexandra's apartment, laughing our heads off.

"He's ugly."

"No, he is not!" I yelled, laughing hysterically.

"He is!" Alexandra insisted. "That's why she left. The no spark thing was complete BS. She thought he was ugly."

"Ok well, I agree he's not the most attractive, but there's no way. All these girls are obsessed with him."

"The girls are always obsessed with the Bachelor until he doesn't pay enough attention to them, and they snap out of it like they've been in a trance or something," Maggie chipped in, throwing a piece of popcorn in the air, trying to catch it in her mouth. She missed.

"And they realize he's ugly!" Alexandra yelled, pushing herself up to a seated position. She looked down at me with a serious look on her face.

"Seriously, Bee, would you kiss this guy? I sure wouldn't."

"I mean… I don't know."

"She's not into the dark hair," Maggie said, trying her popcorn trick again. "Have you seen Eric?"

"Shut up!" I laughed, hitting her with the pillow I'd been hugging.

298

"Ow!" She yelled, and we all burst out laughing again.

When I sat up, the blood all rushed back into my head, making me dizzy.

"Should I sign up for the next season?" Maggie asked.

"As the Bachelorette or as a contestant on the Bachelor?" I asked.

"Either one. I just want to find The One," she replied, smiling into space.

"You think people actually find love on these shows?" Alexandra quipped.

"I mean, I bet some do. I certainly would!" Maggie laughed. "Gosh, I'm desperate. The men the Doctor employs just aren't doing it for me."

"What about Zeke?" I asked, causing Alexandra to perk up a bit. I'd not seen her do that before, let alone for Zeke.

"Nah, I don't really think he's my type." Maggie played with her hair and thought about our suggestions.

"Well, I guess you'll have to look elsewhere. I think Eric is taken," Alexandra replied matter-of-factly.

"I still don't understand why you'd want to date a guy who can literally disappear on you. Talk about ghosting you to the extreme," Maggie laughed. "Kidding!" She yelled as I wailed on her with the pillow.

"But for real," she said, calming down. "How are we supposed to meet anyone when all we do is follow around an old guy with a staff?"

"He's not old," I responded. "He's what, in his forties?"

"Old," Alexandra replied, "And ugly. Just like the freaking Bachelor!"

We laughed and laughed, Alexandra tipping backwards and rolling onto her back again. I could barely breathe. Tears streamed down Maggie's face.

I was so lucky to have moments like this. My life was nothing like I thought it would be, but I loved it anyway. I was dating a strong, handsome, and thoughtful guy. I spent my days training my body and mind in order to better myself and help others. I spent my nights laughing with my friends.

I'd never been happier.

CHAPTER SIXTY-ONE

Jasmine

A thunder-like crack followed by a deafening roar echoed through the room.

"What was that?" I heard myself ask. I didn't direct it to Robert, but he shrugged anyway.

Suddenly, the room shook. The concrete ceiling sprinkled us with dust.

"Robert!" I desperately looked for an exit. But it was too late. The ceiling caved in and we dropped to the ground, covering our heads like we were experiencing a Cold War nuclear drill. Pieces of cement fell around us and I screamed again. Robert moved his body over my head and neck in an attempt to protect me. I couldn't even be mad, I was so overcome with fear.

Rubble! Do not fall on us!

I commanded the cement to steer clear of our bodies, hoping that my Voice could keep up with the destruction. My body was in fight or flight, and running was not an option.

After a few moments, the shaking stopped and the room filled with silence.

The power had been cut. Either that, or all the light bulbs in the room had blown, as it was now pitch black.

I fumbled for my phone in my pocket and turned on the flashlight. Robert did the same next to me. Sitting up slowly, I moved the flashlight around and took in the destruction. The ceiling had caved and rubble littered the floor. The door—the only exit—had caved as well, boulders blocked our escape.

"No no no no no…"

I pushed off the floor and ran to the door, jumping over several chunks of concrete and kicking up dust as I ran. I dropped my phone at my feet and began clawing at the rubble, trying to fight my way through to the freedom that lay on the other side of the pile.

"Jasmine, stop," Robert sighed. I kept digging. A stone cut into my hand, and I quickly yanked it back, my fingers burning.

"Jasmine! Stop! It's not going to work."

"*Rocks, move,*" I commanded. "*Rocks, clear from the doorway!*"

Some smaller rocks floated up and drifted around, but they refused to move away from the exit entirely.

"*I said move!*" I screamed. Two softball sized pieces of concrete flung across the room and shattered against the opposing wall.

"Jasmine, even if the rocks move, the doorway has collapsed. We can't get out."

I turned sharply and took in the sight of Robert with his flashlight and thousand-yard stare at the blocked exit.

"I can't believe this." I said. My tone was somewhere within the crossroads of anger, frustration, and awe. "I can't believe this is happening."

I bit my lip and fought back the tears. I suddenly felt hot and unzipped my jacket. I pulled it off and tied it sloppily around my waist. I wanted to take off more layers, but had nothing left to remove. I was panting like a dog in an overheated car.

"I'm sorry, Jasmine," Robert replied. "I'm sorry you're in this mess and I'm sorry it's with me. I'm probably the last person you want to be trapped here with; I know that. I'm really sorry."

He was right. I was trapped in this room. This building had likely collapsed. Who knew if my friends were even alive. And if no one knew we were here, or that we had survived, would anyone come save us?

I was probably going to die. Stuck in the same room as Robert Arashi.

"I want to scream at you," I said, matter-of-factly.

"You can," he replied, a little too calmly. "You're certainly welcome to. I don't know how it will help, but be my guest."

"I want to scream at you," I continued. "But I can't. I want to be mad at you, but it's impossible.

"I want to tell you that you're annoying and infuriating. I want you to know that you drive me insane."

"Harsh," he replied, but nodded all the same.

"You drive me crazy and you make my head spin. I really, really want to hate you. You don't know how much I want to hate you."

His face, although barely lit by the backside of the flashlight, looked dejected and meek.

"But I can't," I said, tears finally falling for the first time in ages. "I can't hate you. In fact, I can't stop thinking about you. I've tried to be angry about you kissing Alexandra, about the way you've flirted with her. About how you probably like her more than me and that you've played with my emotions like I was a game piece on a board. But I know deep down that my anger is just a coping mechanism. I've been, or at least I've felt, rejected by you and I used anger to cover up the fact that you hurt me. I wanted to be chosen by you.

"I thought you liked me and when you told me you kissed Alexandra, my heart broke. I've never experienced anything like that before because I've never really felt *liked* before, at least not in that way. And for you to rip the rug out from under me kind of destroyed me, Robert.

CHAPTER SIXTY-ONE

But I can't hate you. I want to, but I can't."

"Jasmine, I—"

"I'm going to die here with you. And I don't want to die. I'm so, so scared. But at least now, I won't go to my grave clinging on to these thoughts and feelings. So do with them what you will. Now you can go to *your* grave with my deepest, darkest secret."

I wiped my eyes and sniffed. I took a deep breath and stopped the flow of tears. I'd said my peace. It was over.

The silence of the room was deafening. But soon, a new sound broke through the void. Robert started laughing to himself.

"Stop it," I said, more vulnerability than Voice. "Stop it right now."

"I can't," he laughed harder.

My eyes welled up again, blurring my vision. I blinked them back angrily.

"Please don't make fun of me," I whispered. "I can't handle any more rejection."

I looked up, but before I knew what was happening, Robert had moved across the room, fast. He took my face in his hands and brought his lips to mine.

His phone had fallen to the floor, shrouding the room in darkness. I couldn't see him very well, but it didn't matter. His hands gripped my waist as he pulled me into him. Our bodies pressed together as one of his hands moved up from my hip, dragged up my waist and arm, and settled in my hair, gripping it gently. My arms laced around his neck and my left foot lifted slowly off the floor as I leaned into him.

The fingers of his other hand dug into my hips and my body tingled. All my worries and fears had been brushed away by his touch.

My first kiss: in an obliterated basement, surrounded by concrete slabs, essentially standing in my own grave. But that kiss was heaven on earth.

When we finally pulled apart, I gazed through the darkness at his smiling face, hard to see but so easy to feel.

"I can't believe you don't hate me," he whispered.

"I don't think I actually could."

"I never liked Alexandra like that. I kissed her to scare off Fadel's goonies. I never meant anything by it. I've had my eyes on you since we were trapped in that office in Louisiana."

"Ah yes," I said, rolling my eyes. "The *other* time we were trapped in a room together because of that stupid magician."

"The overall company is better this time," he replied, kissing me again.

"So now we can die happy?" I laced my fingers into his with both hands.

"We could do that. Or we could find a way out of here."

I let go of his hands and leaned down to get my phone. He did the same. No cell service.

Classic.

"We can't call anyone for help. And as you said, the door has caved in."

"Could we yell for help?"

"I don't think anyone would hear us."

We moved over to the door and cleared some more rubble by hand.

"Robert, look!" I exclaimed, moving a few rocks. "There's a crack here."

A gap between the wall and the door had formed, maybe the size of a golf ball.

"I don't know where it goes, but I have an idea."

Fumbling through my jacket pocket, I pulled out a small, crumpled gum wrapper in the shape of a paper crane.

"Is that—"

"Yes," I nodded. "It's yours. My dad used to fold these for me when

I was young. It reminded me of him, so I kept it."

He smiled and took my hand—and the crane—in his.

"If we can find something to write with, we can write a note on it."

This time, when we checked our jacket pockets again, I produced a small lip stick.

I scribbled three words across the crane, one on each wing and one on the body.

Basement. Help. Jas.

I kissed the crane for good luck and willed it to fly.

Slowly, it hovered over our hands and I smiled, remembering that I still had power inside myself.

Find Bianca or Sebastian. Find my friends. Help us get free.

The crane flapped its little wings and approached the crack. Robert gave it a little boost of wind, pushing it through the hole and into the darkness.

"And now," I said. "We wait."

I sat down on the floor, my back against the wall. Robert laid his head in my lap. I stroked his hair and smiled softly to myself.

"I'm so tired," he yawned. "But I don't want to sleep."

"Sleep. I'll wake you if something happens or if someone comes."

"But I want to keep looking at you. If I'm going to die, I'd like to look at you for as long as possible before doing so."

I laughed as butterflies filled my stomach. He thought I was pretty. How beautifully tragic if we really were going to die.

"Sleep," I said again, running my fingers through his hair over and over again. I wasn't using my Voice, but he still drifted soundly to sleep. Our breathing fell into sync as I, too, nodded off against the crumbling wall.

CHAPTER SIXTY-TWO

Sebastian

"Alexandra, we've gotta *go!*"

She stood, motionless. Her eyes stared straight ahead, latched on the spot where Maggie had fallen, where she still laid. Part of me wondered why she hadn't run to her, why she hadn't fallen down by her side. But the fact she didn't relieved me. It would be easier to pull her away now.

Alexandra swayed a bit, like she was going to pass out. I rushed to her and caught her as she fell, still conscious, but barely.

"Allie, I need you to breathe. We need to run, right now. This place is crumbling. We need to get out of here."

She nodded, weakly. I pulled her arm around my neck and scooped her up. She clung to me as I ran down the stairs and after Eric, Penny, and Bianca.

I dodged falling plaster as it fell from the ceiling, shielding Alexandra's head. I jumped over split boards and whipped around corners. The stairs felt uncertain as I ran down them, skipping every other step.

"It's my fault," Alexandra whispered, barely audible.

"It's not," I whispered back, but I knew she couldn't hear me. I knew she wasn't listening.

We burst through the front door and onto the front lawn, and I dropped her into Eric's waiting arms. He nodded behind me and instructed me to go find Fadel.

I grabbed Bianca's hand and we took off down the driveway.

The sound of the house crumbling boomed like thunder in our wake.

Bianca's steps crunched under her, as each blade she touched frosted over.

"Maggie?" I asked, still running. I looked over at her sideways.

She kept her face forward as she ran but shook her head.

"No. The house. It was so beautiful. Why does he always ruin beautiful things?"

I thought about the old hotel in Victory and the town I grew up in. I thought about my parents. My eyes welled up with tears, but I shook them away.

"I don't know, but he's going to pay for it."

We curved around the orchard and looked for Fadel. He wasn't anywhere to be seen.

"Fadel!" Bianca screamed. "Show your face, you murderer! You killed Margaret Andrews! Show your face and fight!"

The grass was no longer icy, it was scorched.

Bianca had a way of releasing her emotions that scared her. She struggled for so long to get them to cooperate, but her issue was a lack of control. But this wasn't one of those times. She wasn't scared. She had complete control. She let the anger wash over her like a tidal wave, letting loose of every other thought, every other lingering emotion.

"Fadel, I will find you and I will kill you myself!" she hollered into the darkness of the orchard.

"Bee, I think he's gone. I don't think he can hear us."

She twirled around, her hands clenched in fists, little flames dancing around them.

"He's a coward. He's a *coward*, Sebastian," she shook with rage.

"I know," I reached for her hand. One of the flames jumped and stung me. I pulled back, shocked.

"Oh my gosh," she snuffed out the fire. "I'm so sorry."

"It's ok. You're mad. That's valid."

"I hate him. I hate him so much. He killed someone."

"I know."

"He *killed* someone. Not just kidnapped. Not just beat and abandoned. He has blood on his hands."

"I know. We're going to find him and enact justice. I promise, Bee."

"I want to kill him."

"We'll talk about it," I replied, gently but cautiously. I tried reaching for her hand again. This time, she took my fingers in hers.

"I really want him dead."

"I know, but first we need to find him. And we won't be able to do that alone, so we need to get back to our friends."

She nodded softly, but before we could move, a *crack* sounded behind us. We turned around quickly, expecting Fadel.

It was Lawrence.

Bee let go of my hand and lit her flame again.

"You," she hissed.

"Hey man," he said, backing up with his hands in front of him. "I don't want any of that."

"You let him kill her."

"No, I didn't. I saw what you saw. He killed her and I booked it out of there before he could kill me too. He took my powers just like he took hers. He doesn't need us anymore."

"Then why have you stayed with him?" I asked.

"Security. You should be able to understand that. But now the most secure thing is getting out of here. I want to go home."

"How do we know you're telling the truth?"

"Do you think I want to end up like Maggie? Did you hear what he said to me up there? He killed Maggie, man. He left me behind after saying those disgusting things. He clearly doesn't want either of us. So much so, he killed her. Who's to say he won't kill me, too?"

Lawrence's hands shook with fear, maybe rage.

"I need to get home before he can find me…before he has a chance to kill me."

He brushed a hand through his hair and let it come to rest on the back of his skull, breathing heavily and looking towards the sky.

"I didn't ask for this," he muttered. "I didn't know."

Bianca's face changed from anger into something else. She understood, better than anyone, what it felt like to be tricked by Fadel and forced to do horrible things. She experienced the weight of guilt that landed on her shoulders once she woke up from his spell. She knew the terror of being pursued by an angry villain, and now both of them had witnessed what happened to supers who got in his way.

Maggie's murder hammered the final nail in Lawrence's coffin, but Lawrence didn't want to lay down and die.

"Where's home?" Bianca asked, lowering her hands.

"Canada. But I'm worried I won't be able to cross the border without him finding me. I think he's hacked some systems to track us. I know he hacked the airlines, maybe he set up other trackers too. He knew where Zeke was, even when he tried to escape. I don't think I can return home yet. I need to find somewhere to hide out."

Bianca took a deep breath, closing her eyes and calming her nerves. When she opened her eyes, she looked calmer, more patient, but still nervous.

"And you swear you're done with him?"

Lawrence looked scared out of his mind. I trusted by the look on his face that he wasn't going to run back to Fadel anytime soon. I think Bianca knew that, too.

"I hate the man. He killed my friend. He tried to kill you all. I think he'll kill me too. Please, just let me go."

"What can you do for us, to ensure you won't change your mind?" Lawrence didn't hesitate.

"You let me go and I can give you all the information you need regarding Fadel's whereabouts. I know all the door codes, secret storage locations. I know his contacts. I know his plans."

"We could just use Zeke for that information, you know," I said, crossing my arms over my chest. He matched me by doing the same.

"The Doctor knew Zeke would betray him. He changed the passwords and locks. He kept things from him. He claimed that Zeke was too emotional to handle sensitive information. He was proven right, obviously."

"You're saying you'd help us if we help you? Scratch your back and you'll scratch ours?" Bianca asked.

"That's exactly what I'm saying. Please, just let me go and I can be your contact. I don't want to fight, but I can be a wealth of information for you."

Neither of us replied. I believed him but still wasn't sure I could trust him.

"Please," he said. "For Maggie."

Before I could reply, Bianca, cut me off.

"I know a place."

"Bee," I questioned, but she kept going.

"It's in Utah. You could hide out there. I can give you a name and address. Tell a man named Charles that I sent you."

"Really?" he asked, grinning.

"Yeah, but if you're lying to us or if you try to hurt Charles, I will come there and kill you myself. I'm feeling particularly murderous today."

"How will I know this Charles when I meet him?"

"You'll know."

Relief rushed into Lawrence's expression. His hands flung together in a gesture of thanksgiving.

"I swear. And I owe it to you. Seriously, thank you."

Lawrence gave Bianca his phone number and she texted him an address.

"You guys don't know how much this means to me," Lawrence said, shaking my hand.

"Just don't give us a reason to hunt you down. You don't want to mess with us when we're really angry," I said in return.

We exchanged goodbyes and Lawrence vanished, teleporting away to who knows where.

"Charles can take care of him," Bianca said to herself. "At least until he can go home."

She frowned and tipped her head back; eyes closed like she was bathing in the moonlight.

"I'm too trusting," she said. "I know that. It's probably my biggest weakness, isn't it?"

She wasn't wrong. She considered everyone trustworthy until they gave her a reason to change her mind. For people like us, that was a dangerous way of looking at the world, but I also couldn't blame her. If she hadn't been so trusting of me, she might not even be here, fighting by my side. I chose my words carefully.

"That was very generous of you," I said, placing a hand on her shoulder.

"Well, if he really wants to go home, I would be a villain to try and stop him."

I pulled her into a hug, which surprised her. She released a small "oh" before she relaxed into my embrace. I stroked her hair and kissed the top of her head, relieved to finally have her back in my arms again.

"Speaking of home," I released her and brought us back to business. "We need to get back to the house and find our friends. And with that, we turned and took off running, back in the direction we came.

CHAPTER SIXTY-THREE

Bianca

As we came running over the hill, back towards the house, I scanned the gathered crowd and made note of each of my friends.

Eric, Alexandra, and Penny were exactly where we'd left them, out under an old live oak. Eric knelt next to Alexandra, who lay on the ground. It looked like she might be asleep. Eric seemed to be talking to her anyway. Penny sat under the tree, looking up and talking to Theo, who had returned from who knows where.

He was originally supposed to meet up with Alexandra and Zeke, taking them to a meet-up location downtown. Evidently, that didn't happen, as Alexandra, and therefore Maggie, ended up back at the mansion. Zeke was nowhere to be seen. Neither were Jasmine and Robert.

"Guys," Sebastian yelled ahead to them. All turned to look his way, including Alexandra who sat up a bit. "Where are Jasmine and Robert?"

"We haven't seen them," Eric replied, pushing himself off the dead grass and starting our way.

"And Zeke?"

"He was here briefly, a bit ago. He explained that he and Alexandra got separated from Theo and then from each other while being pursued by Lawrence and Maggie. Alexandra got turned around and ran the wrong way. Maggie followed her all the way back to the house. We told him what happened to Maggie and since he was her friend, he insisted on going back to town to get the local authorities. They need to… um… you know."

"Understood," Sebastian said.

"Should we also go to town?" Eric asked. "I don't know how much use there is in hanging around here. I guess one or two of us could stay and meet with Zeke and the cops when they get back. Probably not the worst idea."

"You and Theo can take Alexandra and Penny back to town, but Sebastian and I need to find Jasmine. I have to know she's ok." I said, genuinely worried.

Where could they have gone?

I knew they planned to search the cellar and outbuildings. But when the house started crumbling, I expected they'd have come running. The noise was loud enough to be heard across the entire property.

Eric nodded and went back to the group.

"Sebastian, I'm scared something happened to Jas."

But before he could reply, a small paper crane fluttered into my line of sight. I reached up and snatched it from the air, examining it all over.

"Sebastian! It's from Jasmine! They're trapped in the cellar."

"Then let's go," he said, grabbing my hand. "We don't have time to waste."

"If they're trapped," I replied, letting go. "I think you should take Penny. Her powers will be more useful. I'll go wait for the police. I should be the one to talk to Zeke when he comes."

"Ok," he smiled. "Jas is safe. All is well. I'll see you soon."

He flagged Penny over and the two of them took off running

towards the back of the house.

CHAPTER SIXTY-FOUR

Robert

I woke up startled for two distinct reasons. First and foremost, because I was curled around a beautiful girl. Second, because the cavalry had arrived, and boy were they loud.

Jasmine jolted up, looking around, panicked.

"Jas!" Someone yelled from behind the rubble.

"I'm here!" Jasmine yelled back, scrambling to her feet. "We're both here! We're alive!"

"Oh my gosh, I'm so happy!" The voice yelled back. "They're ok! They're alive!"

"Pen," Jasmine replied, clarifying in my mind the face that matched the voice. "Penny! Can you guys move the rubble at all? My Voice isn't cooperating. It's like my powers are weaker here."

"Yeah, it's a whole thing. Too much to explain right now. But Sebastian and I are working on it. We will have you out soon!"

Jasmine and I started moving the rubble from the inside. Soon, a sliver of light began pouring into the room.

The second Sebastian's arm broke through the pile of concrete, Jasmine shrieked with joy. Sebastian kicked the rubble, creating a hole big enough to pull her through. Taking his forearm in both hands, she gripped him tight and he pulled her up and out.

"Stand back, man," Sebastian told me as he began clearing a bit more space around the hole. Within five minutes, I was standing on overgrown grass, looking up at the clear night sky. Jasmine stood wrapped around my waist, crying.

"It's ok," I told her, stroking her hair, like she did to me in the cellar. "Shhh, you're fine. We're safe."

"We didn't find the staff," she told Penny and Sebastian. That was obvious, but she clearly still felt the need to report in.

"I know," Sebastian replied. "He had it with him. He was so powerful, Jas." He stared into space for a moment, as if the scene was on replay in front of his eyes.

"Where's Bee?" Jasmine suddenly asked, her voice shaking.

"She's fine," Penny replied reassuringly. "She's taking care of some things. All of our friends are fine. But Fadel's minion, Maggie… she didn't make it."

"What do you mean, didn't make it?" I asked.

"Fadel," Penny replied, beginning to cry. "He struck her with the staff. The… the… the lightning… She's…"

"Let's get back to the others," Sebastian said, diverting everyone's attention from the tragedy that Penny was referencing. "We can recap later. But we need to get back. They need to know you two are safe."

"Yes," Penny agreed, sniffling. "You're right. Let's go. Bianca will be so relieved to see you guys. Especially together."

Her gaze traveled from our faces to our entwined hands and a sly smile crossed her face as she wiped away a tear.

"Don't you dare say anything cute," Jasmine snapped. But I just laughed and squeezed her tight.

318

CHAPTER SIXTY-FIVE

Theodore

The hugging was a bit much. Yeah, we were happy that no one died, but there were other things to worry about.

Bianca and Jasmine hugged and cried, Penny and Jasmine hugged and cried, I thought I even caught a glimpse of Penny hugging Robert while crying. It was a lot.

"So as much as I'm happy Jasmine isn't buried under the floorboards, we need to talk about what just happened," I said, eyeing Jasmine and Robert, who were now holding hands.

What the heck happened in the cellar?

I wasn't sure I really wanted to know.

"Obviously, Fadel escaped," Sebastian said. "Again. But the good news is that he's alone now. He's vulnerable."

I winced a bit at the mention of his lack of employees. Alexandra was still in shock, sitting on the dirt, staring into space. I couldn't imagine losing a friend and it pretty much being your fault.

"We need to know where he went this time," Bianca said. "We need to get his location as quickly as possible. I can only imagine he fled the city, since… well… you know what he did this time. He won't want the police on his trail. It's likely he's going to board a flight before his name potentially gets flagged by the authorities."

"Shouldn't it already be flagged? I mean geez-louise, this guy sucks. The feds should know about him already," I said, tossing a rock across the grass.

"He removed his own name from the do-not-fly list," Alexandra said, making me jump. I'd forgotten she was still on the ground.

"Maggie… Maggie told me. Back on the plane. He'd hijacked the airline system to track Robert's work travels. That's how he knew that Robert and I would be on the same flight. That's why he sent his… minions… onto the plane that day. He's in their system. He probably didn't even have to *book* the flights through the airline."

"Jasmine," Sebastian asked. "Can you call the Durango airport and see if we can get ticket information for him?"

Jasmine nodded and walked off to go make the call.

"I sent Lawrence out west to Charles," Bianca chimed in again. "He promised us assistance. If we can figure out where Fadel is going, Lawrence can fill in the details and get us where we need to go."

"How do we know we can trust that guy?" I asked. I didn't like that Lawrence kid. But I also didn't want to shoot down any potential help. We needed it now more than ever.

"We offered him protection. He was scared. I think fear of Fadel will keep him loyal to us," Sebastian said.

"So, the plan is to find his location and then go there? Keep chasing him around the country?" Penny looked exhausted, all the bubbly energy she usually had now appeared gone. "I'm sorry, I don't want to be rude, but that's been our exact same plan every time. And it's never worked."

"I think we need to regroup. We need to come up with a more detailed plan. Something new. We need to think things through this time. We need to learn from his patterns and from our mistakes before we jump into things again," Sebastian said. "But yes, I think the ultimate goal would be to follow him wherever he went. But first, I think we need to talk to Lawrence. I also think we need to get Alexandra home, for real this time. Robert can go, too, if he wants. We have a lot of tasks in front of us, and we should take them one at a time. Rushing around and doing too many things at once has only hurt us. We're going to turn over a new leaf and do things right. We're never going to win otherwise."

Sebastian looked dejected. This failure meant more to him than just losing the ability to go back to a normal, Fadel-less life.

"I'm sorry that my plans have never worked. I'm sorry that I've failed as a leader."

Bianca was quick to grab his arm.

"Just because we haven't won yet doesn't make you a bad leader. We're all figuring this out as we go. We're learning and that's what's important."

"And you're right," I added. "We need to try something different. We'll slow down, chat with our super rich friend, Charles, and make a totally awesome, fool-proof plan."

"And this wasn't a total loss," Penny smiled. "He's on his own now. It's all of us versus one of him. He doesn't stand a chance."

Sebastian nodded and thanked us for our support. He took a deep breath and continued.

"Well, if we're going step-by-step, I think we focus on getting Alexandra home first."

"Speaking of Alexandra," Robert said as Jasmine approached us again. "We found something in the cellar."

CHAPTER SIXTY-SIX

Alexandra

"Fadel had some weird stuff in his files, including the deed to this house and property transfer paperwork," Robert turned to Jasmine, who began pulling crumpled papers out of her pocket.

"The deed to this property is actually in Alexandra's name."

My friends all turned to look at me: the girl who just witnessed the death of one of her best friends.

My blood ran cold.

"No, that's not right. I never signed anything."

"I think he forged your signature," Jasmine said, showing me the documents she'd been keeping in her pocket.

"This… this house can't be mine." I scanned them over and over again. Each time it said the same thing: Alexandra Oliver, right there on the dotted line.

"I don't want it." Tears blurred my vision. "I can't take it. Not when…"

None of my friends said anything. Nobody moved.

"If I didn't sign the form, which I didn't, it's not legal. It's not mine. It's still his. Why would he want it to be mine anyway?"

"Maybe he wanted to pass off the liability," Sebastian replied. "He probably doesn't want anything in his name. If it was in your name, but you didn't know it, he could use it like it was his own, but it couldn't be tracked to him."

"I don't want it. It's not legally mine if I didn't sign it."

"Yeah, but legally, that can't be proven. Whether it's your signature or not doesn't matter. The house is technically in your name," Bianca said, looking over the documents again.

"I don't want it. I can't keep the house where Maggie…"

"It's ok," Sebastian cut me off. "You don't have to decide on that right now. We can come back to that later. What's more important is where we go from here. Jasmine, did you find anything?"

Jasmine tucked her hands in her pockets, returning the documents.

"I found a lot. Too much, actually."

"Explain," Theo said, annoyed that she wasn't being forthright enough.

"Fadel didn't just book one flight. He booked five. And they're all international."

"International?" Penny yelped. "Like overseas?"

"Yep," Jasmine said, counting off the locations. "Cairo, Prague, London, Tokyo, and Stockholm."

"He's trying to throw us off his scent," Bianca said softly.

"And he's doing a heck of a good job at it!" Theo yelled. "Wouldn't that get flagged? Wouldn't some alarm go off in the system? Five international flights at once?"

"Remember," Sebastian sighed. "He's in the system. He's doing it internally."

"So how are we supposed to chase him over the ocean?" Jasmine blurted out. "Which flight did he actually take?"

"I bet Lawrence can help us there," Bianca said. "He knows all of Fadel's hideouts. He must know where he is going, or at least where he could hide comfortably. Maybe Fadel has a house or a flat in one of those cities."

"Ok so we call Lawrence next," Theo said, ready to keep things moving. "He's heading out to see Charles, right?"

"Speaking of Charles," Jasmine said. "Fadel actually booked two of the tickets under his name. And one under just a C. Fadel. He thinks Charles is dead, correct? I'm worried he has a fake ID under his brother's name."

"Wait," Bianca said. "C. Fadel. Alexandra, where is that house deed?"

I frowned and pulled the paper out, handing it to Bee.

"The deed is transferred from C. Fadel to Alexandra," Bianca said. "What if C. Fadel, the previous owner of the house, wasn't Chakir?"

"You think it's Charles?" I asked.

"It would make sense," Bee nodded. "I don't think the flight is the first time Chakir has used his brother's name. I think he might have used Charles' identity to buy the house under C. Fadel, so he could blame it on his dead brother if he was questioned about ownership. It gives him an extra layer of deniability. And Charles wouldn't have been notified because he legally changed his own last name."

"Then why bother transferring it to Alexandra?" Penny asked. "Wouldn't it be safer under his dead brother's name and not his living secretary? I don't see the point of moving the deed out of C. Fadel."

"That's just it, he did it under C. Fadel. I think he got paranoid. Think about it! He switched cities! He left people *dead* in Durango. He wouldn't have wanted anything tied to his name. Not even his last name. I think he panicked and signed it over to Alexandra."

"When, though? When he left Durango?"

"No," Jasmine said. "There were other more recent papers with it. Lists of supers he was tracking. I think the safe traveled with him to Victory and back. He could have made that transfer any time."

"But we still don't know when Alexandra signed it. Or didn't sign it," Penny said. "How can you sign something without knowing it? I'd say Fadel forged it himself, but it doesn't look like his handwriting. Even the pen is different."

"It looks more like Eric's scrawl if you ask me," Bianca said, looking closer.

And then three faces lit up with a revelation, including mine.

"Oh my," Bianca said. "Eric, I think it *is* your signature."

"How is that possible?" Sebastian asked, taking the page from Bianca.

"We may or may not have gotten into a bad habit of helping Alexandra finish her paperwork when we wanted to quit work early," Eric flushed red with embarrassment.

"See, so it's not legal! It wasn't me!" I practically yelled. "So it's not my problem."

"Legally it is, though. You can't prove that it's not your signature," Sebastian sighed. "But you don't have to keep it. I have an idea."

I looked expectantly at Sebastian, hoping for both clarity and a way out of this. I couldn't own this house. Not when Maggie…

"It's under C. Fadel. Not Chakir Fadel. What if we transferred it to Charles? For real this time. We could transfer it to Charles Faber, so Fadel wouldn't be able to get it back."

"Yes, please. I don't want it." My entire body ached from grief. I didn't need the burden of anxiety on top of it.

"Next time we see Charles, we can talk to him about it. But for now, let's not stress over it," Bianca said, taking my hand and squeezing it.

"Can we call him and just get it over with?"

"I think we should skip calling him and go see him instead," Eric said. "I think Charles and Lawrence could both be useful as we start to plan ahead. I think it might be good for us to reset and reevaluate the situation."

Sebastian nodded solemnly.

"As I said before, Fadel keeps getting away. And we just keep chasing him with no plan. I think Eric's right; we need to sit down and actually think this through. We're obviously doing something wrong. Before we book a flight across the ocean, we need to make a real plan."

"Let's go see Charles," Theo said. "Let's sit down with Charles and put all our heads together and figure out how to eliminate Fadel once and for all."

"Agreed," Bianca said, smiling. "Charles can help us. He knows his brother better than anyone. And with Lawrence there, too, we can get some up-to-date information on Fadel's motives and potential hideouts."

"So now you want us all to fly to Utah?" Jasmine asked, crossing her arms.

"I think that some of us should, yeah. I think Sebastian's right: Alexandra should go home. She's here in Durango now and she deserves to be freed from this. Robert, you too."

"Not me, man," Robert said, mock saluting. "I'm in it for the long-haul."

Jasmine smiled, realized she was smiling, and plastered back on a fake frown.

"And what about the house?" Penny asked. "I feel like we can't leave this property falling apart. It's a nice place."

"Honestly, I was thinking it could be useful," Sebastian said. "The damage doesn't look as bad as I thought it would be. If Alexandra would be willing to share her new property, before it's transferred to Charles, maybe we could make it a second headquarters."

"Or a third," Eric said. "Charles can tell you more, but he's establishing a safe place for supers out in the desert. You have Utah, Victory, and now Durango. He'd be happy to have another place to protect people like us. Might even make him more likely to accept the deed if we decide we want to establish this house for a greater purpose."

"Yes," I said. "I need a bit of space for a while. But of course, please use the house. I think establishing it as a headquarters for heroes is a great idea. I think it would honor Maggie well."

"Then it's settled," Sebastian grinned. "I hereby declare this house the southern headquarters of the Defenders of Victory— pending Charles' opinion."

Everyone cheered except Jasmine, but that was to be expected.

"It's a dump. The roof literally caved in and there was a landslide in the basement."

Penny didn't hesitate to reply.

"It's actually still in great shape. Like 80 or 85 percent usable! If we can get some repairs going, it will be fine! Plus, it's fully furnished."

"Yeah, that house rocks," Theo said. "And you know who has the literal powers to fix it up?"

He looked at Jasmine, who glared back at him.

"You want me to fix the house? Sebastian, tell him he's crazy." Luckily, she didn't actually use the Voice for her command, so Sebastian disagreed with her.

"Actually, that's a great idea. If you want to stay for a few days, you could help Alexandra settle in and also fix the house. You can tell the boards and drywall and such what to do. It would only be what, three or four days, tops? The rest of us can fly out to Utah and meet with Charles and Lawrence. We then could all reconvene in the mystery city of Fadel's choosing."

"That sounds so lame," Jasmine huffed. "Why do I get the lame task?"

"I'll stay with you," Robert threw out. "I've got quite a bit of experience with construction."

"Fine," Jasmine smiled a little. "I guess I'm in."

Although I wouldn't be a part of it, I liked my friends' plan. The house was beautiful and would make a great spot for them to expand their operations. If they could get Charles to take it back, they would have full control over the property without me even needing to be involved. I could finally go home, and they would have everything they needed.

Grief continued to wash over me, wave after wave. I couldn't bear to look at the house. I couldn't think about my friend without feeling like I was going to throw up. What I'd just witnessed… What I'd just lost…

I was ready to mourn. I was ready to recover from the damages I'd incurred over the last several years of my life. I was ready to go home.

My time with the Defenders of Victory was coming to an end, and that was ok in my book.

They were my friends, they were heroes, and they'd defeat Fadel. I knew that in my heart and soul. And even though I'd be home while doing so, I'd be cheering them on, no matter what.

"It's settled then," Sebastian said. "We've got our marching orders. Let's purchase some flights west and prepare to end this thing once and for all. For real this time."

"Hopefully," Theo added, attracting a nice glare from both Sebastian and Jasmine.

CHAPTER SIXTY-SEVEN

Penny

We were through security and at our gate within two hours.

Jasmine called the airline and booked us tickets, which Bianca's friend Charles gladly paid for. He was thrilled we were coming out as a group to strategize our next move. It was a good plan: we needed to determine Fadel's motives and movement, and who better to help us than his recently turncoat minion and his own brother?

We'd said goodbye to Jasmine, Robert, and Alexandra back at the mansion. Theo and I explored the stable parts of the house and discovered several usable rooms. Robert and Jasmine would stay there and continue to fix the place over the next week, while we made our plans and booked our travel overseas. Alexandra would finally go home to her family.

It was bittersweet knowing that she would be leaving us, at least until she recovered from the tragedy of losing her friend. She'd been an integral part of our lives since we discovered her in Fadel's hotel room a few months ago.

If our time chasing Fadel had given us anything good, it was each other. We'd gained so many friends, each one becoming part of our growing family. Alexandra was now a good friend, Robert was another. Bianca became my sister.

I used to be upset that I didn't have a strong family unit of love and comfort to return home to. Sometimes, admittedly, I continued to let that bother me. But after all the chaos from Fadel, I really did have a family. Especially with Sebastian's latest plans about a Durango 'hub,' to add to our Victory home and Charles' place in Utah, I knew I had places to return to, places to call my own. And I finally knew, wherever my adventures would take me, I would have my friends in the end, ready to welcome me back.

As I hugged Jasmine goodbye, I told her how proud I was of her. I teased her for finally coming around to Robert's obvious affections. But mostly, I told her how much I cared for her. We were very different people, but maybe that's what made us the best of friends.

I would miss her for those few days. It's crazy what only a matter of hours apart can make you feel for your friends.

"We have an hour until boarding," Sebastian said. "Anyone want to go get some snacks?"

Theo volunteered, opening up an opportunity for Bianca and Eric to have some time alone together. I hoped they could finally talk about what was on their minds, so I seconded Theo and joined the boys as they left the gate towards the food court.

"Did I make these decisions too hastily?" Sebastian asked, dipping his waffle fry in his chocolate shake. We now sat at a table in the middle of the food court, letting Bianca and Eric have the time they needed to chat before the flight.

We all wanted to land in Utah with a fresh slate, ready to turn the page and start anew.

"No, man," Theo said. "It makes the most sense to do this right. I think that before, we always jumped right into things. Oh, Fadel is here? We need to rush after him. Oh, he went to a new city? Quick, let's go! It's nice to think things through and Charles and Lawrence will be key to finding Fadel and having a plan."

"I mean," I chipped in between bites of fry. "No one knows Fadel's ultimate motive. We don't know if he's after world domination or just an ego boost of power. What's the point of him traveling city to city collecting powers, anyway?"

"That's what keeps me up at night," Sebastian replied. "I can't quite figure it out."

"I think Charles has some ideas," Theo added.

"Which is why it's a good thing we are going straight to him. We can cross-check his ideas with Lawrence's insight," I said. "If we can get some clarity on his motivations, that might be able to help us stop him."

"Lawrence mentioned that he knows Fadel's connections. I want to dig into that word—connections—a bit more," Sebastian said. "What if he has a network? Or worse, an organization he's working for? He just took an international flight. Does that mean that this is a global thing?"

"Geez I hope not," Theo replied. "I'm exhausted enough being a defender of Victory. I don't need a whole planet to deal with."

"Well, whatever he plans to do with all those powers, we'll be there to stop him," I said, smiling at my friends.

"Absolutely," Sebastian replied. "And then we get to move on to what's next."

"That's what everyone keeps talking about," I laughed. "Everyone is so concerned about what's next. What *is* next, Sebastian? Enlighten us!" I grinned as Sebastian dramatically rolled his head back and laughed.

"Whatever's next," Theo said, grabbing my hand across the table. "We'll be ready to meet it when it comes."

"Didn't Hagrid say that?" I asked.

"Yeah, he said something like that. My goodness, I love that you know that, Pen. But it's true. We're all a team. I don't think there's anything that can stop us."

I liked his words, but I liked the way he brushed his thumb over my ring finger more.

CHAPTER SIXTY-EIGHT

Bianca

Our friends left us alone at the gate and I knew the time had finally come to talk to Eric.

I was more scared to have this one conversation than I was to face Fadel on any given mission. If I wanted to light a fire, it definitely would not work, that was for sure.

We leaned back in our seats, side by side, facing the massive window looking out at the gate and the jet-way.

A plane slowly turned and made its way across our vision, preparing to take off. The glass muffled the roar of the engines, but I still felt the rumble in my chest.

Neither of us wanted to speak, that was clear. But I knew I'd regret it if I didn't say something. I needed to be honest with him. And after everything that had happened back at the mansion, the fragility of our time here on earth was at the forefront of my mind. I wanted to say something to him before it was too late.

"Eric, I think we should talk," I said, turning to look at him. He continued to watch the planes out the window.

"Yeah?"

"Yeah," I said, looking forward as well. It was like I'd entered the confessional. I would speak to the wall and confess everything in my heart.

"I first want to apologize. I should have had this conversation with you sooner. I've been so scared to ruin our friendship that I've acted like a coward."

"Bee, I know where—-"

"No, please. Let me finish. I want you to know everything. I want to lay it all out there."

I glanced over at him. He still faced forward but nodded slowly. I continued.

"It was immature to keep you waiting for an answer. I led you on and that wasn't fair to you or to Sebastian."

"I know this is really about Sebastian. You don't want me because you have him," Eric said. I closed my eyes. This stung even more than I thought it would.

"I know you thought we might be able to rekindle things once we were reunited, but that just wasn't going to happen, whether Sebastian was in the picture or not," I replied, trying to keep my tone steady. "The truth is that we broke up. My heart was shattered when you left, Eric."

I tried so hard not to look at him as my eyes filled with tears.

"I was devastated. I would have come with you if you just asked. You know that. I thought you were my future."

He didn't respond so I kept going.

"But when you left me, I knew that I needed to move on. So even if Sebastian and I weren't dating, I think I still would have to say no. I don't think I could ever be more than friends because I'm not sure I could ever put my heart back together in the same way it was before. Does that make sense?"

I finally turned to look at him. This time, he looked back. His eyes were not filled with tears. In fact, he looked as stoic as ever.

"I'm sorry I hurt you, and not just because it ended up hurting me, too. I shouldn't have left you alone without closure. That was selfish. I was protecting myself and I should have been protecting you, too."

"I'm sorry we aren't going to be together," I said, softly. "I think you're wonderful, Eric. And I know that might make it hurt even more, but it's true."

"Thank you. You're wonderful, too. And for the record, Sebastian is a really lucky man."

We sat in silence for a few minutes, watching another plane taxi and takeoff.

"Do you think we can be friends?" I asked. "Is it possible to be friends with your ex?"

It was a selfish question, like I wanted my cake and to eat it, too. But if we were going to work together, I needed to know if it was possible to mend our relationship, even if it wasn't the same type of relationship it was before.

Eric thought for a moment.

"I think it's possible for us to be friends, but I think it's best if we are friends within a larger context. Like, maybe I'm friends with Sebastian and Theo and we are all friends as a group, but you and I don't spend time alone together if we can help it. Does that seem right?"

"Yes," I replied, smiling for the first time in hours. "I think that makes sense. I don't think it would be appropriate to spend one-on-one time together, since we have history. But I want to still know you, Eric."

"I want to know you, too. But I agree, this is definitely for the best."

I stuck out my hand and he eyed it, confused.

"Friends? But like friend-group type of friends?" I said, making him laugh. He took my hand and shook it.

"Friend-group friends."

"Excellent," I released his hand, relieved that for the first time, our touch didn't lead to sparks or butterflies, or fireworks. We were moving on, and that was a good thing for everyone.

I wasn't stupid enough to believe that he wasn't hurting. This conversation wasn't going to magically fix things overnight. But this was a first step towards a better future for all of us. All would be well and time would heal the wounds between us.

"And for the record," he unexpectedly continued. "I'm happy to be friends with Theo and Sebastian. They're really cool guys."

"They really are."

"And even more for the record? I'm happy you guys came and found me. It might not have turned out the way I'd imagined it would, but I'm happy to be a part of this. I needed to have courage, too. I ran from my problems for so long. Thanks to you, I'm finally facing them head on."

I smiled at him.

"We're all in this together," I said sincerely.

He laughed.

"Ok, I won't pretend like you didn't just make a *High School Musical* reference immediately after our not-breakup."

"You know I used to be obsessed with Zac Efron!"

"Another man you like more than me. Really rubbing salt in the wound today, Bee," He mockingly put both hands over his heart and tipped back into his chair. We laughed.

The others finally approached, Sebastian carrying two milkshakes, I assumed for Eric and me.

"How do you feel?" He whispered as he handed me my drink.

I smiled up at him and lifted my hand. A tiny flame weaved my fingers.

"In control."

He leaned down and gave me a kiss. It was just a quick one, but it flooded me with a warmth that even my fire couldn't produce.

CHAPTER SIXTY-NINE

Jasmine

"I'm gonna head back to my apartment and grab some things," Robert said, checking his watch. "Do you want to come with me?"

"Absolutely. I'd love to see your place."

We got in the rental car—the one we were tasked with returning—and made our way across town. We'd left Alexandra asleep in one of the mansion's many bedrooms. That's where Robert and I would also be living until we met our friends wherever the heck Fadel went.

I wasn't sure how I felt about Robert staying at the mansion, too. But he made a good argument for it.

"I don't feel comfortable having you there alone, in case someone shows up looking for Fadel. Or worse, Fadel faked us all out and returns himself."

Robert Arashi, my hero.

"I just want to pack a bag of fresh clothes and such. Don't need to bring much since we can always go back," he said, turning into the parking garage of the apartment complex. "Oh, and I should probably bring the cat."

"Wait, hold up," I blurted out. "You have a cat? And you're just now telling me?"

He laughed but I continued in utter amazement.

"Scratch that. You have a cat and you haven't returned to your place to collect this cat yet? How has it stayed alive this long?"

He smiled endearingly.

"Don't worry, the cat's fine. My neighbor, Amelia, has been checking on her. She's like seventy-something and her grand-kids come to visit all the time. Pip's been getting lots of attention, I assure you."

"Pip?" I almost squealed. I was starting to both sound and act like Penny. What was this man doing to me?

I tried to pull it together by the time we got out of the elevator on Robert's floor.

"If someone told me a year ago that I'd be dating an older man with a cat while living in a historic mansion in Texas, I'd call them insane. This is crazy," I laughed to myself.

"Ok whoa, what's with the 'older man' talk, huh?" Robert replied, digging in his bag for the keys to unlock the door. "You're what, 23?"

"Yeah. Is that a problem?"

"I'm only 28. You're acting like I'm 35."

"Still," I shrugged. "Older man."

"Ok ok, just move so I can open the door," he pushed the key in the lock and let us in the apartment.

"Welcome to my humble abode," he gestured to the one-bedroom apartment. It was spotless inside, probably meticulously cleaned. What a difference from living with Theo.

"I'll head in the bedroom and pack my stuff. Make yourself comfortable and I'll be out in a few."

I made my way to his love seat and settled in, pulling out my phone to text Bianca, wanting to make sure they all made their flight to Salt Lake City.

A small mewing and a sudden weight on my legs informed me that a new friend had discovered me.

"Hi Pip," I said, stroking her fur. "You're a sweetheart, aren't you?"

"She'll help us catch the mice at the mansion," Robert hollered from the other room.

"You think there are mice?" I asked, surprised I hadn't considered it before.

"No, but if there are, there won't be for long."

I smiled and turned back to my phone.

BIANCA: Made it onboard. I'll call tonight from SLC.

* * *

That night, I curled up in an unfamiliar bed with a somewhat less unfamiliar cat.

I'd claimed the master bedroom for myself, complete with a California king and an en-suite bathroom. The house was honestly perfect, besides the collapsed upper floor and caved in basement, both of which we'd tarped and sealed from the elements. Tomorrow we'd get to work at rebuilding.

Alexandra insisted on sleeping on the couch, not wanting to leave after taking a second nap sprawled across it. Robert took the room down the hall, a comfortable guest room, also with its own bathroom. His cat, Pip, chose to sleep with me, which I considered a major win.

Before bed, I bumped into him in the hallway, both of us in our pajamas, him wearing a flannel robe and glasses. I tried not to smirk, but I smirked.

"What?" He asked, the corner of his mouth curving slightly upwards.

"Nothing. You just look cozy."

"Are you saying I look cute?"

"Absolutely not. I said cozy. Those two words are not synonymous."

"Whatever you say, Kahale," he started making his way back to his room.

I spoke up quickly, in an effort to stop him.

"Are you only dating me because you want to meet my dad?" I asked, partially kidding but partially making one last attempt to protect my own heart. He stopped in his tracks and slowly pivoted around to face me.

"Would you consider what we're doing dating?"

I thought about it for a moment longer than I should have. My fear of rejection was screaming at me to back down. But luckily, I had a certain power to shut it down.

Be honest with him.

"Yeah, I would say we are at least exclusive."

He nodded.

"Ok, well then, yeah. I'm absolutely dating you to meet your dad." He smiled and butterflies flooded not only my chest, but my entire body.

"Excellent. Goodnight, Robert."

"Goodnight, Jasmine." He disappeared into his room.

In bed, I thought about how nice it would be to take him home with me. I couldn't wait for him to meet my dad and go out into the Pacific on our boards together. Ice cream on the pier, sunsets in Malibu, snuggling up together on the couch after a long day in the sun...

CHAPTER SEVENTY

Alexandra

Has the driveway always been this long?

It had been years since I'd seen my parents and younger brothers. I'd been away for so long, and now, after an absence longer than I'd intended, I was home.

The cab crept down the gravel path and my parents' house appeared. It was a simple, two-story farmhouse with a chicken coop on the side and a pen out in the yard for our two goats. I could see their forms walking around, even in the twilight.

I'd spent the day helping Jasmine and Robert clean the house. I wanted to give them as much help as possible before leaving. Once they started using their powers, Jasmine's literal power to control the movement of building supplies and Robert's handyman skills, I knew it was time to say goodbye.

I hugged them both and promised them I'd stay in touch. Robert told me that he would miss me and that he had a wonderful adventure, starting that flight when I rescued him from Fadel's clutches.

Jasmine told me that she and the others would always be ready to welcome me back with open arms. She let me know that she would keep me in the loop as they followed Fadel overseas. She also made me promise two things.

First, she told me not to ignore them or forget them. She worried that I would disassociate completely as I settled back into my normal life. I reassured her that I wouldn't be able to forget them. They were my friends, and even if I wanted to take a break from Fadel, I didn't want a break from them.

The other thing she made me promise was to block Zeke's number. She hovered over my shoulder to make sure I actually followed through.

"Good," she said. "Now don't reverse it. I'm not using my Voice right now, but I sure as heck will be if I find out you've been talking to him. It's not good for either of you."

"I worry about him," I honestly responded.

"Well, he's an adult man. He's fine. His sister is fine. But you don't need the drama and stress tied to that guy. He might have helped us out here and there, but he's not loyal."

I agreed, even though I didn't want to. She was right, though. I needed to keep my distance from anyone who couldn't be totally and completely loyal. True friends were hard to come by, but I had seven and I'd do good to stick to them.

"Goodbye," I said, hugging my friends one more time. "Thank you for everything. Both of you."

And with that, I loaded my bag into the cab and made my way back home.

Now, standing on the front porch with my bags, my heart raced, even more than it did when Fadel came at me in that bathroom or while I ran through the orchard.

What would they even say to me? Did they think I'd abandoned them? I'd gone years without any formal contact and now I was just showing up on their porch, bag in hand. Would I ever really be able to go back to the life I had before, at least in any meaningful way?

I thought about Bianca and Penny and Sebastian, Theo, Jasmine, and Eric. My friends—the Defenders of Victory— I considered what they would do with this moment, this opportunity.

Be brave, Alexandra.

I took a deep breath and rang the doorbell.

The next few seconds were a blur: some muffled footsteps, the door opening, and my mother's cry.

"Oh, Alexandra!"

Then I thrust myself into her arms, held her tight, and cried. Drop by drop, yet all at once, tears of mourning for Maggie, of the reality of my messy life over the last few years, and more than anything, of relief at this homecoming, began to fall.

I was finally home.

Acknowledgments

First and foremost, I'd like to thank my family, specifically Joshua and Lucia, for supporting me on my writing journey. I wouldn't be able to do any of this without my husband's generosity, patience, and kindness. He's the real talented writer in this family; I'm just filling the void until he has the time to release a book of his own. I look forward to the day our works can sit next to one another on the shelf.

Thank you to my sisters, parents, in-laws, and extended family who have encouraged me as I've brought Victory and its heroes to life.

I'd also like to personally thank Sara, who has now helped me edit two full-length books on top of her responsibilities as a full-time employee. She is a busy woman but still has managed to find time to help me. For that I'm immensely grateful.

Thanks as well to Rachel, who did her own edit pass while taking care of her three boys. I don't know how you had the time, but I'm grateful you did!

A special thanks to my friends here in Hillsdale and across the country. They've been my first readers, my ARC team, and my ongoing support. I'm grateful I've gotten to share these adventures with people I care so much about.

Thank you to all the wonderful authors who have inspired me, both as a child and as an adult. To my teachers—my first readers—thank you for telling me I had potential and cheering for me as I grew in my writing. Thank you to my designer, Jo, for bringing life to these pages.

Finally, thank you to you, my dear reader. I genuinely wouldn't be able to do any of this without you. Writing a book is hard, publishing a book is harder. By reading the pages between your hands right now, you're making my dreams come true.

Thank you. I love you all.

About the Author

Rachael Waechter is the award-winning author of the *Defenders of*

Victory series, a YA adventure series of magic, action, and romance. Her first novel, *Playing with Fire*, debuted in 2024. She's also published a short anthology of stories set in the magical world of the *Defenders of Victory*. In her free time, Rachael loves reading, traveling, baking, and attempting to learn watercolor. She lives in her home state of Michigan with her husband, her daughter, and Puddle the Cat. You can find Rachael on Goodreads and on Instagram at @authorrachaelwaechter.

Titles by the Author
Playing with Fire (Defenders of Victory, Book 1)
Stories from Victory (Defenders of Victory, Book 1.5)
Burning the Ashes (Defenders of Victory, Book 2)